# WITHER & WOUND: MOUNT OLYMPUS ACADEMY

# WITHER & WOUND: MOUNT OLYMPUS ACADEMY

## MYTHVERSE BOOK 3

KATE KARYUS QUINN    DEMITRIA LUNETTA

MARLEY LYNN

❀ Created with Vellum

Sign up for the Mythverse Newsletter and you'll receive
THREE FREE SHORT STORIES—all set in the Mythverse!

RAGE & RUIN is part of the Mount Olympus Academy and
features Nico's mom, Maddox.

FIGHT OR SIGHT and TOOTH OR CLAW are prequels to
later books in the Mythverse series, set within Underworld
Reformatory.

# 1

———

L ife is weird.

One minute you're having a heart to heart with your sister in a sea-shore cave, discussing your plans to overthrow the Greek Gods. The next moment you're trying to explain to an angry werewolf that you weren't about to become a traitor...something that he's particularly touchy about.

Dogs are notoriously loyal animals, after all.

Nico, currently in his human form (and only slightly less scary than his werewolf one), stands stiff with fists clenched and his one eye intensely set on my sister, Mavis.

They have history. He loved her once. Then she tried to kill him. Now he loves me. He even sorta proposed, which was hella-awkward. It's a long story.

"You're coming back to Mount Olympus Academy to stand trial for treason," he tells her. "Will you come peacefully, or are you going to fight me?"

Considering that the last time he tried to apprehend her, Mavis gouged his eye out, I'd like to think that my sister is going to fight. But it doesn't seem that way. Right now, she looks like a scared little girl.

That fear doesn't go away when she shifts; Mavis's cat-self is puffy, tail straight up, back arched, every hair on end. She makes a run for it, dashing for the cave entrance.

Lightning fast, Nico grabs her by the scruff of the neck. As he holds her in the air, she writhes, hissing and spitting, taking swipes where she can. But he's got her at arm's length, and from the look on Nico's face, he's enjoying watching her struggle.

Mavis must see it too. She sags and then slips back into human form.

"How did you find me?" she asks, neck craned painfully.

"I followed Edie's scent. I've been keeping track of her to make sure she's safe." His hand is wrapped up in her hair. She's not getting away. And she knows it.

"That's super creepy. You know that, right?" Mavis says. "You used to stalk me like that too."

"Jealousy," he growls, "doesn't look good on you, Emmie."

He focuses on me and something in his expression shifts. Softening, just slightly. "Edie. I trusted you. I introduced you to my mom. Were you just using me the whole time? Using the crazy chemistry between us to blind me with your bitch box?"

I thought I was un-shockable after attending the gods' idea of sex-ed classes, but for a moment I am rendered speechless.

"Wow, still a charmer," Mavis says dryly.

Getting it together, I wag my finger in Nico's face. "First of all, there was no chemistry between us. Secondly, bitch box? And finally, everyone on campus knows that I've got it bad for Val. He strangled me. I set him on fire. Now *that* is a meet cute."

Nico's eye goes all big and puppy-dog on me. "We met in the desert! You saved my life. That is the ultimate meet cute."

"Shut up, Nico," Mavis cuts in. "Edie, why didn't you tell me about Val? I want to hear everything. Have you kissed? Have you done more than—ouch!"

Nico jerks Mavis's hair, cutting that topic short. It's probably for the best. Now is not really the best time to get into the icy/hot kisses Val and I have shared.

Anyway, it was kinda dumb of me to remind Nico of my on-again, off-again vampire boyfriend, especially with Mr. Zee's new rule about no interspecies dating on campus.

Plus, Nico's always hated vampires. The fact that a group of them killed his mom just a few days ago probably didn't endear them to him any further.

But still, I never tried to seduce him. Not for fun or to get secrets out of him. I wasn't even with the monsters when we became friends. No, far from it. Instead I'd stuck my head in the sand, refusing to see all the signs that first my flying instructor, and then my sister, had tried to show me. The gods who run Mount Olympus Academy don't have our best interests in mind. They're using us students as human shields in their ongoing war with the monsters. Monsters that *they* created as their own personal playthings eons ago and now persecute ruthlessly.

I don't know how to explain all that so it would get through to Nico. His mom was a fanatical believer in the gods, and she did her best to raise Nico in her image. Sometimes, I see glimmers that tell me there's a better guy buried under all that fur and bluster. But if there truly is, he's hiding way down deep.

While I'm still trying to figure out my best move, Mavis jumps in.

"I tricked Edie into coming here," she blurts out. "She didn't know I was working for the monsters until I told her. I tried to recruit her, but she wouldn't join me."

I'm shaking my head. This is so wrong. Mavis warns me with her eyes, though. They say, *Let me save you.*

I swallow. I can't bring myself to speak out against her. As always, my big sister is the one calling the shots.

"Edie said that I needed to turn myself in," Mavis continues. "She said I would get a fair trial at the Academy."

"She deserves that," I say. "At least."

Nico looks doubtful. "You were going to bring in your own sister? You know what they do to those who betray the gods, right?"

I nod. Death, by fire or flood. Yes, I know.

"If she's found guilty they'll burn or drown her," Nico says. Still holding tight to Mavis's hair, he gives her a shake. "I can end it more quickly, here and now."

Sick rises in my throat. I know how easily Nico could snap her neck. Or use his teeth to rip it out.

I take a deep breath before speaking again. I can't let my voice tremble right now. "You think the gods will thank you for sparing them their vengeance? Taking away the bloodshed that belongs to them? I'm with the Academy, and Mr. Zee. You know he'd want to witness a traitor's death."

Probably with a glass of ambrosia in his hand and a giant box of popcorn in his lap.

Nico wants to believe me. I can see it on his face. Of course he does, otherwise he's been tricked twice. Otherwise he has to turn his love for me into loathing, like he did with Mavis. I watch his fingers flexing around her throat, and imagine them on my own.

"Nico," Mavis says, her voice small and tight under his hand. "The monsters who tortured you were a splinter cell. I was not working with them; I would never have left you at their mercy. I just wanted to get away. I didn't want to hurt you."

"You took my eye!" Nico spits, and Mavis goes a little gray as her oxygen is cut off.

I want to scream. Or burn him to cinders. Or put my hands around his throat and see how he likes it.

But I can't do any of that. One step wrong and Mavis will be dead.

My heart hammers in my chest as I cross toward the two of them, keeping his focus on me. Slowly, carefully, I rest my hand over his. I hope he doesn't notice the slight tremble.

Beneath my palm, I can feel his pulse beating frantically; confused, panicked. Under that is Mavis's own pulse; thready and scared.

For a moment it seems absurd. None of us want to be here like this. We're just kids. Before I came to MOA, I went to a regular school. A boy decided to start a bunch of rumors about me and it spread all over social media. I thought my life was over.

That all seems so petty now.

"Nico, how about this? Let's bring her in," I give his hand a reassuring squeeze. "You and me. Together."

His eye lights up at the thought, but the confusion is still there. "You really had no idea that your sister was Emmie, the traitor?"

"No." And it's not even a lie. Give or take a week.

I just found out that Emmie—the infamous student traitor—and my sister were the same person. "I thought Mavis was missing, maybe dead." I start to cry; the tears come easily.

I've lost my parents...Dad to a monster, jealous of my mother's love for him. And my mother to amnesia that she brought on herself when she could no longer handle the pain of losing so many people she loved.

Mom's found a new life, here on this island. And a new love, complete with a newborn baby. A replacement family in Greece to wipe away a lifetime of running from the gods and hiding the children she'd helped abduct from Mount Olympus Academy—me and Mavis.

"I want to make this right," I say, looking at Mavis. I hope she understands I'm speaking to her. I won't let her die. Not when I just found her again. "I'll even testify at her trial."

He snorts out a laugh. "We won't need your testimony to sentence her to death. Everyone knows what Emmie...Mavis did."

"Think about it," I say, my hand tightening over his. "One of our own teachers—my flying instructor—was a traitor in our midst. Campus is split in the middle after what happened with..."

His gaze darkens and I realize this was the wrong tactic.

Probably best not to mention our most recent mission, which ended with his mother attempting to slaughter an innocent baby monster. A vampire student—and the girl my boyfriend was supposed to marry—stepped in to stop the murder of the baby manticore. She died for it, at the hands of Maddox Tralano, Nico's mother.

Quickly I recalibrate. "If all the students had just followed your orders, none of that bad stuff would've happened at all." Nico nods, obviously liking this alternate version of history. Technically Nico was leading the mission, but his mother hijacked leadership right from the start. "Nico, you have a chance to draw campus together again.

Unite the students. What better way than a public trial and execution?"

I slide my eyes to Mavis, silently apologizing for making her death an entertainment event. She gives a half shrug, as if to say *What can you do?*

He tilts his head, considers. "I like that. I like that a lot. You and me together." His hand relaxes on Mavis neck, not letting her go, but it's a start. "I'll lead and you'll be there for strong back-up. The students will be inspired and we'll get Mount Olympus Academy back on track."

"Yes, exactly," I prompt.

He grins, fierce and gleeful all at once. If he didn't have my sister's neck in his hand, I'd almost be tempted to smile too. "Let's do it. Let's bring her back and have Zee decide."

I almost collapse, I'm so relieved.

"But first…" He takes out a knife with his free hand and I go tense once more.

"Nico, wait!" I say, but he shakes me off easily. Mavis's wide eyes stare into mine as Nico pushes her head until she's down on her knees.

Tracing the blade of the knife down her cheek, he growls. "First, let's make us even."

Oh gods. He's going to take her eye.

# 2

I freeze.

It's not the first time.

I froze in the hall last semester at the Spring Fling. I stood stock still just long enough for Darcy—a kind mermaid that my best friend was crushing on—to lose his head. The resulting spray of blood made me jump into action. But I was too late to save him.

I can't let that happen again, can't stand here while Nico extracts my sister's eye. It can't be yet another thing I fail at.

Luckily, I don't have to.

"Really, Nico?" Mavis asks, her voice suddenly strong and firm.

This is a tone I know well. One that told me to get my homework done and set the table, warned me that my hair was too greasy to go out in public and that my shorts were too short.

This is big sister tone, and nobody argues with it. Apparently not even a werewolf intent on revenge. The blade in Nico's hand stops short of Mavis's eye.

"Eye for an eye?" Mavis taunts him. "Not very original.

All this time I thought you'd be planning something spectacular to get back at me. But this? *Pfftt.*"

She actually blows a raspberry at him, her hair fanning out from her mouth. "I'm so disappointed in you, Nico."

Wait. That last bit didn't sound like my sister. That sounded like Maddox Tralano, Nico's mother. And Nico almost never went against what his mom said. For the most part, she owned him.

"I mean, if something is worth doing, you've got to do it right," Mavis goes on, straightening her neck as Nico's grip loosens. "You weren't raised to half-ass anything, were you?"

"No," Nico agrees, drawing the knife back from my sister's face. "I wasn't. You make a good point, traitor. I'll ask the gods for special compensation before your execution, a chance to even the score between us. After what you put me through, it will have to be creative."

I relax slightly, relieved that I won't have to stand witness to my sister being maimed in a dark, Grecian cave. But it's a short-lived reprieve, and a glint shows in Nico's eye as he leans closer to Mavis.

"After all," he says. "There's more than one way to skin a cat."

———

I fly back to Mount Olympus Academy with an angry werewolf on my back and a sleepy cat in my clutches.

Mavis put everything she had left into convincing Nico to maybe *not* try out his surgical skills on her face. After her boost of adrenaline wore off, she was clearly running on fumes. Once we reach campus, Nico will be the least of her problems and Mavis will need all the strength she can muster.

Dragon Air (that's me) doesn't have first class seats, but I wanted to make Mavis as comfortable as possible. If she could get a bit of sleep her chances of surviving this disaster will be greatly improved. Like all cats, her preference is to be snuggled up and warm, so I suggested I carry her in her blanket.

Nico wasn't as supportive of my leniency, but I was his ride home, after all.

Mavis wrapped herself tightly in the blanket and I carefully picked her up, cocooning her within my curled talons. I held out my other claw to Nico, but the alpha-hole jumped on my back instead. I gritted my teeth and promised myself that if the words "giddy up" came out of his mouth, there would be fire coming out of mine. Thankfully, once perched on top of me, he mostly kept quiet, although once we reached altitude I could've sworn I heard, "Whoo-hoo! I'm king of the world!"

My thoughts are a mess as we cross the ocean. The mighty power that goes along with being a dragon is not always tempered by my human side. After the carnage I caused at the Spring Fling, I realized I was a killing machine —and pretty much nothing or no one could stop me.

Except myself.

If I wanted to, I could shake Nico right now, toss him into the ocean and see if he still feels like the king of the world as he doggie-paddles to some godsforsaken island. I could save our skins by drowning him. The logistics of killing Nico would be easy.

And if the world revolved only around logic, I definitely should.

But...feelings are a thing. Unfortunately.

I've seen Nico be a decent person. Seen him rein in some of his darker impulses simply because Cassie—my friend and the seer who saved him from the monster stronghold—asked him to. I'd seen him hesitate to attack the baby manticore even though Nico's mother ordered its death. And, most importantly, I'd met his mother.

Even though she was dead, Maddox still held a lot of power over her son, and always had. I don't think Nico had much of a chance to grow up into a loving, caring person. Maddox raised him to hate and to fight, yet there were still glimmers of a good guy underneath the hard veneer. Maybe with his mother's influence gone, that side of Nico could be encouraged.

I spot the coastline of Florida. As I descend over the swamp that holds the lotus stream and Mount Olympus Academy, the clouds break around us and Mavis squirms in my grip as she wakes up, aware that we're approaching our destination—and her imprisonment. Below us, students swarm on the campus green, pointing as I come closer, circling to lower altitude.

Nico leaps from my back in wolf form, landing easily on all fours. It's a relief to have him off my back. For the moment at least.

Identifying Jordan, Cassie, Fern, Marguerite, and Greg in a group, I land beside them, quickly shifting into human form, though Mavis prefers to remain a cat. She curls in my arms, her tail tucked around her nose as if she is suddenly shy.

"Hey kitty kitty," Jordan says, petting her. "I didn't know we could take off-campus trips to the pet store." He says, apparently not identifying Mavis as a shifter. "I would've had you bring me back a puppy."

"Oh, no," Fern says, a horrified look on her face.

"Emmie?" Greg asks, peering closer at the bundle of fur in my arms. "That's—"

"My prisoner," Nico interrupts. Having shifted back into human form, he tears Mavis from my grasp. Her claws latch onto my shirt, as her wide panicked eyes meet mine.

Greg shifts into bat form and flies at Nico, who easily swats him away with a backhanded blow. He doesn't even look in his direction. Jordan, with his quick cat reflexes, grabs Greg out of the air.

"It's okay, little buddy," he says.

Doubly outraged, the rest of the group looks ready to charge too, now.

"Wait, guys," Cassie says, her voice low and urgent. "Let's follow Edie's lead."

Her eyes meet mine as she waits for me to tell her what we should do. If only I knew.

What I did know was arriving with Mavis was going to be bad, but the reality of it is so much worse than I thought. I feel like I'm betraying Mavis as Nico tears her away from me. Mavis lets loose a ferocious yowl and Nico gives her a hard shake in response. Then he walks away with her, holding Mavis in the air, even as she spits and hisses at the students who surround them.

"Make way," Nico yells. "Make way for the traitor!"

Nico leads a parade of curious students in his wake to the faculty building.

I grab his free arm. "Nico, wait."

He softens a little as his gaze focuses in on me. "Edie, you're a true patriot, sacrificing your own sister for what's right. We serve the gods, they come first in all. My mother would've sacrificed me to win this war. No hesitation." He swallows and I wonder if saying that aloud makes him realize how horrible it sounds. But whatever's going on in Nico's mind, he quickly shakes it off. "You've done enough. You don't have to see this."

"What if they...what if there's no trial?" I ask. "I need to be there when she's punished."

"This will only be locking her up. Maybe some questioning. I'll make sure the trial is public," he promises and takes a deep breath. "As public as this announcement."

"EVERYONE!" he bellows, and Mavis lays her ears back, like his volume just knocked them down. "The entire campus needs to know about the hero in our midst!"

The circle of students pulls tighter, curious.

"This traitor—" he gives Mavis a shake again, and she growls, deep in her chest. It takes everything I've got not to cinder his ass right that second.

"We all know who she is," he says, turning in a circle so that everyone gets a good look at Mavis, in her cat form. "Emmie, my former partner—and friend."

There are some smirks in the crowd. Looks like everyone knew Nico would have liked to have been even friendlier with Emmie.

"To be betrayed by her cut out my heart," he says, turning to me. "But it's been regrown in my chest. Regrown, because of Edie's actions. Edie, who is so loyal to Mount Olympus Academy and the gods that she would turn in her own sister."

There are gasps from the crowd and beneath that the simmering anger from this past summer starts to flare up once more. Nico has clearly inherited his mother's oratory skills. She had a real talent for getting people all riled up. In her mind she was turning us into winners, but in reality she divided this campus, turning students against one another. Even dead, she left a lot of resentment in her wake. Nico also has his mother's tendency to ignore anyone who doesn't think the same way as he does. So when he hears some boos, he instantly assumes they're against me.

"Hey, c'mon. Don't hold it against her that disobedience lurked in her bloodline," Nico says, warning the crowd. "Edie has purified herself by denouncing Emmie. No one can question where her heart—and her loyalties—lie."

Some cheers follow that, eyes landing on me, indecisive mouths turning into smiles. But other gazes narrow further. No doubt those people are wondering what kind of asshole turns their own sister in. Before I can decide how to deal with that, I'm surrounded by people squeezing my shoulder and clapping my back. They're the type of fanatics whose eyes gleam as they say, "Good soldier" and "For the greater good."

I'm pulled away from Nico and Mavis as I try to evade my new admirers. But the time I extract myself, Nico and Mavis are gone. I twist around in time to see Nico carrying her up the stairs of the faculty building. Mavis's gaze latches onto mine as the doors close behind them.

"Be strong," I mouth, and just like that, she's gone.

Jordan's hand clamps onto my wrist, pulling me into my small circle of friends. "Has Nico officially lost his mind?"

"Greg, are you okay?" I ask. "Nico hit you pretty hard."

The whole left side of his face is swollen, but Greg just scowls at my question. "Yeah, he used me for batting practice. But it's fine. Okay. I can take it."

This school is full of guys with chips on their shoulders, but Greg isn't usually one of them. I glance at Cassie, wondering what's going on with him, and she just shrugs.

"Hey, let's focus on Edie here," Fern says softly. "And Emmie." Fern, in tears, rests her head on her girlfriend, Marguerite's, shoulder. This is dangerous; Marguerite is a vampire and there isn't supposed to be interspecies mingling. But Fern is so upset that Marguerite seems willing to take the chance.

"Oh, poor Emmie," Cassie says softly. She and Mavis were roommates before I came to the Academy, and they became close.

"Somebody has to feed that cat," Jordan goes on, ticking things off on his fingers. "And litter. She's going to need litter. Probably some toys, too. Our kind can't stand to be without stimulation for long."

"You seriously still don't know what's going on?" Greg asks, rolling his eyes. "That's bad, even for you, roomie."

"Oh, and catnip!" Jordan says. "I know where there's some growing wild—"

"Jordan," I say. "That's my sister."

He stops, eyeing me curiously as pieces fall into place...slowly.

"She's a shifter," Greg adds, helping his roommate with the puzzle.

"You have a shifter sister?" Jordan asks, then laughs. "That's hard to say. Shifter sister. Try it, Edie."

"Jordan," Marguerite asks. "Did *you* have some catnip today?"

"Yes, I may have had a quick nip. But that stuff doesn't really affect me at all." Jordan crosses his arms and tries to look offended, but it doesn't work. Instead he starts laughing again as he tries to say "shifter sister" three times fast.

Greg turns his back to Jordan and faces me. "You should have told me," he says, and for the first time in our friendship, I think Greg might actually be mad at me. "You should have told me that Emmie was your sister."

"I'm sorry," I say, and I mean it.

"I know I'm not smooth like Val, or strong like Nico," he goes on. "But I'm your friend, and you could have trusted me. I might have been able to help."

"I...I...I just found out." I stammer, eyes going to Fern

still weeping on Marguerite, who has one arm protectively around her.

"Let's not fight," Fern says, wiping her eyes. "We've got enough problems. Emmie—sorry—*Mavis* will be tried as a traitor, and with the prophecy being discovered, the gods aren't going to go easy on her. She'll be put to death, for sure." Her face twists into grief again, fresh tears falling onto Marguerite's shoulder.

"It will be okay, baby," Marguerite whispers to her. "Don't cry."

Cassie's face tightens in determination. "We have to do something. We need to take a good look at that prophecy."

"What prophecy?" I ask.

Greg answers. "While you were off playing with Nico, Merilee found something in the Archives," he says. "A prophecy declaring that Mr. Zee will die—"

"Mr. Zee can't die!" I interrupt. "He's a god."

Cassie shakes her head. "The prophecy says that Mr. Zee will die by the hand of one of his own children, a Moggy."

"A Moggy," I repeat. A mixed blood. A creature born of two different types of supernatural creatures. Zee has always disliked Moggies, and believed that interspecies relations only weakened bloodlines. Now, he'll have even more reason to hate them.

"He's wants us vampires to bite test everyone, which no offense, but..." Marguerite sends Fern an apologetic look. "My parents would have a fit if they knew. That's healer stuff and it's an insult to expect vampires to do it."

"An insult?" Fern demands.

"My parents' words. Not mine." She leans in close to Fern. "Baby, you know that."

"Themis wouldn't allow them to be executed," Cassie adds as Marguerite whispers something into Fern's ear that makes her smile in this dreamy sort of way. Despite every-thing, seeing them so happy together makes it all seem a little less hopeless. "But she is keeping a close eye on all suspected and known Moggies."

"I don't know if Mr. Zee can die or not," Greg continues. "Hepa says he's incredibly sick. They're working day and night to figure out what's wrong with him, but—"

"But it looks like someone knows how to kill a god," Cassie finishes for him. "And it's probably one of us." The silence is almost frightening, pregnant with possibility.

But then Jordan shouts "Not it!" and looks at everyone else in the group. Cassie smacks him in the stomach, but has to shake her hand afterwards. Jordan isn't that bright, but he does have washboard abs.

"I don't mean one of *us specifically*," Cassie clarifies. "But it's got to be a student. Who else would have that kind of access to Mr. Zee?"

It's a good question.

And I don't have the answers.

## 3

Two weeks later, Mavis is still alive.

Fern has told me that Mavis refuses to say a word. Literally. The only sounds that come out of her are screams of pain. But she holds her silence, refusing to confess or incriminate anyone else.

I'm refusing to give my witness testimony as well. At least not until Mavis is officially granted a trial. It's the only leverage I've got.

Well, that and Themis. Mr. Zee has been on the verge of setting Mavis afire multiple times. Only Themis has been able to step in front of him and convince him that the Academy is in a fragile place right now, and such a move might scare away already spooked parents.

Honestly, I don't know if practicing good PR is really what sways Mr. Zee. He's not his usual robust self these days, so Themis is also able to physically steer him away from Mavis. His mind seems even worse off than his body, so once Mavis is out of sight, he usually forgets all about her for a while.

But he still hasn't officially committed to a trial and until he does, I live in fear that a day will come when Mavis won't have Themis to stand between her and Mr. Zee.

Which is why today, like every day, I come and knock at Themis's door, hoping she'll tell me Mr. Zee has finally relented and will grant Mavis a trial.

Actually, today I don't have to knock. As I approach, the door opens and Hepa comes flying out. She's in such a hurry that she slams into me. I grab hold of her to steady us both. But she quickly jerks away.

"I'm not in the mood to dance right now," she snaps and then hustles away down the hall. Hepa can be a little bitchy at the best of times, so I shrug it off.

"Edie, I was expecting you," Themis says dryly from where she's waiting by the door.

"With good news, I hope?"

"Perhaps." She hesitates, then gestures for me to enter. "Please do come in first so we can talk freely."

Once she's settled behind her desk and I'm seated in what I've come to think of as the 'student supplicant' chair, Themis says, "I believe we may be able to tip Zee over the edge today. Three vampire students were pulled from the school late last night. It's very unusual for such a thing to happen on the eve of a new term. But after Larissa's death..." Themis sighs.

"Hades clearly saw an opportunity and has been wooing the vampire parents, assuring them their undead offspring will be better appreciated at his Underworld Academy." A look of annoyance crosses her face. "As if education is about appreciation. Do you know what they learn at UWA? Nothing. It's a dark smelly frat house that will over time actually leach whatever brains they might have right out of their heads. I mean, Hades won't even lend us a handful of zombies for the war..."

At the mention of the war against the monsters, Themis sighs, falling back into her chair. "Of course, that hardly matters now that Mr. Zee has called a halt to all missions. He wants to keep all of the students on campus, ready to rally to his side in case he's attacked. Luckily, Maddox's last raid really took the fight out of the monsters. They never thought we'd stoop to killing civilians. Well...I might not have, but Maddox Tralano certainly didn't hesitate. Of course, I don't condone such an action, but it can't be argued that the monsters seem less interested in taking the offensive these days. They actually seem content to be left alone. But you can never trust—"

I clear my throat, because Themis seems to be getting started on a rant and I can see it might go on for a while.

She blinks and focuses in on me once more. "Edie, yes." Themis clears her throat. "As I was saying—" Before she can finish that sentence her door smashes open and Mr. Zee himself staggers in.

"Whaddya want?" he demands, scanning the room several times before his eyes finally lock onto Themis. "There ya are, old Missy. A regular gnat in my ear these days, aren't cha?" He squinches his eyes shut as if in pain. One of his giant fists comes up to pound his chest...and I can't help but notice the skin visible around his toga doesn't look its normal healthy color. He's almost a bit grey. Mr. Zee's eyes open wide once more as he releases an enormous burp. The smell of it makes me gag, though I try to cover it with a cough.

"Zee, yes," Themis says, smiling cheerfully, not at all disturbed by his messy state. "So glad you could make this meeting with Edie." Themis sends me a significant look, which I can't quite interpret.

"Right, right. You're honored. She's honored." He lurches

toward the sideboard and grabs the decanter sitting there, which I assume is filled with ambrosia. Ignoring the glasses laid out alongside it, he simply brings the carafe to his mouth and chugs.

If Underworld Academy really is like a frat house, I'm tempted to suggest that Mr. Zee might like it better there.

"Now, Zee," Themis says, as he finishes and wipes his mouth with the hem of his toga—I quickly look away, focusing on Themis as soon as it becomes clear he's about to flash the room. "I know we both agree that it is of the utmost important that we keep Edie here at Mount Olympus Academy."

As Themis's eyes lock with mine, I finally understand where this is going.

"I appreciate that," I say. "But having been raised among humans and as an American, I have a strong belief in maintaining a fair system of justice. I can't see myself staying at an institution that doesn't have those same values."

Themis gives me an approving nod. Mr. Zee meanwhile replies with...raspberries.

"Thhhhbbbttt."

Themis wordlessly hands me a handkerchief to wipe the stray spittle from my face.

"Yer not going anywheres," Mr. Zee slurs. "Cush you don wanna die. And to attend the Underworld Academy, you's gotta be dead."

Oh. I honestly hadn't been aware of this. I guess that explains why Hades was focusing on recruiting the vampires.

Themis, though, seemed ready for this line of attack. "Actually, Zee, I believe it's Athena who's attempting to recruit Edie here. For Amazon Academy."

This gets Mr. Zee's attention. He stands tall and looks as

if he was struck by his own lightning. "Born right outta my head and gettin' craftier every day. Damn Athena."

"Yes, that's what Hades said," Themis says dryly.

Mr. Zee's eyes go wide and he wheels toward me. "It's a trial you want? Even though we all know she's guilty?"

I nod. "Yes sir."

"Fine then. Fine! We'll have it. But it'll be a trial combined with a luau. Did you know they have luaus all the time at Underworld Academy? Apparently, it's a big selling point. Well, our Academy can have luaus too. There will be a big roasted pig and hula dancing and everyone will get lei'd." He snickers at this and is smiling as he adds, "And then we'll declare your sister guilty and kill her. It'll be a great time—the Mount Olympus Academy way!"

And with that he disappears, teleporting away.

"Well there we go," Themis says, folding her hands and trying to look pleased. "You'll have your trial."

———

I hurry back across campus to catch up with my friends about this latest development. There should be a sense of relief—I've convinced the highest authority in the land that my sister deserves a trial over torture. But somehow I don't feel like this is a story with a happy ending. I'm hoping someone—probably Cassie—will be able to put a good spin on it.

But just as I near the dorms, Val steps out of the shadow between two buildings.

"Edie, I heard about your sister. Are you okay?" There's an expression of concern on his face, which isn't really like him. Usually Val appears slightly mocking or else totally unreadable.

He's been off campus during the break between terms, visiting Larissa's family in Russia. When Themis mentioned vampires getting pulled from the Academy, I did wonder if it was Val and his twin sister, Tina. Relief flares inside me as I realize he's still here. I want to throw my arms around him and sob onto his shoulder like Fern did to Marguerite.

But Val led a bunch of other vampires to kill Nico's mom, Maddox. He didn't say so outright, but he didn't exactly deny it either. And Maddox was powerless at the time. Her ability to shift had been stripped as punishment for her murder of Larissa.

A long time ago Cassie warned me that vampires lived by their own code. She didn't mention, however, that revenge was such a cornerstone of that code.

I stick my hands in my pockets and just nod. "Yeah, I'm okay. Actually, I just found out they're gonna give Mavis an official trial. So that's good news."

Val frowns. "How is that good news? It'll be a circus and at the end, the gods will still kill her."

Yeah, that's exactly what I was afraid of—count on Val to reinforce my fears. But I refuse to agree with anyone predicting Mavis's death. "Maybe before then I'll figure out a way to bust her out."

Val shakes his head. "No way they'll let her escape a second time." Finally, Val seems to notice that his pessimistic attitude isn't helping. "Sorry, Edie. After everything with Larissa." His eyes go dark and I can see anger simmering there. "My parents were ready to transfer us, but Tina begged to stay. For her résumé. Everyone knows Underworld Academy is just a party school. She wants to be a vampire ambassador and those positions go to Mount Olympus graduates."

"Oh," I say, realizing how close I'd come to possibly

never seeing Val again. "And what about you? Did you want to stay?"

His eyes lock with mine. "This place is poison. But I've got to watch out for—"

"Tina," I cut in. Feeling disappointed, although I have no reason to be.

"No." Val's hand softly cups my cheek. I gasp from the cold and a puff of smoke escapes my mouth. "Not just Tina," he says.

"Edie!" From behind me, I hear Fern calling. I turn and the ice of Val's hand slips away. "Wait," I look back, but he's already gone.

Fern is out of breath as she approaches. For my sake— and Mavis's, too—she's been running herself ragged lately. Literally.

As one of the top healer students here, and one of the most likeable people on the planet, Fern has access to parts of the school that are closed off to me. Namely, Mavis's prison cell. Fern had volunteered to be the healer in charge of prisoners, and so for the last two weeks she's been allowed to go in everyday to assess Mavis's condition.

Fern tries to spare me the worst of it, but from the pained screams that sometimes escape the walls of the cells, it's obvious that the gods are doing more than just asking questions. Still, each day Mavis writes me a note telling me she's okay. And for me to be strong. And she ends it with a joke. Yesterday's was: "Why did the chewing gum cross the road?" She answers the joke the next day on the back of her newest note. At first I thought she was just trying to keep my spirits up, but then I realized this was a way for me to know the notes were coming in order and that she was the one writing them.

Now Fern gives me a hug and at the same time presses a

piece of paper into my skirt pocket. I knew she was a spy for the monsters, but I never knew how good she would be at it.

"I just heard the news about the trial," Fern says with a hopeful smile.

"And luau," I add wryly.

Her smile falters slightly. "Yes...but I think we can use that to our advantage as well. Tell Mr. Zee that the luau needs to be top-notch and have Merilee research and Themis order the proper supplies. We can drag it out for quite a while that way."

This is the dose of optimism I needed.

"Come on," I say to Fern, my spirits lifting as I hook my arm through hers. "Let's go tell everyone else the good news."

**4**

"Welcome back, students! I'm so happy to see all your smiling faces once more. Now, as you know, we've had some difficult times the last few months at Mount Olympus Academy. Let's not focus on the past, though. Instead, turn your young faces to the future. For many of you this is your last year at Mount Olympus and I can already see so many of those futures will be bright."

That's how Themis begins her fall term speech. She's definitely understating the problems by categorizing them as "difficult." Several students burned to death. Then there was the Spring Fling dance being invaded by monsters. And finally this summer's disastrous raid which left even more students dead. If things keep going this way, they're gonna need new brochures that read, "Mount Olympus Academy: We Sure Hope You Survive Until Graduation."

There are definitely fewer students at this all-campus speech than last term. Not just because of the deaths. I've heard that parents are pulling their kids out left and right. MOA was the premier school for paranormal offspring.

Being taught by actual gods is a pretty good selling point. Select students getting chosen for the gods' official army after graduation was the cherry on top. But a diploma isn't much good to a dead kid.

As Themis goes on about how things are totally gonna be super great and awesome from here on out, Fern sidles up to me and presses a piece of paper into my hand.

Speaking of Mr. Zee, as Themis wraps things up, he comes to the stage. His gait is a little unsteady, like a drunk wandering home. And he looks...wrong somehow. I squint and get a better look.

"Fern," I ask. "Is Mr. Zee wearing foundation?"

She takes a hard look herself, then has to cover a smile. "Oh my gods," she says. "He is crap at blending. His neck doesn't match his face."

Three healers accompany Mr. Zee. Metis, a goddess and the head healer, Hepa, and a snooty looking warlock I always try to avoid. Mr. Zee tugs a chain and Mavis stumbles on the dais behind him.

"No," I breathe.

Fern grabs my arm. "Don't freak out. You won't help Mavis or yourself."

I calm the fire rising in my belly. Mavis looks bruised and battered, but at least she's alive. She has a gold collar that glows eerily. Zee is using the chain like a leash, pulling her in. She falls to her knees before him. Nico stands behind her, his face stoic.

Apparently he's making up the credits he missed for the year he was imprisoned by doing an independent study class with Kratos. I've heard it's called, "How to Keep Someone Alive Until You're Ready to Kill Them." Tina was actually the one who told me. Although not gleefully, as she once would have. After she was sick over the summer, we sorta bonded. Also, like all the vampires, she hates Nico. So after telling me about the class, she added, "Whenever you decide to kill him, I'm in."

Themis grimaces as she stares at Mavis. "Honestly, is this necessary?" she asks.

"I'm not letting this traitor out of my sight," Mr. Zee says. He's not slurring his words as much, so he must not be sloshed. Maybe he's taking this seriously at last. "Not until her trial...ridiculous notion that that is. I should just fry her with a lightning bolt and have done with it." Or not. I gasp.

"He won't." Fern assures me. "There's too much pressure to do this the right way. He's just making a show of his power."

I will my thoughts to Mavis, to let her know I'm here and to try and give her strength. For a brief moment her eyes catch mine and I see a look of defiance before she bows her head again. Nico also catches my gaze and gives me a little nod. I force myself to nod back.

Mr. Zee orates loudly about the grand history of Mount Olympus and himself. Mostly himself. He uses the word "pure" so often it starts to lose meaning.

"Oh no, they're doing it now," Fern whispers.

"Doing what?"

Her eyes meet mine as she urgently pulls me closer. "All the Moggies are gonna be outed. If you even suspect you might be one, you need to get out of here. Now."

My heart speeds up. I honestly don't know if I'm a Moggy or not.

My parentage is a huge mess. I was raised by two Mount Olympus Students who took me and Mavis because our lives were in danger. I still don't know why. But those students weren't my birth parents. I still haven't been able to figure out who my bio-dad is, but my mother's portrait hangs in the Hall of the Dead. Adrianna Aspostolos died in childbirth. Having me.

Adrianna was a shifter, but not a dragon. There's never been a dragon before me. So it's pretty certain that some sort of weird mix created me. Which would, in fact, make me a Moggy. I don't even understand why the whole Moggy thing even matters, except that Mr. Zee has a bug up his butt about it. As the head of Mount Olympus Academy, and king of the gods, Mr. Zee lives by his own rules. And then makes the rest of us live by them too.

Frantically, I crane my neck, looking back toward the two exits. Two vampires stand at each door. Almost as if they're blocking them. Each is shadowed by a healer.

I suck in a breath. This was planned.

I lean toward Fern. "There's no way out. What's gonna happen?"

"A magic spell. Only a select few have been working on it. Somehow it will detect and mark all Moggies. I'm not sure how."

I bite my lip, thinking hard. "Could I shield myself somehow?"

Fern grips my hands. "Yes. That's it!"

"Why is there so much whispering over here?" Greg asks, sidling up next to me. Cassie is behind him.

"Is it about Mavis?" Greg looks to her on the dais, where she kneels in humility.

"It's disgraceful," Cassie says. "She hasn't even had her trial yet and Zee is parading her around in chains."

"No, Edie's in trouble and we need a distraction," Fern explains. "Now!"

"Oh!" Cassie's eyes widen. "I volunteer."

I can't help but smile despite Mr. Zee's voice growing louder and angrier as he launches into the evils of Moggies.

Cassie was in bad shape after being kidnapped and then witnessing the slaughter of monsters during our mission to retrieve her. But after helping rescue that baby manticore, she seems like her old self. But even more so, because now she's got this whole social justice warrior attitude.

"And Greg will help too," she adds.

"Of course, I'll help, Edie," he agrees with no hesitation. Cassie grabs his hand and pulls him through the crowd.

"Hurry!" Fern hisses after them.

Nervously, we turn our attention to Mr. Zee.

"There's been enough student deaths. I guess. That's what Themis says and honestly, I haven't had time to personally look at the numbers myself." He blinks a few times and seems to lose focus, gazing out into the middle distance. Hepa steps forward with a cup of ambrosia. Grabbing it from her, Mr. Zee gulps it down greedily. When he finishes there's a new light in his eyes. He tosses the goblet over his shoulder and Hepa runs to fetch it, shooting Mr. Zee a nasty glare.

Jordan gives a wolf howl as she bends over to get it, which is really inappropriate since he's a panther. He's been trying to get back into her good graces ever since the no-interspecies dating rule last semester made him question whether or not he should be attracted to her. Which in turn, had made her question if she liked him at all. Now that she was most definitely unavailable, Jordan was hopelessly in love.

"We will not kill our own students," Mr. Zee says, as if that were somehow redeeming. "Even if they're Moggies and as such a threat to us all. Myself included."

There's a gasp from the crowd. The prophecy hasn't yet become common knowledge. We got the scoop early only because Cassie's mom, Merilee, is head of Archives and the one who discovered it.

"Yes, an ancient prophecy has come to light that forewarns of my own death at the hands of a Moggy." There are murmurs and shaking heads. Breathing hard, Mr. Zee grips the sides of the lectern tightly. "It's alarming, I know. Which is why we need to know who the Moggies are so that they can be watched at all times. I hereby deputize every pure-blooded student to stop a Moggy if they are acting suspiciously. If you see something, kill something." He clears his throat loudly.

"If you see something, say something," Themis corrects, her voice easily carrying.

Mr. Zee swivels to glare at her. "You say too much, woman." He turns back to the crowd and the sudden movement seems to make him dizzy. "There's too much talk and not enough action. The Moggies in our midst cannot stay hidden. We will have their names. We will know their faces. Starting—"

"I love you, Greg. I love you and I don't care who says it's wrong!" Cassie stands on a chair in the middle of the room. Greg in bat form flaps around her. "Kiss me, you batty boy!"

Greg squeaks, shifts into human form, and throws himself at Cassie trying to look passionate. They collide awkwardly.

"My nose!" I hear her yelp in pain. And then they both topple off the chair and disappear into the crowd.

At the podium, Mr. Zee's chin rests on his fist. Themis is at his side, whispering something in his ear.

"Now," Fern says to me. Chanting, she circles her arms around me and raises them over my head and then brings them all the way down to the floor at my feet. A feeling of warmth envelops me. Like I've been wrapped in a fuzzy blanket.

Meanwhile, Mr. Zee roughly shoves Themis away. "We're doing it now! It's *my life* at stake!" He gestures to the waiting healers behind him. "What are you waiting for? Do the thing!"

I'm safe, but panic fills me regardless. "Fern," I grip her arm. "What about Tina? And Val?" Fern's eyes widen a little. She knows that Tina is a Moggy after last semester when Tina caught the shifter plague. And since Val and Tina are twins, I'm sure she did the math and figured Val was a Moggy as well. But we never talked about it.

She gives me hand a quick squeeze. "Stay here. I'll try to reach them."

I watch as Fern begins to push through the increasingly agitated crowd, feeling helpless. At least Val and Tina are together; I can see them with a few other vampires at the other end of the room. I try to catch their attention. Tina is standing straight and tall, staring at what's happening on stage with her chin lifted high. I recognize it as her battle stance. She knows she's about to be outed.

Val, however, turns. His eyes meet mine.

"Run!" I mouth at him.

In response he shakes his head lightly, while a mocking smile lifts the right corner of his mouth. Then he turns forward again, his back straight as Tina's.

I can't see Fern anywhere in the crowd and it's not looking like she'll make it in time.

On stage, the healers each uncap a jar. The ones blocking the exits do the same. Almost immediately, a glowing green mist is everywhere. Around me, students breathe it in and then exhale a darker shade of green.

Except some exhale red. The color hangs in the air above them, like an arrow pointing at its victim.

Both Tina and Val have red overhead. They lock eyes, and hold hands. Exposed now, for everyone to see. I know Val—he's never been as absorbed with the (false) tale of how pure their vampire blood is. But Tina was obsessed with proving how pure she was...even though she knew she wasn't. With shifter and nymph blood in both of them, the twins have been found out.

Beside me a breathless Fern reappears. "I'm sorry, Edie. I couldn't reach them in time."

"Thanks for trying," I say, as we scan the room, seeing who else has the red over their heads.

I count one other vampire. Several shifters. And a handful of healers. Beside me Fern doesn't look surprised. "Witches have always had more of a free love type of life-style," she says.

The green mist surrounds Zee in a swirl, seems to caress Nico, then wafts over to Mavis, turning red above her head. Shit. I had hoped...but I don't know if Mavis is my bio sister or not. We know we have different bio moms, but have no clue who either of our dads are...or if they're the same person.

Zee glances over at her. "Not very surprising. Moggies can't be trusted."

The mist is already starting to dissipate—the red and green both.

"That wasn't so bad. Is that it?" I ask. Sure, those students will probably be treated poorly by the more enthusiastic Zee supporters but...

Even as Fern shakes her head, a new god takes the stage. Artemis. She's actually one of my favorite teachers. She's tough, but fair. But right now, she has a flock of ugly birds behind her. They look like mutant vultures, small and twisted and evil. About the size of a large parrot, their beaks are bronze and the feathers have a metallic gleam.

"Oh gods," Fern says. "Stymphalian birds."

"Not a thing I know, Fern."

Her eyes meet mine. "Man-eating birds. Artemis keeps them as pets, because, well because...Artemis."

"There she is, my favorite bird lady," Mr. Zee booms. "Quickly now, before the trails disappear." He gestures to Artemis.

She strides forward and then with a single uplifted hand, the birds take to the air. Each one finds the lingering remnants of red and hovers over it.

"Moggies," There is a note of regret in her voice. "These birds will be your constant companions for the rest of your time here. They will do you no harm so long as you obey curfew, stay within your assigned areas, and never display a threatening attitude to any gods or your more pure students."

Voices of outrage swell, with ones raised in jubilation mixed in as well.

Yep. It's gonna be another great semester at Mount Olympus Academy.

## 5

Turns out Stymphalian birds shit. A lot.

I get back to my dorm room to find my roommate, Tina, sitting on her bed, staring down the bird who is perched on the footboard. Just as I walk in the door, the bird lets loose another stream of gluey gray shit.

"Oh my gods," I say, covering my nose. "That's awful!"

Tina doesn't even respond; she's giving the bird the stink eye. But he's definitely winning any competition involving stink.

True to its mission, it doesn't even look at me. He's honed in on Tina, his eyes locked onto her for the rest of her time at the Academy. The only living thing in the room that even acknowledges my presence is Vee—Tina's self-aware Venus Fly Trap plant. She turns her head towards me, then back to Tina, clearly alarmed at her owner's predicament.

"It'll be okay, Vee," I say to it, walking over to the window. I crack it to let some of the stench out, and I swear Vee gives me an up-nod of thanks.

"Did you have much trouble getting back to the dorm?" I hazard the question.

I saw more than a few students with Stymphalian shadows getting razzed as they left the assembly. Tina hasn't exactly been the friendliest vampire on campus, either. She touted her blood like it was ambrosia, all in an effort to cover up her true Moggy identity. Even if she escaped some ribbing today, she'll have to face it in the morning, for the first day of classes.

"Hey," I try again, even though she didn't answer my first question. "I think I'm going to go down to the Archives, see if Merilee has any more information about this prophecy. Wanna come? Knowledge is power, right?"

Tina seems to believe that the silent treatment is power, because she gives me nothing. Not even a shake of the head. I've done my best to help her out in the past, even covering for her when she came down with the shifter plague—which as a full-blooded vampire she *should* have been resistant to. And she still can't even acknowledge my presence? Whatever.

I slam our door on the way out. It reverberates in the hall, followed by the sound of a very large Stymphalian turd splatting against the floor.

Down the hall, Cassie's door pops open. "What's going on?"

"Nothing new," I tell her. "Just reinforcing my very strong roomie bond with Tina. I was just going to come get you. Feel like visiting your mom?"

"Yes!" Cassie actually does a fist pump. "I love my mom!"

There's a pang in my stomach at her words, a reminder of what I've lost. The memory potion that my mom took means she doesn't know who I am anymore, even if I can remember perfectly. And my bio mom...I never even knew her.

Cassie links arms with me as we make our way to the Archives. "So, any big Moggy surprises today? Other than Val and Tina, I mean. That one...woah!"

She whistles and makes a motion, slicing her hand above her head. Cassie's been raised her entire life on campus, and her attempts at real-world interaction often go this way.

"No," I correct her. "That's *over her head*. Like...she didn't get that joke, it went right over her head. I think you want *mind blown*." I mimic an explosion on either side of my temples.

"Oh, definitely," Cassie says, doing it back at me, but still whistling instead of making a bomb noise.

"Thank you, for the distraction today, with Greg," I say.

She nods. "I just wish we could have helped all the Moggies."

"How's your face?" I ask. "It looked like Greg headbutted you pretty hard."

"It's fine. Fern fixed it up." She touches her nose as if to check that there's no pain. "He felt so bad about it he kept apologizing. He really is sweet."

I look at Cassie, who has a slight smile. Maybe it's time for Cassie to move on from grieving Darcy. Maybe Greg is just the boy to help her do it. I push that to the back of my mind as we arrive at the Archives.

Merilee is nowhere to be found. Actually, it's hard to locate just about anything here, even the Archivist. Merilee's filing system is more of a stacking system. Piles of paper surround us, small unimportant slips of paper like doctor's excuses from class resting on top of *Annals of the Histories of the War: Volume 1 Where Monsters Went Wrong*. All of this might make it seem like Merilee is scatterbrained, but the truth is exactly the opposite. She can remember everything she's ever read, and files it away in her mind. She doesn't need to refer to any of this stuff; all anyone has to do is ask her. Merilee figured out a long time ago that her skill made her irreplaceable on campus, and how to use that to her advantage—and Cassie's.

When Merilee dies, all of her knowledge will pass to Cassie, guaranteeing a job for Cassie here on campus. She'll never have to wander into the real world, which—let's be honest—would eat her alive. Unfortunately, that's also why she was kidnapped by a splinter cell of monsters, to try and gain that knowledge. At least they never got a chance to hurt Merilee.

"Mom?" Cassie calls, her voice soaring out above piles of paper and stacks of books. "Where are you?"

There's a sudden flutter, and some loose pieces of paper float through the air. Merilee comes around the corner, red-eyed and crying. She's followed by a Stymphalian bird.

"Mom!" Cassie cries out, going to Merilee. The older woman sobs into her daughter's shoulder.

"I'm sorry, honey," she says. "I didn't want you to know."

"Wait," I say. "But if you're a Moggy, why isn't Cassie one, too?"

Merilee shakes her head. "Cassie's dad was a seer, like me. As long as your immediate parents were the same, you're safe."

"I don't care that you're a Moggy," Cassie says, rubbing her mom's shoulder. "I'm proud to be your daughter, so I wouldn't care if I were one, too."

"Don't say that!" Merilee lifts her head suddenly, eyes sharp behind the tears. "The birds are only the beginning. Zee has marked us, publicly humiliated us. Who knows what will come next?"

Nothing good, that's for sure.

I wander away into the stacks, letting Merilee and Cassie have a moment alone. All this talk of blood and Moggies has me wondering about my own parentage. I can still feel the presence of Fern's spell around me, like a soft film of cotton that I'm moving through. But it's fading. If Mr. Zee employs any further experiments to test for Moggies and I'm caught unaware... I shiver, and my wings erupt as a bright silver. I wrap them around myself for comfort. It's better for me to know for sure what I am.

Pages continue to settle around me, blown in the draft from the bird's wings. They waft down as the now unfortunately familiar smell of Stymphalian bird poop fills the air. I snatch a piece as it drifts past my face.

*Some cat shifters have secretly been growing catnip in their dorm rooms...*

Ugh. Boring. It's about to be legalized in the shifter community anyway.

I sift through some random piles, but find nothing more interesting than a student's musings on whether Hermes was sleeping with Themis or not, and a bulletin from the Pure Prairie Vampire League: Mavens of the Midwest meeting.

No, if I want to learn more about my own parentage in this mess, I'm going to have to go to the source. That means interrupting Cassie, Merilee, and her Stymphalian shadow.

I wander back through the piles, following the easily identifiable scent of the bird. Merilee is drying her eyes, and Cassie is patting her mother's shoulder. Again, I feel the stab of pain that I don't think will ever dull. I've lost both my parents, and the bio-mom I never knew.

Time to find out who my real father was.

"Merilee?" I ask. "Can you recall the exact wording of

the information we found regarding the day my dad fled campus?"

"Of course," she says, wiping her nose and then tapping her temple, like she's clicking on a link.

"*Student Daniel Evans fled the grounds last night. He carries with him two secrets that could ruin the Academy forever, if their existence was known. Steps must be taken.*"

I wince a little when she says my dad's name, still remembering his face as Leviathan, a water monster, swept him away to his death, all because of a jealous love for my mother.

"I'm sorry, dear," Merilee says. "I've cross-referenced his name, but no more mention of him, your mother, or the secrets they left with have been found."

"I'm pretty sure the secrets were me, and my sister Mavis," I tell her. "But I don't understand why our existence could ruin the Academy."

"Because you're a Moggy?" Cassie hazards.

"She could be," Merilee agrees. "But just being a Moggy wouldn't ruin the Academy. Until recently, Moggies were tolerated on campus. No, there's got to be something much more sinister in Edie's past."

"Great," I say.

"Being a Moggy is sinister enough these days," Cassie says, giving Merilee's bird a glare. "At least you don't have one of these tailing you."

"No, I've got one pooping where I sleep, though," I tell her. "It is beyond gross."

"Stay with me," Cassie offers. "I don't mind."

"Thank you. If it gets to be too much I will, but I don't want Tina to think I've deserted her." If everyone were half as good-hearted as Cassie the world would be a much better place.

"I wish I could help you out more, Edie," Merilee tells me.

"What about the prophecy concerning Mr. Zee? The one that said he'd die by his own child, a Moggy. What were the exact words?" Cassie asks.

Merilee taps the other side of her forward, her eyeballs sliding back and forth under the lids while she speaks.

*"He who throws the lightning will die by one born of his own diluted blood."*

"That's it?" Cassie asks. "That's like, twelve words. Twelve words and he's got the whole campus in an uproar?"

"It's fifteen," Merilee corrects, eyeballs rolling as she counts. "But remember, it's Mr. Zee. He's a god. He's *the* god. There are some ancient texts that refer to him as the very root of the entire universe. Any threat to the safety of the gods is taken seriously."

I snort. "So seriously that they created an entire Academy in order to draw young paranormals to fight their battles for them."

"Exactly," Merilee nods in my direction.

"But can gods die?" I ask. "I mean, I know Mr. Zee is rattled but..."

I'd seen Hermes heal himself from a fairly serious burn once. The blink of an eye and his skin was fresh, eyebrows grown back in. It had taken only seconds.

"It's...difficult," Merilee admits. "In order to kill a god they'd have to be weakened first, drained of some of their power and faculties."

Cassie locks eyes with me and I know we're thinking the same thing.

Mr. Zee has always been a little off, but lately his behavior bordered on the mentally ill. And he'd been wearing some sort of stage makeup during the big production where the Moggies were identified. I'm willing to bet that under that foundation, his skin is as gray as my wings are right now.

I'm pretty sure somebody is poisoning Mr. Zee.

And I've got a good guess who it is.

## 6

W hen I arrive at Themis's office, Hepa is leaving. This is the second time we've run into each other here. Weird.

I haven't really seen her much lately; she's been cloistered with the other healers, working on their secret project. Not so secret now—it was obviously the fog that outed all the Moggies.

"Hepa," I say when she tries to walk by me. I grab her wrist and she spins back to me, looking...ashamed.

"I didn't want to do it," she tells me. "I hate all this Nazi bullshit. I just...I have to stay on Metis's good side." Metis is the goddess in charge of the healing arts, mother to Athena and, weirdly, Zee's ex-wife. The family tree of the Greek gods is incredibly complicated, and terribly violent. A healer who wants to do well after the Academy will need Metis on her side.

"I understand," I tell her. "We're all trying to get by."

She looks grateful. "If I can do anything to help you...or Mavis."

"Thanks," I tell her. As Hepa turns to go, I add, "Hey, what's with all the visits to Themis lately?"

Hepa goes still for a moment, but then forces a sickly smile onto her face. "Just getting some guidance on my schedule for next term. I like to think ahead."

And with that she whirls around and quickly strides away.

Okay, definitely weird. But right now, there's so much else already going on, I shrug it off and push into Themis's office. As I do, I make my own promise to myself. I'm not leaving here without answers.

She looks up and I'm about to go full out dragon on her when I see the look in her eyes. Sadness, regret, and a little fear. She rushes to me and enfolds me in a hug.

"Edie, I'm so sorry Mavis is being treated this way."

Despite myself I relax into her hold. I think of Mavis being paraded around like a pet on a leash, the barely hidden bruises on her skin, the green fog turning red as she inhaled it.

"Why is he doing it?" I ask. "Why torture her?"

"To show he can," she says, releasing me. "The collar keeps her from shifting and the chain is impossible to break." She goes to sit behind her desk. The scales she usually keeps immaculately balanced are askew. They're supposed to indicate how the war between the monsters and gods is going, but right now they are precariously tipped in favor of the monsters. With everything going on here, the war has been sidelined.

Themis follows my eye, and sighs heavily.

"The monsters have regained territory that we drove them out of. I shouldn't even say they've regained it; we didn't even put up a fight. With enrollment perilously low, we can't afford to send students on missions that might prove fatal. And with the new threat on Mr. Zee's life, well..."

"He's more concerned about his own skin than anything," I finish for her.

"Things at Mount Olympus Academy have not been right for some time," she tells me. "I try to keep it balanced. This Academy is my life. But Zee is so reckless. He's always followed his impulses. If we could just get him to step down, the Academy could thrive. But that will never happen."

I remember during summer term, at the faculty dinner when Themis slipped something into his wine glass. And Hepa had handed him his ambrosia on the stage the day that he outed the Moggies. His memory loss, his ashy appearance, his lack of appetite, his impotence.

"You're poisoning him." It's not a question but Themis answers anyway. "And Hepa is helping."

"Yes, in a way. I'm decreasing his power. I've been doing it for years. It makes him less predatory, more docile. But with this prophecy, he's gone full blown Zeus. He's paranoid. He's distrustful. He's suspicious of everyone. Only those who absolutely have proven their trust can get near him."

"You want him dead?" That one is a question.

"No, of course not!" Themis actually covers her mouth for a moment at the thought. "I don't want anyone dead, least of all the leader of the gods. Think of the chaos that would ensue! Minor gods would run amok. There'd be earthquakes and volcanoes and gods know what else. But I would like him to leave the Academy. Step down, if you will. Maybe go into permanent retirement at the real Mount Olympus, in Greece. Wherever he goes, he's done more than enough harm here at the Academy."

"What can I do to help?" I ask. "I've heard the prophecy.

The one about Zee's diluted blood coming back to kill him. I can try to find out who it is. If he's faced with that threat—

combined with his weakening powers—maybe he'd go away."

*And if he goes away*, I add silently to myself. *Mavis has a better chance of being freed.*

Themis leans over her desk, her hands clasped. "Edie, do you really want to help?"

"Yes!" I practically shout. "If it will help Mavis. If it will get Zee gone."

She sits back. "Zee has always had an eye for mortal girls," she tells me. "Most of the male gods do."

"Yeah, I know. That's why you told him I might be a Moggy, so that he wouldn't be interested in me." Even a good-looking pair of legs isn't enough to get Zee past his Moggy-hatred.

"About twenty years ago, Hermes got a young shifter pregnant. I hid that pregnancy and took the baby, caring for Bella's child as my own."

"Wait..." Mind reeling, I remember the portraits in the Hall of the Dead. "Bella Demopoulous was Mavis's mother," I say aloud, piecing it together. "Are you telling me that Hermes is Mavis's *father*?"

But Themis continues. "After Mavis was born, I spoke with Zee. I strongly argued that students were off-limits to the gods. Not only because of the moral reasoning— teachers should never put a student in that position—but also because these demi-god births are always hard on the mothers. They often die.

"We don't allow students to become pregnant; that's why we make all our students use magical birth control. But that doesn't protect against a god's...seed. Zee was aware that Hermes had fathered a child on the student and that the mother had not survived the birth. But he also thought the baby died."

It's all making sense now. The puzzle pieces coming into place.

"I wasn't naïve. I knew that Zee had his own"—she clears her throat— "*dealings* with students. But I thought after speaking with him that he could control himself. But it happened again." She raises her eyes to mine, her stare burning.

"Another student pregnant. Another poor girl dead in childbirth. Another baby for me to hide."

I shake my head, an uneasy feeling in my stomach. "No..."

"Edie," Themis tells me, "that student was Adrianna Aspostolos."

"No," I say, backing away until my heels hit the wall.

Themis picks up a rock from her desk. It's the same one she had me hold the first time I was in this room. It showed me my inner dragon. And scared the hell out of me. I wasn't ready to handle that information yet.

There are some undeniable parallels to this current situation. "What will I see if I touch it?" I ask Themis.

"Only the truth," she answers.

I take a deep breath, and hold out my hands, receiving the rock from Themis.

The room spins and I feel dizzy as a darkness settles around me, swirling until I see something other than these walls. It's Adrianna, my birth mother, in her dorm room, holding a pregnancy test. Mr. Zee suddenly appears behind her, and she whips around, hiding the test behind her back. His arms go around her, his robes falling off his well-muscled chest. She drops the stick, kicking it under her desk as she leans into him, her head tilted back, ready to meet his kiss.

That vision rolls and changes, showing me the same scene—Adrianna in her room. But this time she's sitting at the desk, writing madly, tears falling onto the ink, smearing it. I peer over her shoulder, anxious to catch the words: *Metis, I've found myself in some trouble, and fear I will need the help of a master healer in about six months' time...*

One arm is curled protectively around her stomach, where a bulge is just visible. That pregnancy will kill her. That pregnancy is me.

I drop the stone back onto Themis's desk.

"Just for the record, that stone is an asshole."

"Well, yes, that's quite possibly true. It was one of Hermes's little inventions." She pauses and then adds with a significant look, "And you are apparently one of Zee's little inventions."

I bury my head in my hands. "I don't want this."

"You are his daughter," she tells me firmly. "And you have the power to threaten his life."

## 7

With my thoughts and emotions in an uproar, I've still got to get to class. Campus has been a mess. A low enrollment rate this term has all the gods on edge, and I don't want Artemis using me as the example for what happens to students who are tardy.

As I rush to the clearing where we're meeting, Artemis is already calling the class to attention. It's an interdisciplinary class, so spies are mixed in with the trackers and the assassins.

Artemis addresses us. "You'll remember from spring term the exercises we did pairing a tracker with an assassin. This term we will take that same exercise to the next level. Now quickly pair off so we can begin."

I wave to Greg where he and Cassie are standing off by themselves. Greg and I worked together last semester and while we were never top of the class, we made a pretty good team. But Greg doesn't even seem to notice me hurrying toward him. I see him and Cassie point at each other and realize that this time the two of them are pairing up. I stop, suddenly feeling like a third wheel.

What exactly is going on between Cassie and Greg anyway?

An arm comes around the back of my neck and suddenly I'm pulled snugly up against Nico. "The two of us teaming up is almost unfair to everyone else," he says with a laugh.

I pull away. "Yeah, you're probably right. Let's split up."

He grins at me. "Nah. Let's show them how it's done."

I swallow back the scream building inside me and turn to see who everyone else has partnered up with. Of course, my eyes go to Val first. I don't even need to scan the crowd for him; I could feel his eyes on me as Nico pulled me close.

Now I meet those eyes. Val said that he's watching out for me and even though I'm an independent woman with an even more independent dragon on standby inside of me, it's nice to know that he's got my back.

Except now I realize that having Val and Nico stare daggers at each other with me in the middle isn't really doing anything to alleviate the on-campus tensions. I've already heard rumors that Nico's been going around asking shifters to choose sides: us or the vamps.

It's common knowledge that the vamps were responsible for Maddox's death. Merilee told me and Cassie it wasn't too long ago that much of the warring took place on campus—between vamps and shifters. They were like rival gangs fighting, each claiming their own turf. Themis worked hard to bring both sides together, but now with these new tensions, it seems impossible that everyone will continue to get along.

"Does everyone have a partner?" Artemis demands, thankfully before Nico and Val go for each other's throats.

Someone clears their throat and then I hear Tina quietly say, "I don't."

She stands tall with her head high, but there's no missing the red blush coloring her usually freakishly white complexion.

Val steps forward, "Go with Jordan, I'll work alone."

"Yeah, me and you, Tina!" Jordan happily agrees.

"No." Tina holds a hand out. "Go back to my brother. I'm not having a pity partner."

Jordan lopes back around only to stop again when Val says in a low voice, "Tina, just take him."

I've never seen tensions between the two of them before. They always seem to be in sync—even if they disagree with what the other is doing, they understand it.

But now Tina looks ready to kill her twin. Shoving Jordan aside, she stomps toward him.

"Hey, excuse me, I'm sorry, I'm late." The tension is broken by the high-pitched voice of a young boy crossing the clearing to stand before Artemis. The kid is tiny, even smaller than Greg. And he seems to still be in the midst of puberty as his voice cracks on the last word. "My roommate told me class was at the woods on the west side of campus, but I discovered there are no woods on the west side of—"

Nico growls low and soft in the back of his throat. Almost like a warning.

The boy stiffens, obviously hearing it. He throws a glance at Nico and then turns back to Themis. "That is, oh, um—look! There's my roommate right there." He visibly gulps as his eyes briefly meet Nico's. "Hey, Nico. I, ah, probably misunderstood him—"

"Fine," Artemis cuts him off with a wave of her hand. "You're with Tina. Don't be late again." She looks down at the boy. "Small, right?"

"Ahem, uh, Little actually. Chester Little."

"Chicken little," Nico snickers.

The tips of Chester's ears go red. "Rooster. I'm a rooster shifter."

Eesh. I want to send the poor kid a sympathetic glance. That's a tough card to draw, but to give him credit, he seems proud of it. I went through a period of time when I first arrived at MOA dreadfully afraid that I was an ostrich shifter. Bird shifters don't have a ton of options, but that particular one turned me right off. A rooster isn't that bad, by comparison.

But Nico won't let it go. "Then why do you look like you're about to lay an egg? You claim you're a rooster—are you sure you're not a weak little hen?"

"Whoa, man." Jordan says. "Don't equate femininity with weakness. That's just wrong."

"Yeah." To my shock, Tina strides forward and puts a hand on Chester's shoulder. He takes one look up at her and his Adam's apple visibly rises and falls with a gigantic gulp. "C'mon, Rooster, let's kick some ass."

Grabbing hold of his shirt, she drags him to her place in the circle of students surrounding Artemis, as Chester protests, "Actually my name is—"

"Nico." Artemis pins him with a look. "I don't know whose bright idea it was to put a wolf and bird in the same dorm room, but let me make one thing clear to you. I have a fondness for winged creatures. I am, in fact, having a very hard time with having my beloved Stymphalians loaned out. I am also a woman. And as Jordan put it in a moment of uncharacteristic wisdom, do not mistake femininity for weakness. I'd have thought your mother would've taught you that."

Nico holds Artemis's eye contact throughout this speech, but at the mention of his mother, he visibly wilts.

"No, ma'am," he agrees.

"Good." Artemis turns her attention to the rest of us. "Now that's settled. Each of you will go to the chest"—she jerks her head in the direction of a huge wooden box filled with smaller wooden boxes—"and choose one container per team. When I give the signal, you will open it. An animal will leap free. This is not a real animal, so I don't want to hear any moaning from any of the cruelty-free vegetarians in the crowd. This is a magically simulated animal created for the purpose of this exercise. Staying together, you will track the animal and when it is cornered, the assassin will kill it and return its body to me. Any questions?" Artemis waits half a second, and then claps her hands. "No? Good. Begin!"

Everyone rushes toward the chest, including Nico. Snagging my hand, he drags me behind him. "C'mon, Edie. You know your bitch of a roommate is gonna want to show us both up."

"Actually," I start to say, but then realize it's probably not helpful to tell Nico that Tina and I get along pretty well now. But still, I have no intention of letting him run this show. I dig my heels into the ground, grinding us to a halt.

"Wait, Nico."

"What?" He snaps, fur covering his face and teeth elongating.

I snatch my hand back from him. "Wow. Lose it much? What's going on with you? You're super on edge. And the way you're picking on your new roommate. I don't get it. He's a shifter. You like shifters." I pause and then add, "He doesn't have a bird, so he's not a Moggy. So that can't be why you don't like him."

Nico hunches his shoulders. "Yeah, my roommate is pure-blooded. He's got a whole brood of chicken and rooster family back home. His parents write every day, these tear-soaked letters about how they miss him. And they send care packages weekly. With enough food to feed twenty little chickens."

Oh. I understand it now. It's gotta feel like salt in the wound to have this new roommate accidentally flaunting his loving family while Nico is still grieving his mom.

"I get it," I tell him. "Sometimes when I see Cassie with Merilee, I feel so jealous and angry and sad all at once."

Nico scoffs. "I'm not sad. I'm pissed off and I'm gonna make the vampires pay."

And there's the Nico I'm used to. "Okay, fine." I walk toward the chest, but Nico grabs my hand again.

"Edie, wait." He looks around and then pulls me further away from everyone else. Speaking in a low voice, he says, "Just so you know, I don't care about the Moggy thing. I know you're probably one too. I don't know how you avoided being assigned a Stymphalian bird, and I don't care. I would never out you. I mean, if being a Moggy makes a dragon like you...well, what would happen if a werewolf and dragon mated, right?" He smiles so sweetly and hopefully, I forget for a moment how hopeful he is. Then he adds, "I still want to marry you, Edie. Once you're done mourning your traitor sister, I think we should—"

I shove him away, not bothering to disguise my anger. "Traitor or not, she's still my sister, Nico. And she's not dead yet." Stalking over the box, I snatch up a silvery-grey smaller one and hold it out to Nico. "Let's just get this done already."

Nico shakes his head and then gives me the puppy dog eyes. "Edie, I'm sorry. We'll wait until after Mavis is de—er, after the trial—to discuss our future. Okay?"

Remembering that I can't afford to have Nico as an enemy, I force myself to nod. "Okay."

He jerks his chin at the box. "You open it."

The box shakes and trembles in my hands; whatever's inside is rearing and ready to go. I flip the latch, the top pops open, and a little face with a pointed nose stares back at me.

"Oh my gods," I say.

It is quite possibly the most adorable thing I've ever seen. A tiny fox with the same silvery gray fur as the box that held it. Opening its mouth, the fox emits a tiny little yelp and then leans forward and—

"Ouch!" I slap a hand over my face. "It bit my nose."

With that opening volley the fox jumps out of the box and disappears beneath a bush and into the forest.

Already shifted, Nico is on its heels. "Edie, let's go!" He yips over his shoulder.

Unable to keep up in human form, I shift and rise above the treetops. It's hard to stay with Nico as the forest covering is dense. But he's good at finding clearings so I can stay nearby or howling when I lose him for too long.

In the thrill of the chase, I lose sense of time. And I forget how awful Nico is. Right now we are a team with a common purpose.

Finally, Nico herds the fox into a clearing he'd already passed through several times. The fox is running low on speed, and Nico has expertly taken it through this spot before—one with an opening in the foliage that a dragon can easily dive through to snatch its prey. The fox passes directly below me and in a moment, I'm upon it, snatching the tiny bit of fluff up in my one of my talons.

It immediately goes limp, playing dead. But I'm not fooled. One squeeze and the hunt will be over. Our assignment finished.

Instead, I shift back into my human form. With the fox in a hand instead of a talon, I can feel its little heart beating furiously. I look down into its small face, trying to remind myself it's not real. But it feels real. It looks real. The fox lets out a pitiful cry. It sounds real too.

"Edie," Nico says. He's also shifted back and waits at my elbow.

"Just give me a minute," I say.

He comes around so he's standing in front of me, also looking down at the fox in my hand. "I know you didn't kill the baby monster," he says.

I'm so shocked I almost drop the fox. "What?"

Nico looks right at me. "I know. I saw Cassie run away with it."

"But..." I shake my head. "Why didn't you...?"

He turns away. "My mother..." He hesitates for a long moment before finally saying in a rough voice, "Wasn't right about everything." He stands with his shoulders bowed as if the concession was painful.

"She thought the only way to win the war was to kill all monsters. But that's crazy. There's too many of them. What we need is for the monsters to fear us, but also to know we can be compassionate rulers when necessary." He spins, turning back to me, the fanatical gleam I've come to know so well making his one eye bright. "You instinctively under-stood that, Edie."

I stare at Nico, wondering how he can see an Edie totally different from the girl who stands in front of him. Partially, I've misled him, but mostly, I've simply allowed him to believe what he wants, to imagine I'm his perfect girl, the kind he'd be proud to bring home to his mother.

I open my hands, releasing the fox. It hesitates and then leaps to freedom.

The tiny fox takes two leaps and then Nico's paw comes down on its back.

The snap of its spine is no louder than that of a twig

breaking underfoot. And yet my whole body jolts as if a gun went off near my ear.

Nico grabs the lifeless body in his mouth and drops it at my feet. He grins up at me with his friendly doggy smile. "Sorry, Edie, my fault for distracting you with all that talk. But no worries, I got it. That's why we make a great team. Right?"

I don't trust myself to answer, so shifting, I gently scoop the fox's body into a talon and lift off into the sky.

**8**

------------

I can't get the image of Adrianna—my mother—writing
that letter to Metis out of my mind. Her hand resting
over her belly, the absolute fear on her face.

She knew she might die giving birth to the child of a
god...but she took the chance and did it anyway. She chose
to have me. I've been wrestling with that so much that I've
zoned out. I'm so far lost in my own thoughts it takes the
smell of a fresh Stymphalian turd to zap me out of it.

"Oh my gods," Tina moans from her own bed, pulling a
pillow over her face to block the smell. "When will it end?"

I'm thinking it won't end until Mr. Zee steps down as the
head of the Academy, and about to say so, when Cassie and
Hepa burst through the door. They're followed by Fern and
Marguerite, their faces red, their gait suspiciously awkward.

"Are you..." I hesitate to even say it, but then Cassie goes
down hard, landing on her hands and knees, barely missing
the bird poo. She giggles.

"Guys...I almost ate shit. Like, literally." Hepa thinks this
is the most hilarious thing ever, and bursts out with a giant
guffaw. I don't think I've ever heard her laugh before. Fern

and Marguerite help Cassie to her feet, though they almost fall a few times before they get her upright.

"Yep," Tina mutters from under her pillow. "They're drunk."

Marguerite and Fern pop onto Tina's bed, and Marguerite—a fellow vampire, and therefore bold enough to challenge Tina's crappy mood—pulls the pillow off her head.

"Where's that pretty pout I know so well?" she asks, pulling the edges of Tina's mouth down, then back up into a forced smile. I have to laugh, as Cassie and Hepa join me on my mattress, handing over the bottle. I'd never considered the option of just manually making Tina smile.

"What's in it?" I ask, looking down at the bottle.

Cassie giggles. "It's ambrosia! We lifted it from the kitchens. It's watered d—" She hiccups. "Down," she finishes. "Safe for human consumption."

Which is a good thing, because if humans drank the nectar of the gods straight, it would probably drop us to the floor in a second. Maybe even melt our brains. Come to think of it, I don't think I'd mind too much if my brain melted right now. At least it would get Adrianna's tears out of my mind.

Fern puts her arm around Marguerite, and Marguerite puts her arm around Tina, pulling her into a sitting position. "Look Tina," Marguerite says. "You've always been a bitch. And that's okay. I mean, if you're going to do something, do it right. So, you went full-on mean girl, and I respect that."

"Thanks," Tina says. She actually looks amused.

"It must be hard, not being able to be yourself. With this interspecies dating ban, we know better than anyone else." She looks lovingly at Fern, who gives her a squeeze.

"Let's get this Moggy drunk," Hepa says, taking the bottle from me and handing it over to Tina. "We thought you could use it."

Tina slides out from under Marguerite's arm, and I think she's about to kick everyone out but she surprises me by taking a swig. She gulps, then wipes her mouth. She catches me eyeing her and shrugs. "What have I got to lose?" she asks.

She puts the bottle in front of my face. "C'mon, Edie, join us."

"Mavis would want you to have some fun," Cassie tells me sincerely. "Actually, Mavis would want you to have a drink. Or like, ten. In fact, the last time I got drunk on ambrosia was after she came back from the mission where Nico was killed. Or not killed, as it turns out." Cassie frowns. "It's very confusing, isn't it?"

I grab the bottle from Tina, clutching it in my hand. The mission where Nico was supposedly killed, is also when Mavis thought I was dead. And after our mother went to the cockatrice to have her memories wiped. Yet Mavis came back to campus and immediately started whooping it up with Cassie. I am seeing red, when suddenly I remember that Mavis is now in a prison cell. All my anger drains out of me.

I look down at the ambrosia in the bottle and imagine Mavis doing the same thing. It's been one Hades of a week and I don't need a vision from Cassie to tell me it's only gonna get worse.

I take a sip.

The sweet liquid rolls down my throat and warms my stomach. Immediately I feel better. Not better in an 'all is right with the world' way, but things don't seem as bleak.

Cassie is right; Mavis probably wouldn't begrudge me a night off.

I take a bigger sip, then pass the bottle. Cassie glugs, then passes it to Hepa. "It's spelled to never empty," Hepa explains.

"OMQ," Cassie says.

"Do you mean OMG?" I ask.

She giggles. "Yeah, that one. We should play Dare or Truth. Just nobody ask me what happened to the magical little baby fawn that Greg and I were supposed to kill for Artemis's class."

"Oh Cassie," I say. "Please tell me it's not in your dorm room."

"Who cares?" Tina says. "We have an actual shitting bird in our room. She has a magical whatever that will fade away in a few days."

"It will?" Cassie's bubbly mood suddenly falters and her lower lip trembles. I shoot a look at Fern; it's a little early for the drunken crying phase.

"Cassie, I'll spell you a magic animal for a graduation gift, okay?" Fern promises. "Whatever you want."

"Oh, yes, please!" Cassie's face lights up once more as she claps her hands with excitement. "Okay, let's do Dare or Truth now."

"It's Truth or Dare, and is it even fair to play that with a seer?" Tina asks her but her voice lacks her normal edge. "Don't you have an unfair advantage?"

"Honey," Cassie says, leaning toward Tina, "Right now I don't even know when I'm telling the truth." She slides dangerously to the side, and Hepa props her back up.

"I'll go first!" Fern turns to Hepa. "Truth or Dare?"

"I don't want to play," she says.

"Booo!!!" Cassie gives her a double thumbs down, then flips her off. Except she uses her pointer finger.

"Fine. Whatever." Hepa relents, covering up a smile. "Truth, I guess."

"How do you really feel about Jordan?" Marguerite asks.

Hepa looks thoughtful. "It's complicated. I mean, I like him, but he dropped me like a hot coal when Mr. Zee announced the dating ban. Jordan didn't even fight for me. So I turned my back on him, and now he says I'm the only girl for him."

"Typical boy," Tina says, swiping the bottle from Fern. "Only wants what he can't have."

"He's been trying to win me back," Hepa says, a slow smile spreading on her face. "He keeps trying to save me from really mundane things in order to be my hero. Yesterday he took off his shirt and held it over my head while I walked to class because UV rays are harmful to the skin. Except he kept saying SUV instead of UV, plus his shirt did *not* smell awesome."

"Jordan is yummy!" Cassie exclaims. "Especially his tummy. He's got a great six-rack."

"Girls have racks," I correct. "Boys have six-packs."

"Yeah, but Jordan's is an eight-pack," Hepa inserts with a smug smile.

There's a knock at the door and we all startle. "Come in," Tina calls.

"Gug," Cassie says, clumsily hiding the ambrosia behind her back.

"Relax," Tina says as the door swings open. "It's Val."

The room swims around me and I'm pretty sure it's not ambrosia as Val enters the room, his Stymphalian bird riding on his shoulder. He takes in all of us girls as half of his mouth curls into an amused smirk. "I didn't realize Tina was having a party tonight."

Tina shrugs. "It just sorta happened." She snatches the ambrosia from Cassie who has turned her back to Val and is trying to surreptitiously take a sip. "Have a drink."

Val shakes his head. "Not tonight. I've gotta take Kevin out for a game of night tag and then if he's a good boy, I have some soup bones from the kitchen stashed away as a treat. But only if he's a good boy." Val holds a hand out and his bird delicately steps onto it. He and Val look each other in the eye, and the bond between them is so obvious I'm almost jealous. "You're a good boy, aren't you?" Val asks, running a hand down the bird's back.

Tina folds her arms over her chest. "I can't believe you named your bird. Also, there's a line of shit running down your back, Val. I don't think he's that good of a boy."

Val breaks his intense eye contact with Kevin. "Yeah, we're still working on potty training."

Tina turns to the rest of us. "My brother is apparently an idiot."

"Tina, we've discussed this." Val voice hardens, while the rest of us sit and quietly watch them squabble like it's our own personal soap opera. "We can leave or we can make the best of it."

"Or," Tina counters. "We can wait for the moment when we can kill these birds and maybe Mr. Zee too."

"Tina!" Hepa gets to her feet. And looks around, as if she's not sure who's in the room. "You can't say stuff like that."

"Why not? Everyone knows about the prophecy. Someone with Mr. Zee's blood will kill him. Who's to say it won't be me? I'm a Moggy. My mother was a mix of who knows what. Some of Mr. Zee's offspring could be mixed into my family tree somewhere."

"And you'd actually kill him?" Cassie asks in a small voice.

Tina smiles her vampire smile. Fangs fully out. "Gladly."

I don't say anything. I don't know what to say. After finding out Mr. Zee was my father, I was sure the prophecy was about me. But Tina's right—anyone with Mr. Zee's blood could be the one...and the dude has definitely gotten around over the years. I expect to feel relief, but my feelings are as mixed up as ever. Even if I'm not the one who's supposed to kill him, do I let him die? Would I fight Tina to defend Mr. Zee?

"Okay, well, I'll let you ladies get back to your party." Val backs toward the door, but Tina grabs his hand.

"Wait. Remember, I told you to come and get your new T-shirt." Tina turns to rummage in her wardrobe and then tosses the shirt to Val, who easily catches it. Unrolling it, he holds it out in front of his body so we can all see.

It's a chart with the words "Bird Identification" at the top. Below are pictures of all different types of birds with their names beneath them. Blue Jay. Robin. Nightingale. The final bird on the shirt is, of course, the Stymphalian. But instead of having that name, below it says, *Epic Asshole.*

"Oh wow! Tina made a funny!" Cassie exclaims. "I never saw that one coming!"

This cracks the rest of us up, even Tina.

"It's great, Tina," Val says, rolling the shirt up.

"You should try it on," Cassie says. "Make sure it fits."

Val pauses and throws a glance Tina's way. "She buys the T-shirts in bulk. It'll fit."

"No, Val," Tina steps forward. "Cassie's right. Try it on."

He frowns at her and then darts a glance at me. I quickly look away, trying to hide the

blush heating up my face.

"We were just discussing Jordan's eight-pack," Hepa says. "I think it's pretty rare for a man to have that level of musculature. Perhaps just for comparison's sake..."

Smirk in place, Val shrugs and with one smooth move whips his shirt over his head. Even Fern and Marguerite watch. His smooth torso looks like carved marble. A living statue that would make Michelangelo weep.

As he lifts his arms to pull the new shirt on, I see it. A wound, deep red and angry, that wraps around his side and half his back.

"Val," I gasp. Without even thinking about it, I'm on my feet, my hand on his bare shoulder. "You need to see a healer."

"He has," Fern says. "I've healed it several times. It just comes back. Someone sliced him with a spelled knife."

"Someone did what?" My head spins and not just from the ambrosia. Then suddenly the answer is obvious. "Maddox. You got hurt when you killed her."

Val looks straight at me but says nothing—neither denying nor confirming.

But Tina isn't so tight-lipped. "Nico's getting all the shifters on campus all worked up, saying we attacked his poor helpless mother after her shifting powers were taken." She scoffs. "That woman was never helpless in her life. She would've been a danger to every vampire until her dying day. We just moved that day up a little, is all."

"Um, Tina," Marguerite says softly. "We're not supposed to admit it, remember?"

Tina frowns and looks confused for a minute—it's not often she screws up and she seems to be struggling with the feeling. But then putting her chin up she says, "I meant in theory, Marguerite. Of course, we didn't kill anyone. It was probably actually Nico wanting to get away from his beast of a mother."

"All right then," Val opens the door. "On that note, I'm going to say goodnight."

"Find me in the infirmary tomorrow," Fern calls right before the door snaps closed once more.

There's a silence after that. The party mood has dissipated as reality intruded once more. It's a bummer to be reminded that my friends and my...um, Val, killed someone in cold blood. Although maybe Tina does have a point. Even without powers Maddox would've remained a formidable opponent. But going after her when she was leaving seems wrong. On the other hand, is it honorable or just plain stupid to wait until she has time to regroup and attack again?

My head hurts with the questions. Or maybe it's the ambrosia.

But then Tina thrusts the bottle of ambrosia into the air. "One more round!" she declares.

Or maybe I just need *more* ambrosia, I decide as Tina passes the bottle my way.

After taking a long swig, I pass it to Cassie who does the same. Once the bottle has gone around the whole room and returned to Tina, we are loose once more.

Marguerite gives Fern a big wet kiss and stumbles to her feet. "Maybe we should get back to our rooms," she says, never taking her eyes off Fern.

"Nuh-uh," Tina moves to block the door. "We're finishing Truth or Dare first." She points a finger at me. "It's my turn and I pick Edie." She levels her eyes at me. I'm sure she's going to ask me about her brother Val and what my intentions are toward him but she surprises me. "What's going on between you and Themis?"

Hepa and I exchange a glance. She's tight with Themis too. How much does she know? Cassie passes me back the bottle and I take a long drink, for courage.

"All of you in this room are my friends," I say.

"Well, I just kind of put up with you," Tina says. "You're kind of like this bird. I'm stuck with you both." She takes a swing at her Stymphalian bird, but misses by about three feet, the momentum rolling her off the bed and onto the floor. "And you both stink."

I reach out, pulling her up. "I would die to protect anyone in this room."

"That got dark fast," Marguerite mutters.

The ambrosia is flowing freely through my body, my blood light with the feeling, my head dizzy. I'm warm and happy, ensconced here with my friends. The fear from earlier has evaporated, and I think of how much better I would feel if I could just tell them everything, let it all out. I'm sure this awesome group of girls would know what to do.

But I can't, and I know it. As much as I want to share my biggest secret with them, my parents both died to keep it safe. I can't disrespect them like that. But that doesn't mean I have to keep everything from my friends.

"I need you all to promise that what I'm about to say will not leave this room. That you won't tell anyone."

"What about Jordan?" Hepa asks. "I mean, I need to have something to talk to him about so that he stops swatting all the mosquitoes that come near me, while informing me about the latest statistics of West Nile virus."

"Oh yeah. You can tell Jordan," I say. "I trust him completely."

"And Greg?" Cassie blushes for some reason. "I can't have a secret from Greg."

"Well, of course Greg can know," I amend. I mean, if I trust Jordan, I can certainly trust Greg.

"Wow," Hepa says with an eye roll. "A secret that only half the campus can know. I feel really privileged to be in on it."

Tina opens her mouth but before she can speak I clarify. "Look, I need you all to promise that you won't tell anyone except for Greg, Jordan and" —I glance at Tina— "Val." They all nod solemnly. I take another swig and pass the bottle on.

"I'm a Moggy," I admit.

"What?" Marguerite asks. "No way!"

"Well," Hepa says. "Honestly, I kind of suspected. I mean, you're a freaking dragon shifter! What kind of weirdo combination made that?"

Cassie's eyebrows come together at Hepa's question, and I can only hope she's not thinking too hard about the answer. Tina's the only one who looks even remotely upset. "Wait...if you're a Moggy, how did I get stuck with this stupid bird and you didn't?"

Fern raises her hand. "I did a thing." She swallows, the booze definitely getting to her...or, I realize, it's guilt. "A spell," she explains, crossing over to Tina and hugging her. "I tried to reach you, the day of the announcement. I really did. But I failed you."

Tina pats her on the back awkwardly. "That's okay. You tried, I guess." She turns to her bird, which cocks its head at her. "It's just so annoying. I mean, it watches me twenty-four seven. At least the non-vamps get some time off when they're sleeping. I can't even apply my sunscreen without it creeping on me."

"Ugh," Marguerite says, wrinkling her nose. "Pervy bird."

"It *is* a perv," Tina says. "*You're* a perv," she repeats, shaking her fist at the bird. She's got the bottle in her other hand and is about to take a swig when she changes her mind. In a lightning fast motion she grabs the bird by the throat, shoves the bottle in its beak and upends it.

It flaps madly, feathers flying around the room as the rest of us dive for cover to avoid its talons. It makes a strangling sound, but Tina isn't letting go anytime soon. The bird's eyes roll, then it gives up, and swallows. She releases it, and it flies around the room, weaving. Cassie screams and I pull my cover over both of us, while Marguerite throws herself on top of Fern to protect her. The bird hits the window with a tremendous *thunk*, and falls to the floor, one wing sticking up in the air, as if in surrender.

"Is it dead?" Cassie asks.

"I hope so," Tina mutters.

"I think it's just sleeping," Hepa says, turning it over onto its side. A healer to the core, she pulls a blanket off Tina's bed and covers the bird up, tucking it in.

Marguerite crawls off of Fern. "Are you okay?" she asks, running her hands all along Fern's body. "You didn't get scratched or anything, did you? I would die if anything happened to you."

"Vomit," Tina says.

"I'm fine," Fern tells Marguerite, giving her a peck on the cheek.

"Guys," Cassie says.

"Is it your turn for Truth or Dare?" I ask.

When it's my turn I'm gonna ask her if she's crushing on Greg, because I have my suspicions.

"I really don't feel good." She grabs her head and I think

she's about to lose all her ambrosia, but instead her eyes roll back in her head and she goes starkly white.

"A weapon, one in three to defeat the king of the gods. Three places of learning. One child of his loins. Three in one to wound. Three in one to kill."

Cassie's eyes go back to normal. She leans forward and barfs between her feet.

Nobody moves as we eye each other. I'm feeling suddenly sober.

Cassie just told us how to kill Zeus.

## 9

The mix of bird poop and Cassie's ambrosia puke is enough to drive me from my room. We did our best to clean everything up, and Fern even cast some sort of air-freshening spell, but Tina and I have still been dealing with the lingering scent of stomach acid. Plus, a hungover Stymphalian bird is not the best roommate. It was beating its head against the window when I woke up this morning, apparently believing that the best way to get rid of a headache is to bash your head the rest of the way in.

The night before brought a nice reprieve; I haven't thought about my parentage for twelve full hours. But daylight—and a hot shower—brought everything back into perspective. I couldn't drown my sorrows in ambrosia, and I couldn't forget Adrianna Aspostolos—or the letter she'd written to Metis, asking for help in delivering her child.

The child of a god. Me.

I find a bottle of good old ibuprofen at the bottom of the bag I brought here what seems like ages ago. There's also a handful of old photos and I can't resist quickly flipping through them. Some of them are old, of Mavis and I as little kids in Thing 1 and Thing 2 Halloween costumes. Another is one of those cheesy posed family pictures done in a studio. We all look stiff and unnatural.

I pause on the final one. It's just Mavis and me again, posing together as we got ready to leave for a middle school dance. It was my first real dance. I was nervous and scared and excited all at once. Mavis was in eighth grade and of course had a date. But she ditched him to hang out with me and my friends. They were so impressed with my cool sister. My feet hurt the next day from all the dancing.

My throat thickens. I thought I'd lost her once and I'm not losing her again.

Shoving the pictures back into my bag and then under my bed, I get to my feet.

I need to find out if the person in the prophecy is me. And I want that letter my mother wrote to Metis; maybe it will have a clue.

I visit Merilee first, but after taking a moment to mentally scroll through the information in her head, she shrugs. "Often the gods hold onto their personal correspondence instead of passing it along to me. They're not supposed to, but..." Merilee shrugs again. "Gods, you know? What can you do?"

Discouraged, I leave Merilee, unsure where to go next. I've met Metis once before and she's pretty intimidating. I'm not sure how she'll react to visiting her office and asking for a letter from my long dead mother.

But then I remember that picture of Mavis and me. Now is not the time to hesitate.

I turn toward the infirmary.

I find Metis in her office. As head healer, she spends most of her time working, even the weekends. I knock on her door, and she invites me in with a brief, sharp, "Come!"

I step into her office, which is very different from Themis's. Healing plants hang from the ceiling, there's a small cauldron boiling in one corner, and multi-colored vials suspended with string hanging on the walls. In one corner there's also a hospital bed and a small metal table with a microscope and some glass lab equipment.

"Um...hi," I say, as Metis looks up at me from behind her desk. Her shimmering silver hair is pulled back into a braid. "I'm Edie. I'm not a healer, but we've met—"

"Yes," Metis says, leaning back in her chair. "You're the girl who found the scorpion last semester. Saved us a lot of time, too. It was much easier to cure the shifters once we knew the source of the plague. Please, sit down. What can I do for you, Edie?"

"Well...I'm not really sure how to start," I begin. I'd walked over here only half expecting to find her in, and now that I'm here, there's no easy way to tell my story.

"The best place to start is usually the beginning," Metis says, smiling at me.

The beginning...my mother hiding a pregnancy test behind her back when Mr. Zee appeared in her room.

"I...do you remember a student named Adrianna Aspostolos?"

Metis doesn't hesitate. "Yes, a shifter. Her portrait hangs in the Hall of the Dead." Her eyes on me are bright, like she's just discovered a new specimen.

"Yes, it does." I nod. "Do you happen to know how she died?"

"Of course I do," Metis says. She leans forward. "I was with her when it happened. Right here, in this room."

The breath goes out of me, and I grip the sides of my chair for support. "Here?" I ask, my voice light and shuddering.

"Yes," Metis says, standing and coming around her desk to my side. "She came to me for help, knowing that she was carrying the child of a god, and that the delivery would likely kill her."

"Then why is she dead? Why didn't you save her? You're a god and a healer."

Metis nods. "She was mortal. I did everything I could, but in the end the delivery was too much. She did, however, hold you before she died."

My eyes well with tears, one slipping down my cheek. Metis pushes it away with a thumb. Her touch is cool and comforting, and I wonder if my mother found some solace in it as she died.

"She wanted her baby, Edie," Metis whispers to me. "She wanted you." She looks strangely triumphant, like she was working on a puzzle and the final piece just clicked into place.

I turn my gaze to hers, cold and blue, the secret inside me reaching out, seeking a connection. Everything I was afraid to tell my friends, everything I wanted to say to alleviate some of the pressure. I feel like I can now. I can, here.

"I've been keeping an eye on you."

"For Themis?" I ask.

"Yes. Themis. Of course," Metis says, pushing my hair out of my eyes. "Mr. Zee has done endless damage to this Academy, and its students. Themis and I want nothing more to see him gone. He has no place here, drawing the young to him, for his own amusements. If it had gotten out the Academy would be done." Metis shakes her head. "We had to hush it up. Keep it secret. No responsible parents would send their children here if they knew what might happen."

She hands me a tissue, and I blow my nose.

"It would destroy the Academy," I say, realizing. "I found

some information in the Archives that said my father—Daniel Evans, the man I thought was my father—had stolen two secrets that could ruin Mount Olympus Academy. Me, and my sister Mavis."

"Yes." Metis nods. "And the Archives gave up another secret too, didn't they? The prophecy that Zeus would die at the hand of one born of his own diluted blood."

"Me," I say, my head hanging. "I don't want to kill him. I know Themis has been weakening Mr. Zee with poisoned ambrosia, and she doesn't want him killed, either. She's just hoping to scare him into leaving."

"A wise choice," Metis says. "And you are the weapon we need to do exactly that."

A weapon. Cassie's words from last night roll through my head. *Three in one to wound. Three in one to kill.*

"Now that we each know where each other stands," Metis says, crossing back over to her side of the desk. "What can I do for you? Why have you come to me, Edie?"

"My mother wrote you a letter," I say, wiping the last of my tears away. "I was hoping you might still have it. I never met her. Never knew her. I didn't even know she existed until recently. I'd just like to have something of hers."

"Of course," Metis says, leaning forward. "It only makes sense. One second, it won't take long to find it. Merilee organized all my old papers a while back. Now I need only think of what I want..."

She rummages through some drawers, and I take a moment to get myself back together. "Ah, here we are," Metis says, placing a rolled scroll on her desk. I reach for it, but her hand closes over mine before I can take it.

"I'm glad you came to me today, Edie," she says. "It gives me a chance to talk to you about something."

"What's that?" When she releases me I put the scroll in my bag, to read when I'm alone.

"Themis and I have been working for a long time to ensure that the Academy—and its students—are safe. Themis has more cogs in her machine than you know. In fact, it's best if you don't know all the moving parts."

I nod, thinking of Hepa, and how many times I've spotted her slipping out of Themis's office.

"But Zeus has his own spies and suspicions," Metis continues. "We need to be sure that those who are under our protection stay safe. That means being cautious. You spend a lot of time with Themis, and it hasn't gone unnoticed."

I shiver, my heart gives a jolt. "What? Who said something?"

Metis shakes her head. "Whispers in the wind, child. You can't believe all of them, but that doesn't mean you shouldn't be listening. I think it's best if you don't see Themis for a while, to stay safe. She asked me to pass that along to you, as well as—" Her voice drops suddenly. "Can you please make sure the door is locked?"

My pulse pounds as I flip the lock and return to my seat. "What?" I ask, my voice high and tight. "What did Themis want you to tell me?"

"Well," Metis glances around her office, her voice slackening into a whisper. "She's perfectly right that killing Zeus could spell disaster."

"She said minor gods might revolt," I remember. "Cause earthquakes and all kinds of things."

"Quite right," Metis says. "But...Zeus won't ever step down unless there's a true threat. One that he knows is real. One that actually makes him fear for his life."

My eyebrows come together. "Even if we're not going to actually kill him?"

"Exactly!" Metis says. "But how can we threaten a god if he doesn't believe we have the power to truly hurt him?"

"*Three in one to wound, three in one to kill,*" I mutter.

"Ah, you do know," Metis says, almost to herself. "You know about the sword that can kill a god? The sword that can spill ichor?"

Ichor, the blood of the gods.

"Yes," I say. "My friend Cassie had a vision last night." I don't mention that she was three sheets to the wind at the time. I mean, obviously I can trust Metis with the biggest secret I've got, but I don't think she needs to know about my underage drinking, too.

"Tell it to me," Metis says, eyes narrowing.

I repeat the prophecy, word for word. "A weapon, one in three to defeat the king of the gods. Three places of learning. One child of his loins. Three in one to wound. Three in one to kill."

"Yes," Metis says when I've finished. "A long time ago, Zeus and I were...together."

My mind races, running back over everything I've learned about the gods since coming to Mount Olympus Academy. "That's right," I say, hitting on it. "You were married to Zeus once!"

"Good thing that's ancient history. He was a lying, cheating, immoral, depraved...but I digress. Let's just say he was a bastard in the figurative sense of the word. When we parted ways I asked Hephaestus to forge a weapon for me. It took an incredible amount of magic and..." She shakes her head, her composure slipping. "You don't need to know everything that went into crafting a blade that can kill a god. All you need to know is that my husband found out what I was doing, and had it broken into three parts."

"I think I've narrowed down where they might be," I say. I'm pretty sure the part of Cassie's prophecy about *Three places of learning* must have referred to Mount Olympus Academy, Amazon Academy, and Underworld Academy.

"The pieces are at the other Academies," I say. "He spread them out."

"Yes," Metis says. "One is here for him to watch over. One was given to his brother, Hades, to keep under his care. One he handed to his daughter to guard. I can help you find that one when the time comes. It will be the easiest, so you should save that one for last.

"If the pieces are retrieved, you can re-forge the blade. With a child of his blood on our side, and the sword that can kill him in her hands..." Metis's face becomes sharp, all traces of the kindly woman who had wiped away my tears shoved aside as she is lit from within, illuminated by rage against her ex.

"Um...but we're not going to kill him, right?" I ask, worried by this sudden change.

Metis's eyes narrow on me. "Are you not in the assassination class?"

"Yes, but..." I hesitate. "You said we were just going to use the weapon to threaten Zeus."

"Yes, of course," Metis says, her composure coming back. "We would never want the lesser gods unleashed on the world. I mean, the poor mortals!" She laughs, her throat rippling. "They're so funny...all those broken bones."

"I guess," I say, realizing yet again how different gods are from everyone else. Metis continues to laugh at something that's decidedly not amusing. "So, uh, just so we're on the same page. I'm definitely not killing Zeus."

The only times I've killed have been in defensive situations. And the monsters I took down were strangers. Or maybe I should say the monsters my dragon took down. I'm honestly not sure if I could look Mr. Zee in the eyes—knowing he's my bio-dad—and kill him.

Metis steps back, disappointment dimming her face. "Well, Zee isn't at the top of his game. I suppose the weapon alone may be enough to convince him."

Metis rises, holding out her arms to me as she comes back around the desk, steering me to the door. "The location of the sword shards may be somewhat difficult to manage. I suggest you start with the piece here, at our own Academy. And keep me updated. Remember, your association with Themis has been noted. It's best that you come to me from now on."

"I will," I say. "But how do I know where to look for the sword piece?"

"Perhaps your seer friend..." She trails off, waving her hand in the air.

"Cassie," I supply.

"Yes, Cassie," she says. "It is so embarrassing, what a few thousand years does to the memory. Ask Cassie if she might be able to narrow things down a bit. She might find this helpful."

Metis drops something small but heavy into my hand. I glance down to find a Seer Stone.

"But last time she used one of these, it—"

I look up, but Metis has closed her office door in my face. I'm on my own again.

## 10

I put the Seer Stone in my pocket and rush to the dining hall. I need to talk to Cassie, who looks weirdly perky. I sidle up to her and Greg on the green.

"Hey, aren't you hung over?" I whisper.

Greg sticks his head in. "*I'm* not hungover at all. You know why? Because I wasn't invited."

I shove his head out. "It was girls only."

"I heard Val was there and you were all ogling him."

I stare at Cassie. "How does he already know all this?"

Cassie blushes red. "He, uh, stopped by my room so we could have breakfast together, but I felt too sick, so he brought in some toast and then we...talked...just talked, that's all."

"Uh-huh," I say.

"Yeah, and then Fern interrupted our *talking*," Greg adds with a wink, "when she came by with her hangover cure."

"Ha, yes, wasn't that nice of her? Fern made this wonderful potion to help with being over hung." She rustles around in her bag. "I mean, no one wants to be hung, right?"

"It's not all bad," Jordan says, slipping past us.

Greg sighs. "Cassie, we discussed this. Being hung means something totally different. Remember?"

"Ohhh, that's right. Well, anyway, I've got a vial of the *hangover* cure for you too, Edie..." Cassie rummages in her purse. I take the vial she gives me and slip it into my pocket, even though I don't need it. Having an instant hangover cure on hand seems like a good idea, at the rate that ambrosia flows around this place.

"I'm actually okay, I had some human medicine leftover from home that I took."

Cassie's eyes widen. "Wow. Human medicine. That's amazing."

"Yeah, magic medicine. Super lame." My sarcasm goes right over Cassie's head.

We enter the dining hall and Greg sniffs the air. "Smells like sloppy joe day." He looks to Cassie. "Hey, remember when you used to predict lunch? I kinda miss that. I mean, I know it wasn't some amazing magical reveal, but it was more like common sense, every day, useful information."

"Those were the good old days," Cassie agrees. "Before I touched that awful Seer Stone."

The stone that Metis gave me is burning a hole in my pocket. I have to get Cassie alone to talk to her, but she and Greg are joined at the hip.

"Is it really that bad?" I ask. "Having more important visions? I mean, when I first met you in the swamp, you were bummed out about no one ever taking you seriously."

She looks at me. "I don't know, really." We sit at the table and she holds up her cup. "It's like before I was handing out grape juice. Nobody ever got hurt by drinking grape juice, you know? And now, there's stuff coming out of me that could get someone killed." She shudders. "I feel like I might accidentally hand out poison every time I open my mouth."

Fern, Marguerite, and Hepa slide in beside us, Jordan trailing Hepa like a puppy. She takes the cup from Cassie's hand and guzzles the liquid. "Those potions you made are a lifesaver, Fern, but I still feel super dehydrated. I'm gonna have to see if I can tweak it for better hydration. I am parched."

"I'll get you a refill!" Jordan jumps up and jogs away.

"So, instead of being your boyfriend, he's basically your servant now?" Marguerite asks.

Hepa shrugs. "It seems to make him happy. And I'm not complaining."

I look around the room and realize something. "Where are all the birds?" Not one Stymphalian bird is in the dining hall.

"You didn't hear?" Fern says, lowering her voice. "Moggies aren't allowed in the dining hall anymore. It's unsanitary."

"That's horrible," Greg says. "Can't Artemis just order the birds to wait outside while the Moggies eat?"

"Of course she could," Hepa rolls her eyes at Greg. "But the point is obviously to humiliate the Moggies and make their lives miserable."

"That's not right!" Cassie says, slamming her fork down.

"Yeah, that's pretty messed up," Greg says and I completely agree.

"Zee made a proclamation," Marguerite says. I feel guilty. I'm a Moggy. I should be suffering with Val and Tina. And Mavis.

"Jordan, I can feed myself," Hepa snaps, bringing me back to the present. The two of them are wrestling over her fork.

"But I like doing it for you," he protests. Leaning closer to Hepa, he adds in a low voice, "It feels intimate."

Hepa goes red and the rest of us can't hold back our giggles.

Jordan gives the rest of us an outraged look. "Not cool, guys. I'm making myself vulnerable here."

That only makes us laugh harder, but Jordan ignores us. He picks up Hepa's sloppy joe and brings it to her lips. "Take a big bite, baby, so you'll have lots of energy for your afternoon classes."

From between clenched teeth, Hepa answers, "I *am not* a baby."

"Right. Sorry." He waggles the sandwich a bit. "You're a big strong girl and you need a big strong lunch. Now how about you—" The sandwich, true to its name, falls apart, covering Hepa in sop.

"Oh, shit." Jordan says, looking stunned by this outcome. But he quickly recovers. Grabbing a pile of napkins he reaches for Hepa's chest. "Don't worry, I'll clean it up."

Hepa shoves him away with two hands. "I think you've done enough."

Fern, ever the peacemaker, takes the napkins from Jordan. "Let me help her."

"You don't need me?" Jordan asks, crestfallen.

"I can honestly say I don't," Hepa tells him as she takes a handful of meat from her lap and dumps it back on the tray.

"Ouch," Jordan grabs his chest and falls out of his chair onto his knees beside her. "A mortal wound!" He lurches forward. "My heart has broken!"

"I doubt that," Hepa's words drip sarcasm but there's a smile tugging at the corner of her mouth. "Get up, you idiot."

Marguerite looks at Fern. "I'm so glad we're past the courting stage."

———

After lunch, I grab Cassie's arm and steer her towards the shade of a tree.

"The vision you had last night, it's about a weapon—a sword—that is capable of killing a god. Of killing Zeus."

"Woah...Edie." The light is gone from Cassie's eyes. They're dark now, apprehensive. "You're not seriously—"

"No," I shake my head. "No, of course not. But if someone had the weapon, it might be enough of a threat. If he just knows it exists, and has been re-forged—"

"Right," Cassie says. "Okay, so...no killing?"

"No," I repeat emphatically. "I'm just going to convince Mr. Zee to step down."

"And then Themis takes over, and of course she'll free Mavis," Cassie says, nodding along. "Okay, I'm in."

"Great!" I say, hoping she means it. Because there's a big ask coming up next. "I need you to help me find the first piece of the sword. According to the prophecy, it should be hidden here, at the Academy."

"Three places of learning..." Cassie muses aloud. "Right. But that's all I've got. The prophecy wasn't specific, and this campus is huge."

"I know," I say, taking a deep breath. "That's why I need you to use a Seer Stone to locate it."

"Oh..." Cassie's face falls, her enthusiasm fading.

"Listen," I say, leaning in. "I know what I'm asking is huge. I know the last time you used one it...changed you. But wasn't it for the better? Aren't you glad that you see important things now?"

"Glad!" Cassie pulls away from me, her face twisting. "No, Edie! I'm not glad I get to see things like Darcy's head being cleaved from his body!"

She starts crying, and I immediately feel terrible. My wings burst from my back, a deep, dove gray to match my mood. I wrap one around Cassie, and she leans into it, hiding her tears from students passing by.

"I'm sorry I asked," I whisper. "Truly. Never mind. I'll figure something else out. I'll—"

"No," Cassie pulls away, holds her hand out. "I'm being selfish. I'm the only seer you know, and I can help you save your sister. Not doing it would be cruel."

I hesitate, but Cassie's head is thrown back, her shoulders squared. "Are you sure?"

"Yes," she says, and I try to slip the stone into her hand. But she shakes her head. "Tonight," she says firmly, then walks away to her next class.

She doesn't look back.

## 11

Tina wasn't kidding when she said that she doesn't need sleep. Adjusting to being a roommate with someone who never needs shut-eye has been hard enough. Having a bird following her constantly hasn't made things any better. At first, Tina experimented with trying to exhaust the poor thing. Her endless vampire energy never flags, so she'd run everywhere she went around campus, and had even taken to morning jogs in an effort to wear her bird out.

But the bird had seemed unfazed by all her tricks—until she got it drunk.

Now, it wants more.

"Oh my gods," Tina cries, once again burying her head under a pillow as the bird alights on the headboard.

"Gawk!" It calls, its voice harsh. Vee actually folds her leaves around either side of her head.

"Gawk?" This time it comes out as a question, and the bird nudges into Tina's pillow.

"Go away!" Tina yells, shoving it off the bed. Feathers fly, but it doesn't seem bothered by the treatment. Instead, it hops over to me, head cocked to one side.

"Gawk?"

"I don't have any booze, buddy," I tell it, and I swear, it looks disappointed. I almost feel sorry for it, until I remember that it's a living, breathing sign of Mr. Zee's bigotry. "Hey, Tina?"

I'm answered by a groan from under the pillow.

"Do you want me to see if I can find some—"

"Gawk! Gawk!" The bird flies at me, encouragingly. I put my arms around my face to protect my eyes.

"Some *ambrosia*?" I yell, which pushes the bird to such heights of anticipation that it craps on the floor.

"Whatever," Tina moans, and the bird goes back to her bed. It pulls the pillow away from her, then settles down and begins grooming its feathers, pausing every now and then to pull its beak through Tina's hair.

"Get off me," she growls at it, but I intervene.

"Wait," I tell her. "Maybe if we give the bird what it wants, it'll get off your back. Like, literally."

"Great, so now we're enabling an alcoholic bird?"

"A sort of evil magic bird. Yes." I turn to the bird. "Good birds don't shit all over our room. Good birds get ambrosia."

"Gawk!" It cries, then goes to the window, positions itself just right, and poops...outside.

"Oh my gods," Tina says, looking at me with astonishment. "Did you see that?"

"Tina," I say, not breaking eye contact with the bird. "I think we can housetrain this thing."

"Do it," she nods firmly. "Get this bird its—"

"Gawk!"

———

I slip into Cassie's room after dark and find her sitting cross legged on her bed. She doesn't look ready to go—much less have an epic prophecy.

"Edie, don't be mad at me," she says quickly.

"Why?"

"I know that I said I'd use the Seer Stone and I will. There are three parts of the sword, so I'll probably have to use it eventually, I promise. But for MOA, well, I thought maybe my mom could find some sort of written clue."

I rush over to Cassie. "Of course, that's fine! You know I trust Merilee! I should have thought of it first."

Cassie immediately brightens. "Mom says that since Mr. Zee has been getting sort of loopy, he's taken to writing everything down. She found a lot of scattered scribblings, but we both thought this one might be it since it specifically mentions a sword. Though, um..." Cassie blushes. "It's possibly not the sword you're looking for."

She holds a paper out to me, where I see Merilee's neat handwriting replicating Mr. Zee's note.

*Remember those who die*
*Though some I wish would rise*
*One girl I'd again prick*
*Upon my sword so thick.*

"Gross." I drop the paper. And then to my horror, I feel tears start to spill down my cheeks.

Cassie throws her arms around me. "Edie, I'm sorry. I know Mr. Zee's bad poetry about his sexual exploits is awful and probably has nothing to do with the actual sword piece. I'll use the stone now, okay? I'm sorry for making such a big deal about it."

"No, Cassie." I wipe away my tears, amazed at her generosity. I know I can trust her with anything. "I'm crying because I'm pretty sure that poem is about the sword *and* also about Mr. Zee's sexual exploits." I hesitate for a moment, and then spill it. "The thing is, I found out the other day that Mr. Zee got my birth mom pregnant. She had the baby, knowing it could kill her. And that baby was me."

Cassie's eyes go round as she stares at me. "Edie. Oh my gods."

"Yeah." We both absorb the enormousness of this. I don't know if I'll ever fully accept it.

"If he hid the sword with your bio-mom, he must have loved her," Cassie offers kindly.

I nod, hoping it's true. That my mother knew love before she died. But then why did she keep me a secret? Because she knew Zee would expel her regardless, would probably kill me in her womb. I shudder.

"Do we know where she's buried?" Cassie asks.

I shake my head. "No. It would have to be somewhere on campus." But wait, I know a place to start. "Maybe Zee hid the sword behind my mother's portrait," I suggest.

"Let's go and find out," Cassie jumps to her feet.

"Cassie, it's okay, you should get some sleep..." I start to say, but she waves me off.

"I'm not letting you wander around campus by yourself, with everything that's going on," she says. "Everybody has their blood up about the Moggies, and with Nico telling everyone he's planning something to get back at the vamps... no way. I'm sticking with you."

My heart swells with love, but I don't have time to say anything about it. Cassie is already out the door, headed for the Hall of the Dead.

It's even creepier than the first time I was there, with

sconces burning in between each portrait of students who have died while attending the Academy, although the tradition was short-lived...much like the people it was built to memorialize. When we get to Adrianna's—my mother—my breath catches in my chest.

She's exactly as I remembered...it would be almost impossible to forget, after all. The same face looks back at me in the mirror every morning. Underneath her portrait are the Greek words Hepa helped me translate: *died in childbirth.*

My throat closes up. The first time I was here it stunned me. Now, I know more. Know how my mother died...and why. I still have her note to Metis, rolled and tied shut. I haven't had the gumption to read it yet. Haven't had the guts to look at my mother's handwriting. And it's no wonder. I can hardly raise my eyes to hers, even though it's only a photo. This woman—girl, really—died giving me life.

"Hi...Mom," I say, my voice coming out weak and empty here in this dark stone corridor. Cassie takes my hand, and her fingers intertwine with mine. I clear my throat, and go on.

"So, I...I know what happened to you," I tell Adrianna. "I know about—" But I can't finish, can't say it out loud.

"I know that you hid a secret," I say instead. "And I think you're still hiding one now."

My fingers go to the portrait, running around the edges, looking for a clasp or a lever, something that will indicate that there's more to this portrait than meets the eye. But there's nothing.

"I thought..." My finger catches something sharp and I pull my hand back. A perfect round drop of blood beads up on my finger. Suddenly I remember the "prick" part of Mr.

Zee's poem. I press my finger to the corner of the portrait, avoiding my mother's face.

I needn't have worried, though. When I pull my hand away, I see that my blood has left no mark. The portrait seems to have absorbed it. Or accepted it as payment, because suddenly there's a small *click*. My mother's picture swings outward, revealing a dark hole in the stones behind.

"If Zee put a blood spell, and it worked for you," Callie says, her eyes wide, "you really must be his daughter."

"I guess there's no denying it now." I reach inside, my hand closing over metal so cold it feels like it's burning my fingers. I gasp.

"Okay?" Cassie whispers.

"Yeah," I say. "Just...surprised."

I pull the hilt from the shadows, a heavy, ornate thing with no blade attached and a large, gaping hole in the center.

"I wonder what that's for," Cassie marvels.

"I don't know," I say, swinging Adrianna's portrait back into place. "The prophecy says there are three pieces. So maybe it's the hilt, the blade, and something that goes there?"

"Like a gemstone, maybe?" Cassie suggests, but I can only shrug. I slip the hilt into my belt loop. It hangs heavy against my hip.

Kratos taught us to never pick up a weapon unless we were prepared to use it. But this is only part of a weapon, so maybe it doesn't count.

"Back to the dorm?" Cassie asks, a smile of relief on her face.

"Actually...no." I open Adrianna's portrait once more and put the hilt of the sword back inside. "Mr. Zee hid this here and he's paranoid right now, so possibly he'll check on it. We'll let Adrianna hold this secret just a little bit longer."

Cassie nods. "Good call. I was gonna offer to hide it under my mattress, but—"

"You've already done more than enough for tonight," I tell her, then add, "Thank you."

"No problem. I like being the breeze beneath your wings."

I sling an arm around Cassie. "Wind beneath my wings. And yes, you are. Now if you don't mind, I do have one last errand. I promised Tina I'd bring back some ambrosia for her bird."

"Um, what?"

"We reached a deal," I tell Cassie. "We get it drunk; it shits outside."

"Nice," she nods appreciatively as she touches me elbow, guiding me back toward the infirmary. "They use ambrosia as the base for a lot of healing potions," she tells me. "I'm sure we can find some in here."

The few patients are still asleep, the night nurse no further along in her reading, since she's joined them in la-la land. We're making our way down the hallway when we hear footsteps coming around the corner. I grab Cassie by the elbow and we duck into an alcove just in time as Hepa appears, a cup in her hand. Jordan is tailing her, in his pajamas. Or at least, apparently in what he sleeps in. It's not much. Just boxer briefs.

"Can I carry that for you?" he asks.

"It's just Zee's tonic. It's not heavy," she says, waving him off.

"What's that anyway?" he asks. "Zee's been looking pretty crappy lately. Shouldn't his medicine help?"

"It's a placebo," Hepa tells him.

"Ew. That's gross." Jordan wrinkles his nose.

"No, you doof. It's not medicine. It's just watered-down ambrosia," she explains. "Why do you care?"

"I don't," Jordan tells her. I just thought that I could I carry you, while you carry it?"

Hepa sighs, and shakes her head. "Why don't you—oh, bless the gods," she says, now truly frustrated. "I forgot to lock the door to the potions cabinet."

"I'll do it!" Jordan says, highly invested in pleasing her.

She gives him a dark look. "I am not handing over my keys. Metis only entrusts a few healers with them." Setting the cup down on the windowsill, she turns to head back the way she came, Jordan pivoting immediately to follow.

"I'm coming with you," Jordan calls, shadowing her all the way.

Cassie and I watch each other over our hands, trying to stifle our giggles. "I think they're gone," she finally whispers.

"Yeah, and I think we just scored our ambrosia," I say, swiping the cup.

We head back to the dorm, sneaking into our respective rooms. Tina sits up in bed, her chin resting on her hand as the bird perches on her shoulder.

"Gawk!" It greets me, flying to me when it spots the cup in my hand. It perches on my wrist, immediately sucking up as much as it can.

"Took you long enough," Tina says. "Were you meeting my brother?"

"What? No!" I say, a blush rising to my cheeks as I remember the rustle of feathers I'd heard as I left the dorm. Had that been Val? There was definitely another Moggy running around campus tonight.

"I mean...I don't think I saw him, was h-he h-here?" I'm stuttering, trying to find the right words.

When the bird on my wrist lifts its head, looks at me oddly and asks.... "Gawk?"

Then it falls to the floor, dead.

Tina looks at me. "Well, shit," she says.

I glare at her. "It's your bird. You deal with this."

"Fine," she agrees. "Vamps don't mind dead things." She flashes me her fangs.

I hide under my blanket and hope the bird's death isn't a portent of something worse.

## 12

———

The next morning I wake up before the sun rises, hoping to catch Metis before everyone else is up. The dead bird is gone—or at least out of sight—so Tina has taken care of it, but I really don't want to know how. I have too much shit to deal with to worry about that.

As I hurry across campus, the sound of running feet comes from behind me. I duck behind a giant Kratos statue, depicting him strangling the life from two monsters simultaneously. A group of maybe twenty students thunder past. Some of them are shifted into wolves or other animals, but others are in their human form. They wear masks, though, so it's impossible to identify who they are. There's no mistaking Nico's voice at the back of the pack, urging them on.

"You have to be fast to beat a vampire. Only the strongest will survive if they decide to come for all the shifters!"

His voice carries back to me even after the group disappears over a small rise. Nico has taken to training some volunteers, claiming that—with the war on hold—MOA students need as much activity as possible. Funny, though, how he only invited shifters to participate. I shake my head, certain this will end badly for everyone.

But there's nothing I can do about it now, so I continue on my way.

When I arrive at Metis's office, she doesn't look happy to see me. "You can't possibly have collected the other two parts of the sword."

"No, I wanted to see you about something else."

She sighs. "Edie, I don't have time for daily chats with you."

"This isn't a chat. I need a favor. Normally I'd ask Themis, but you told me to stay away from her." I look over my shoulder where the sky has begun to lighten through the window. "It's early still, though, maybe no one will see me if I go to her now—"

"No, no," Abruptly changing her mood, Metis pulls me into her office. "There are eyes everywhere. Let's not risk it. Why don't you tell me—quickly—what you need."

Since Metis doesn't invite me to sit, I stand. "I found the first piece of the sword last night."

Metis's eyes light up. "Wonderful."

"Yeah, I guess. But the thing is...holding it...I realized I'm not sure I want to find the other pieces."

"Oh." Metis nods and looks pissed, but also like she's trying to hide it. "But dear, we discussed this the other day. You don't need to use the sword—"

"But once it's out there someone else could use it. A sword that can kill a god would probably also do a lot of damage to non-gods. And what if I'm not the person in the prophecy, what if someone else uses it to kill Mr. Zee? Themis said that'd be bad."

"Hmmm." Metis walks around her desk and sinks into her chair, looking pensive. After a moment she gestures for me to sit as well. "So you need a pep talk of some sort? That's why you're here? And..." She sighs heavily. "This will be a regular thing?"

"No, that's not why I'm here." I hesitate. Since Metis seems pretty annoyed with being bothered again, I decide to sweeten the pot. "Actually, if I can get this one thing, I promise you won't hear from me again until I have the second sword piece."

Metis leans forward. "What is it you want?"

"I want to see my sister. I want to talk with her and find out what she thinks about all this."

I hold my breath afraid she'll say no. But instead the concern melts from her face. "Is that all? Good lord, I thought you were going to demand immortality." Metis laughs. "Yes, yes. I'll arrange for you to sneak into her cell. Come back after breakfast."

I stand, and a shaky laugh escapes me. "That's it, then? I can see her tonight?"

"Didn't I just say so?" She pulls some papers closer and bends to them. "Close the door on your way out, won't you?"

"Thank you," I say softly as I close the door behind me.

―――――

Later, as I make my way back to Metis, I run into Greg. "Edie." He stops me, studies me. "Cassie wouldn't tell me what is going on but I know something is up. I want to help."

I shake my head. "You can't help, Greg."

He starts to protest but I brush past him. I hate leaving him in the dark, but it's safer for him. When I push my way into Metis's office I'm surprised to find Fern there as well.

She gives me a little wave as Metis hustles us down the hall to her lab.

"Fern tells me the two of you are friends," she says to me. "That's good. It will make this all a bit more comfortable, I'm sure."

"Make what more comfortable?" I ask.

Fern looks at me and shrugs. So she's in the dark as well.

Metis doesn't answer until we're in the lab with the door closed and securely locked. Then moving toward a giant cauldron at the center of the room, she answers, "You'll need to switch faces, of course. It's really quite simple. Fern has access to your sister and you do not."

"Oh." Fern's hands go to her cheeks, like she's protecting her face from whatever this process is going to be.

"Um...does it hurt?" I ask.

"Well," Metis says, tossing a piece of dried leaf into the cauldron. "It will essentially reshape your facial structure so...yes. Come here, dear," she says, smiling sweetly at Fern, who gulps.

"You don't have to," I say, quickly.

"Oh, it won't hurt *her*," Metis says, smiling. "You, on the other hand..."

Metis submerges a dipper in the cauldron, and pours a steaming, bright pink liquid into a flask. Handing it to Fern, she instructs her. "Take a mouthful, swish it around, then spit back into the cup."

Ewwww. I mean, I like Fern a lot, but I didn't know back-wash was going to be part of the deal. Still, when Metis hands the flask over to me, the foaming liquid smells pleasant, like bubble gum.

"Bottoms up," I say, nodding to Fern before draining it down.

It pools in my belly, warm and heavy. I belch, and a bit of

colorful mist exits my lips. "Excuse me," I say, bringing my hand to my mouth. But under my fingers I can feel my face shifting, moving...stretching.

"Ouch," I cry, my hands now traveling over my whole face, where I can feel my hairline rearranging itself, my cheeks tightening, my eye sockets shrinking. It feels like my skin should be torn open but it's not; it only rolls under my fingers as the bones beneath my face travel.

The pain drives me to my knees, and my hair falls across my face...but it's not my hair. It's Fern's long and straight locks. I think I'm about to pass out—or maybe even puke—when it's over. Shuddering, I climb to my feet, and Fern gasps, her hands once more going to her own face.

"Whoa," I say, when I glance into the mirror.

I'm not there. It's Fern's lips matching my words, even if it's not her voice.

"I've never seen it done before," Fern says, coming over to me, running her hands wonderingly through my hair.

"It's a terribly complicated spell," Metis says, with a sniff. "I've had graduates attempt it, only to turn themselves into a pile of arms and legs. Took forever to sort that out. I never was sure we got the pieces put in entirely the right places. You humans all look so funny on the inside."

She slaps her knee, once again amused at something rather hideous.

"Well, hurry along," she motions me forward with both hands. "That spell will only last so long. Fern, stay here with me so no one spots you together. Besides, I need help organizing the fingernail clippings from this year's crop of healers."

Only too glad to leave, I slip out the door. I knew that fingernail clippings and hair play a big part in some of the healing arts, but I mostly try not to think too much about everything my witch friends go through to practice their skill.

I slip across campus, reminding myself that I don't have to stick to the shadows. I'm not Edie anymore. I'm Fern, and Fern has the night shift. Checking in on a prisoner would be entirely routine. A shifter guard—one I've spotted before in Nico's training pack—gives me a nod but doesn't meet my eyes. Fern draws no remark from him, so I move forward, remembering the instructions she had given me.

Mavis is being kept in the dungeon. The smell of damp stones and mildew grows heavier as I descend, the walls on either side of the twisting stone staircase getting wetter. There's a light below, sconces lining the hall of the deepest level. I come to the bottom, the smoke from the fires making my eyes water. Which is all for the better, I'm already tearing up at the thought of Mavis being kept down here.

"Here for the cat bitch?" another guard asks. There's two flanking the staircase, both of them decent-sized. I want to strike out at them, shift into a dragon and ash their asses right now. But that wouldn't get Mavis out of her cell, or the magic collar from her neck. Killing them would just put two more bodies on my count, and I'm dedicated to not raising that any higher.

I simply nod, turning to the right, where Fern told me Mavis was being kept in the very last cell. The guard's voices fade as I make my way, the flickering light of the sconces barely lighting a path for me.

"Fern?" Mavis's voice is dull, scratchy, like she's had a sore throat her whole life. Of course, it probably feels that way—all the screams...

I shake my head. "No, it's me, Edie."

"What?" Mavis comes to the bars, her hands closing around them, the chains clinking together. "How?"

There's hope in her voice, but also suspicion. Mavis wasn't an excellent spy for no reason.

"Why do fish live in salt water?" she asks, prompting me with the joke from her latest note. Like all the others, they're from our dad's never-ending treasure trove of middle school principal jokes. He used to read them over the morning announcements every day, making the kids laugh. Although it was usually at him, not the joke.

"Because pepper makes them sneeze," I say. And relief floods my sister's face. She reaches through the bars, running her fingers over my cheekbones.

"Fern looks good on you," she says.

"Don't tell Marguerite," I shoot back, and she smiles through her tears.

"Edie, what are you doing down here? That spell can't last forever. It's not worth risking your—"

"Mr. Zee is my father," I tell her, and her smile immediately falls. "Did Fern tell you—?"

"The prophecy, yes, of course. Zee is worried that some long-lost bastard child is going to come along and kill him." Mavis laughs, but there's no mirth in it. "Edie..."

"There's more," I say, talking fast. She's right, I won't look like Fern forever, and this is supposed to be a quick medical checkup, not a heart to heart. The guards at the end of the hall will get curious if I take too long.

"Cassie had a vision, a prophecy from long ago about three parts of a weapon that Metis had Hephaestus forge in order to kill Zeus, after he left her. Nothing like a scorned woman, I guess."

Mavis's hands are fists now, clenched tightly on the bars of her cell. "And?"

"Those three parts...they're at the three different academies. I found the hilt of a sword, behind" —I swallow thickly—"behind my mother's portrait in the Hall of the Dead."

"And the other two?"

I nod my head. "Metis knows where the one at Amazon Academy is. I haven't looked yet for the one at Underworld Academy. I don't know if I want to." I gulp, knowing my sister won't like what I'm going to say next. "Mavis, I don't think I can kill anyone."

"What?" Mavis pulls away from the bars. "You did a pretty good job at the Spring Fling."

"Yes, but..." I struggle, looking for words. "When I'm a dragon it's easier. I'm myself, but also something else entirely. An animal with a much less nuanced view of justice. Killing just makes sense when I've shifted."

Mavis nods. She knows what I mean about becoming an animal; I've seen her lick her own rear end clean in cat form.

"But you don't think you can when you're human," Mavis finishes for me. "And you have to be human to wield a sword."

"Well, I mean yeah, there's that," I say, surprised that she's still not getting the point. "But also...I don't think I really *want* to kill Zee."

"Why the Hades not?" Mavis asks, her voice rising high enough that I shush her while glancing back down the hall toward the guards. "Edie." She drops her voice, but emotion throbs in every word. "He might be your father, *biologically*, but he's the real monster here, not the ones we've been fighting for years."

"We're not even really doing that anymore—" I start, but Mavis interrupts me.

"Do you know the things he's ordered?" she asks. "The lives ended just because he didn't like someone's comment at dinner? And that's if you *say* the wrong thing. You can also *be* the wrong thing. Just wait. He'll kill all the Moggies before he's done."

I nod. I know she's right.

Now, she can't resist slipping back into all-knowing big-sister mode.

"Dad told me about MOA when I turned eighteen," she says.

"Yes, Mavis. I know," I control the urge to roll my eyes. But just barely. It's amazing that she's behind bars, suffering, trapped, on the verge of death—and yet, Mavis can still push my buttons. "Dad told you first. We've covered this already."

"Right, but he didn't tell me everything. I knew we were shifters, but that was all. I vowed to come back here and do everything I could to free the students from being used as human shields for the gods."

Her voice is low, but intense. And her eyes nearly spark with passion for her cause. Clearly, life behind bars has only increased her desire to stop the gods. And I don't think at this point that it's all about justice for the monsters—or the students. It's pretty clear that for Mavis, her cause is now more personal than ever.

I don't understand why I don't feel the same way. After Dad and Grandma died, I was all about vengeance.

Or maybe that was just the handy excuse I needed to come here. If I'm honest with myself, what I really wanted was to find out why Dad died. As if that would bring him back. Instead, it sometimes feels like the more I learn, the further away I get from him.

But it's not like I have some fantasy of Mr. Zee becoming my new dad. Of wiping away my tears or walking me down the aisle someday or shit like that. He's obviously horrible. Epically horrible.

And yet...aren't the Greeks famous for stories about mistaken parentage? It always leads to killing, which pretty quickly gets ugly and messy in a way that can chop the family tree down until only a stump is left. Those are the tragedies. And I'd prefer to move into the comedy portion of my life sometime soon.

I don't say any of this to Mavis, of course. I'm still trying to sort it all out for myself.

"Edie, if you can't do this, then find a way to get me out of here, and I'll get that sword and put it right through Mr. Zee's black heart," Mavis says, breaking into my thoughts.

I raise my head, unsure which part of this to tackle first.

"You can't do it, Mavis. You're not Zeus's bastard child," I tell her. "My mom was a student—Adrianna Aspostolos. She had a thing with Mr. Zee." I clench my fists, remembering what I saw. Then I look up at Mavis. This is the part I've been dreading sharing with her. "Your mom was a student too. Her name was Bella Demopolous. You look a lot like her. But the thing is...Mr. Zee isn't your father. We're not sisters. We're not even related."

I'm crying now, the last word coming out as a sob. I stifle it with my hand, my fingers closing over the unfamiliar contours of Fern's lips.

But Mavis's face has gone hard, the glitter in her eyes is now a cold flicker. "And who is *my* father?"

"Hermes," I whisper, and she backs away from the bars, into the shadow of her cell.

"That son of a bitch," she says, and I can hear tears in her voice. I give her a moment, wiping my own cheeks dry.

"Besides," I go on, hoping to build my case. "Themis says that if Mr. Zee dies, nobody will have control over the minor gods. There'll be all sorts of natural disasters and stuff. Like, end of the world scenario."

There's a huff from the shadows. "Bullshit. Have you seen the state Zeus is in right now? He couldn't control a flock of sheep, let alone all the other gods. That's just propaganda. A rumor I bet Zee started to protect himself."

I'm quiet, mulling that over.

"Edie." Mavis's voice comes from the darkness, heavy and cold. "You have to do this. You have to kill Zeus. Do it for your mother. Do it for the Moggies. Do it for me."

"I can't," I tell her, shaking my head. "I just can't."

Mavis steps back into the light, her sleeves pushed up past her elbows. "Tell me that again," she says, holding her arms out. I can see burn marks, old and new, scarring and scabs lining the soft inner flesh of her arms.

She lifts her hair, turning in a circle so that I can see the bruise around her neck, evidence that she'd been hanged... but not for long enough to kill her. Just torture her. Her ruined voice makes a sudden, horrible sense, and I reach for her through the bars.

"No," she ducks past my reach, and her tone isn't the older sister I know. It's something deeper, and harder. It belongs to the person who could dig out Nico's eye and leave him for dead.

"You have to do this, Edie," she says, pulling back into the dark once more. "He's already ordered my death."

"You'll get a trial—"

"Oh yes," she laughs, a scratchy, horrible sound. "A trial that he will preside over. He wants me dead. And if you do nothing—soon, I will be."

I back away trying to avoid her words. But they find me. The hit me like an arrow to the heart.

"Are we no longer sisters? Is that it? Mr. Zee is your blood now. So what does that make me?"

"Mavis, no," I protest, tears now falling in earnest. "Of course, we're still sisters. Always. Forever."

Mavis says nothing for a long moment. She just studies me, as if weighing my words. "If I'm still your sister, prove it." She reaches through the bars and grabs my shirt, pulling me close. With her breathe warm on my face, she whispers the truth.

"You kill Zeus, or you kill me."

**13**

———

"**O**h my gods," Cassie says an hour later, her arms around me as I cry on the floor of her dorm room. "That's horrible."

"I know," I say, wiping my eyes—returned to their rightful shape and color now that Metis's spell has worn off. "I don't know what to do."

Cassie's mouth goes into a thin line. "Wrong. You know exactly what to do. We have to get the rest of the weapon pieces. You said yourself, you don't have to kill Mr. Zee. Just get him to step down and agree to let Mavis go."

I wipe my nose. Everything Cassie says seems to make sense, here in her warm, brightly lit room. The dungeons got to me in the small amount of time I was there, making everything seem bleak, all my choices bad ones.

No wonder Mavis seemed so different. She's been down there a long time. The whole being tortured thing probably hasn't helped her attitude either.

"So..." Cassie reaches under her bed, producing the Seer Stone.

"No," I say, emphatically shaking my head. "You said—"

"That I didn't like how it made me feel, and what it made me see," Cassie says. "It's still true, I don't. But you know what else I don't like? Everything that is happening to my best friend. I can't just sit here and hold you while you cry, Edie. I have to do something."

"Are you sure?" I ask.

"Yeah," Cassie says, but her voice has lost some of its conviction. Even so, she closes her fist around the stone.

Immediately, her mouth drops open, and her eyes roll back.

"Wait!" I shout. I hadn't meant for her to do it right away. But she's already gone, in a trance. I thread my fingers with hers, holding both her hands tight. A small sigh escapes her, and a familiar voice comes out of her mouth, one I haven't heard since that terrible day of the tsunami.

"If you touch my granddaughter, I'll tear you to pieces!" It's the voice of my grandmother, a harpy in disguise who gave up her life to protect me. She died in an elevator fall on the same day my dad was swept out to sea.

This isn't the prophecy I need. This is something else.

"Cassie!" I cry, shaking her. The stone rolls from her hand, and her mouth snaps shut, eyes rolling to the front. She sags against my shoulder, barely able to keep herself upright.

"You shouldn't have touched me," she says weakly. "I saw a flash of something—but then you grabbed my hands and it was...I could hear you, Edie. I could hear you yelling. There was the ocean, and a great face made of water. Levi, just like you always said. He took your Dad and you..."

Her eyes clear for a second, focus on me. She puts her hands on both sides of my face. "You were so scared! I'm so sorry you had to see that. I'm so sorry that happened to you."

"My grandmother," I prompt her, grabbing her wrists. "You were speaking in her voice."

"Yes," Cassie nods, her eyes clouding, not with the opaque white of a trance, but with regular, human worry. "I saw her too. I saw it all."

"Tell me," I urge her. I've long suspected Grandma's elevator falling that day wasn't connected to the tidal wave. There's just no way it was a coincidence. Not with all the secrets I've learned since then.

Cassie is crying now, tears spilling over her lashes. "He instigated Levi to take out your dad. Then he went after your grandma," she says. "She was trying to protect you, trying to keep him from coming for you. She knew that if you didn't have anyone left in your life—you'd take the invitation. You'd go with him and you'd come to MOA. And once here, you'd be in danger."

Cassie falls forward, clearly exhausted.

"Who killed my grandmother?" I ask desperately. "Who did you see?"

Cassie looks up at me, circles already under her eyes. "It was Hermes."

"Hermes?!" But even as I say his name, I realize how much sense it makes. I should've figured it out on my own a long time ago. "Hermes," I say again, this time accepting it.

Cassie nods once and mouths the words, *I'm sorry.*

"Not as sorry as Hermes will be."

———

When I get back to my room, I don't feel like explaining to Tina how I just found out the god who brought me to MOA in the first place wasn't doing so out of the kindness of his heart—if gods even have those.

No, Hermes was keeping tabs on me, and had been for who knows how long. What did he suspect? Did he know I was Mr. Zee's child?

There are a million questions in my head, and more in my heart, and Tina can immediately see that something is troubling me.

"What's wrong?" she asks when I walk in, wiping tears from my eyes. "You know what? Never mind. I really don't care. I've got bigger problems. Like a dead Stymphalian bird."

"Right," I say, eyeing the feathery corpse, which she'd propped it up in the window, more to have it out of the way than anything else, but the sunlight isn't doing it any favors. A few feathers fall out even while we're talking.

"What am I going to do?" Tina wails. "I can't go to class without a bird. And I already missed breakfast."

"And you can't report him dead, either," I remind her. "We talked about this. He kicked the bucket right after drinking from the ambrosia Hepa was about to deliver to Mr. Zee. She's helping Themis to poison him, and we can't blow her cover because of your stupid bird."

"We don't know that for sure," Tina counters. "Mr. Zee is the head of the gods, you know. It could have just been undiluted ambrosia. It might have knocked us dead too, if the bird hadn't downed it all first."

"I guess that's true," I say, but inwardly, I don't agree. I've seen Hepa coming and going from Themis's office too many times to buy into Tina's simpler explanation. "Regardless, how would we explain a dead Stymphalian bird? Do you want to tell Themis we've been stealing ambrosia on the sly? Or face Artemis after she finds out one of her beloved pets is dead?"

Tina goes a shade paler than she already is, which is

saying a lot for a vampire. "No way," she says. "Themis has no tolerance for drinking on campus. And Artemis..."

"Is an unforgiving battle ax," I finish for her. "They'll just issue you a new bird, anyway," I say, as I join her on her bed.

We both look at the dead bird as a fly settles on its beak, then crawls into its mouth.

"Ugh," Tina says. "I bet it's laying maggots in there."

"More food for Vee," I say, trying to find the bright side.

The Venus fly trap turns its head towards me when it hears its name. It's bizarre how life-like it is. Even when Tina's bird was alive, I think Vee was the more sentient of the two. And now...

I go still, my mind churning. Vee tilting her head, studies me almost like she can read my thoughts.

"Tina," I say. "I have an idea. And you're not going to like it."

————

"I can *try*," Fern says. "But I can't promise excellent results. Life is an incredibly difficult thing to mimic. That level of magic is way above my abilities."

"But you can try," Tina repeats. "Right?"

Fern looks at me, unsure.

I sigh. "Look, I know we're asking a lot. And I know that I just took your face earlier today, so it's a big ask on top of a big ask."

"Um, her face?" Tina asks, but I wave it away.

"But we don't have a good explanation for a dead Stympahlian bird that doesn't get everybody into a lot of trouble."

"So if you'd take a swing at it, we'd really appreciate it," Tina finishes for me. Unfortunately, she allows her fangs to erupt as she speaks, which makes it come off more like a threat than a favor.

"Okay," Fern nods. "Shut the door. This could get loud. And possibly very smelly."

She isn't kidding. It takes most of an hour, three rune stones, five very fresh piles of Stymphalian poop (happily donated by Val's bird), a little of Tina's blood, one of Vee's leaves, some fire and enough chanting that Fern nearly loses her voice.

"Well," she says hoarsely, lifting her hair off her neck as the smoke clears. "What do you think?"

"Um..." Tina watches as her bird performs a bizarre, lurching walk around the room. It runs into her bed, then falls over onto its back, legs still valiantly moving. It's like a weird mix of a wind-up toy with low batteries and a drunk turtle stuck on its back.

Fern picks it up, rights it, and the bird takes off again, this time marching into the closed door. It keeps walking in place as its beak repeatedly bounces against the door.

*Thunk.*

"Guys," Tina says.

*Thunk.*

"I don't think—"

*Thunk.*

"This will work."

*Thunk.*

"Oh sons of Zeus, will someone please stop that thing?!"

Fern goes to the befuddled bird and picks him up, lovingly cradling her new creation in her arms.

"He can't help it," she says. "It's not his fault I'm not good at this yet. It's complicated magic. I put a spell on him that should keep him from rotting for a good long while, and you won't have to worry about him eating—"

"Or pooping?" Tina asks, hopefully.

"No, he won't do that either," Fern says. "He *is* dead. I can't resurrect him—that's seriously dark magic. All I did was make him *seem* alive."

"Kind of," Tina says, eyeing the bundle in Fern's arms as his neck goes completely limp, and he stares at her upside down, unblinking.

I squint at him. "I don't know, now that's he's not pooping, he's kind of cute."

"Cute?" Tina looks at me like I'm crazy.

"I think we should name him," I add, reaching to pet his feathers. They're slick beneath my fingers and the body beneath them is cold. Even colder than Tina and Val. "Hey, he's kinda like a vampire," I say with a grin.

Tina's fangs come out for real this time. "I have killed people for lesser insults."

I ignore this. Tina threatening to kill me just doesn't have an effect on me anymore. "I think we should call him Bernie."

"Ugh," Tina sighs. "First of all, we're not naming him. Second of all, he's my dead bird and if anyone's naming him, it will be me. Third, just because you have an old person name, doesn't mean everyone else should too."

I laugh and it feels good to know that I still can...even as Hermes's name nibbles at the back of my mind. "I actually picked Bernie because of this old movie. My dad loved it and made me and Mavis watch it. This old guy named Bernie—"

"Ha," Tina interrupts. "I told you it was an old man name."

"Not the point. Anyway, Bernie dies and these two young guys—for reasons—spend a weekend propping him up between them so people think he's still alive."

"That's horrible," Fern says. "Why would your father make you watch this horror story?"

"No, it was a comedy," I correct.

"I'm naming him David Bowie. Bowie for short," Tina declares in a 'subject closed' tone. "'Cause I wish Fern could've reanimated him instead."

"Yeah, I'm definitely not reanimating anyone else," Fern says. "But I think this one went pretty well, all things considered." Fern crosses the room to sit next to Tina on her bed. "The good news is that muscle memory is very strong, even in animals. And the anti-decomposition spell means that his muscles will be in good working order for quite some time."

"Uh-huh..." Tina eyes Fern warily as she settles in next to her and then raises the bird to Tina's shoulder. Bowie moves over to Tina with a shuddering step and latches on.

"See?" Fern exclaims. "Muscle memory!"

The bird utters a half-hearted squawk and falls forward, claws still embedded in Tina's shoulder as he does a face-plant into her boobs.

"Hooray for muscle memory," she says, dryly.

## 14

I'm surprised when Fern offers to walk with us to Kratos's class. "Are you the healer today?" I ask. Kratos's classes always have a healer on hand since he likes to keep his student demonstrations very realistic.

"Yep," she nods, patting the satchel at her side. "Got everything I need in case you set someone on fire again. They actually assigned two of us here for today," she says, nodding toward another girl.

"But you permanently fire-proofed Val," I remind her, smiling to myself at the memory of my first class here at the Academy...and the first time I saw Val.

"Not everyone here is so lucky," Fern says, her gaze sweeping the classroom. "I'll make you a list if you want any recommendations on who you should smoke next."

Wow. The anger on campus is bad enough that even kind-hearted Fern has a kill list.

Fern and I slide into seats on either side of Cassie. On my other side, a Stymphalian bird hovers over his prey—the healer Fern nodded to earlier, whose face is bright red as she tries to act like it's not there. It's an attitude that is impossible to maintain, especially when it settles onto her shoulder, talons digging in. She cries out in pain, which only makes some of our classmates titter in amusement.

"Those absolute a-holes," I mutter under my breath to Cassie, who nods in agreement. A familiar fire burns in my gut, and I want to let it reach full force, let it erupt from my throat as I shift into a dragon, burn all the birds, and carry the Moggies somewhere they won't be persecuted simply for having the wrong parents.

But my heroic daydream is interrupted when Hermes blows through the double doors, sending the four Stymphalian birds in the classrooms into a flutter. Since the Stymphalian response to any sort of stimuli is to shit, they of course, immediately drop most of their lunch onto the students below them.

All except for Tina's bird, who tries to take off, but lands unceremoniously on the floor instead. "Easy there, Bowie," she mutters, picking the bird up and dusting him off.

"Hello beautiful students," Hermes croons as he strides into the room. He eyes all of us before him in the usual way —like he's undressing us and likes what he sees.

Funny, the first time I met him, I found it almost flattering. He's so handsome and was so obviously interested in me. Then, later, when it became clear Hermes would bag anyone or anything, it became more of an annoyance. The kind I've learned to roll my eyes at along with everybody else.

But now it pisses me off. The entitlement of this jerk. The way he goes through life using his power to just take and take and take.

He took me here, to Mount Olympus Academy, feeding me a bunch of lies on the way.

He took Mavis's mother and then let her die giving birth to his child. I bet he never even gave her a second thought.

And he took my grandmother. A badass harpy who disguised herself in human form so she could help raise me.

"Alright, class," Hermes says. "I know you're all expecting Kratos to be your teacher for *Torture: The Transition from Lies to Truth* class, but he's been reassigned elsewhere for the time being."

There's some shuffling in the classroom, and Cassie leans into me. "Fern says Kratos has been assigned to guard Mavis in her cell. Apparently, the guards there haven't been doing a great job. I guess Zeus found out Mavis had paper and pencil, and he threw a hissy fit."

"That's ridiculous!" I sputter, furious with despair.

Without pencil and paper, our notes will be at an end. They were the only thing keeping me from going crazy with worry. And for Mavis...I can only imagine they were an important lifeline for her as well.

"She's got a magical collar that keeps her from shifting," I add. "And she's locked inside a cell that has multiple spells reinforcing the bars. Why does she also need a completely ripped jailor?"

Cassie shrugs. "I think Mr. Zee is super scared, Edie."

"Good," I say quietly, the fire in my belly reigniting as I think of the burns I saw on my sister. "He should be."

"So," Hermes says, glancing around. "Who can tell me what this class is about?"

We all look at each other, blankly. A vampire slowly raises his hand. "Um...torture?"

"Yes," Hermes agrees. "Torture. And when do we employ these techniques?"

"As sparingly as possible," Fern cries out, coming to her feet. "Testimony given under torture is highly questionable.

A victim will say anything to stop their pain. That doesn't make those statements reliable!"

Quite a few applaud her words, but this is an assassin class. Most of the students boo her back down into her seat.

"Torture is a tried and true method," Nico says, standing behind his desk. "Believe me. I would know." There's a collective gasp as Nico raises his shirt to show off a criss-crossing of silvery, scarred skin.

There's also a really decent set of abs under that, so I'm not sure that all of the gasps are purely sympathetic in nature.

"Wait!" Cassie jumps into the argument. "I was there when the monsters hurt you, Nico. You didn't share any information. You stood firm against the pain and said nothing. That means torture doesn't work."

"It only means that it doesn't work on the son of Maddox Tralano," Nico says, his eyes sweeping the room. Quite a few vampires stare back with equal amounts of antagonism.

Hermes clears his throat. "I think that's enough debating about whether or not torture is a viable—"

"No!" Fern says, coming to her feet again. "Torture is wrong, period. It doesn't gain any information from our enemies. If anything, it encourages them to make up something, just to end the pain. Then we chase down false leads, all because some bloodthirsty torturers wanted to get their rocks off."

Hermes immediately brightens. "On the subject of getting your rocks off, I can certainly say that—"

"Oh gods," Cassie says. "I don't think Kratos gave him any lesson plans."

Around us the rest of the class seems to have come to the same conclusion. Hermes has no idea what he's doing and no idea how to control us.

Students at my old non-magical high school were the same way when a clueless substitute teacher walked into the room. Once it's clear that the old rules won't be enforced—anarchy rules.

Suddenly the torture discussion gets a lot more heated. Nico and a few shifter friends begin exchanging angry words with vampires. They're threatening to use each other as a torture example.

We're seconds away from a full out brawl and Hermes is sorta half-heartedly calling for everyone to, "Settle down. Nobody is going to be used as an example right now."

Suddenly, I have an idea. It comes straight from the churning in my gut. Which probably means it's the kind of idea best ignored.

Hermes laughs. "Okay, if you guys are gonna fight each other. I think we should put some money on it, to make things really interesting. It will be like a math lesson too."

I stand up so fast my chair falls to the floor.

"Hermes?" I say, walking over to him with a big wide fake smile. "I have an idea for a project that will take up the entire class period."

"You do?" he asks. His gaze swings toward the students ready to fight, then back to me, clearly torn.

"Absolutely," I say. "And I'd hate for Kratos to be annoyed if we strayed too far from the lesson plan."

This gets Hermes's attention. I'm not surprised. He's the silver-tongued type, who's gotten through his centuries of life floating by on his charm. Kratos, on the other hand, is a man of few words. He'd rather use his fists to express himself. And if he decides that Hermes messed up his class, he will happily communicate that by temporarily separating Hermes's head from his body.

"What are you thinking, my pretty girl?" he asks.

I bite my tongue to keep from telling him I'm *not* his girl. Instead, I blink up at him as if I'm the Edie of old. A girl who has no idea she has a dragon inside of her. "Well, the other students gave me an idea. Kratos really does like us to have hands-on activities. But in a controlled way, of course. So, I have an idea for us to settle the argument as to whether or not torture is effective."

"By all means," Hermes says, pressing me forward with a hand on my lower—much *lower*—back. "Please, share with the rest of the class."

I make my way to the front of the room and lift a pair of manacles from the wall.

"May I?" I ask Hermes, one eyebrow raised suggestively.

"Oh, please do," he says, giving my legs a sweeping look as I close the first manacle around his wrist. "Is this in relation to getting my rocks off?"

I only smile and take him by his chained hands, leading him to an empty desk. He takes a seat, looking up at me expectantly.

I turn to face the class. "What is something we can all agree is true?"

"Cat-shifters are perverts!" someone yells.

"Moggies belong in Hades!" comes the suggestion, followed by a muted but angry rumbling from some other students.

"Stymphalian birds stink!" Val says, reaching up to mock-affectionately give his bird's nose a boop.

There's a smattering of applause, which sends a few of the birds in question into a quick, circular flight pattern around the room, before returning to their captives' shoulders.

"Stymphalian birds stink," I repeat, looking over the room. "This is a true and indisputable fact."

All the heads are nodding. This is one thing we can agree on, Moggy-lovers or not. Vampires or werewolves. We're all being forced to smell these crap-tastic birds in tight quarters.

"Very well," I say, turning back to Hermes. "Don't you think that the aroma of these birds is particularly pleasing?"

"I...what?" Hermes asks. "No, they smell like a harpy died and ate its own body and crapped it out and then died again."

"That's what you *really* think?" I ask, leaning towards him.

"Hades yeah," he says, nodding emphatically.

"Okay," I say, and walk over to the wall where Kratos keeps the class weapons. I turn to the classroom and point to each student with a Stymphalian bird as companion. "Please come up here and select a weapon."

Tina is the first up out of her seat, bird reattached to her shoulder, but the rest come as well. If I'm not mistaken, each one of them is almost certainly looking to hit something. Hard.

After everyone else has chosen a weapon, I select a mace.

"I'll go first," I tell my fellow Moggies. Val's gaze catches mine and he raises his eyebrows in question. Doubt trickles through my stomach. I've been keeping my distance from him because he killed Maddox and now I'm plotting to overthrow Mr. Zee.

It's hard to take the high ground with a mace in your hands. And even more difficult as I approach Hermes, who smiles up at me guilelessly.

"Hello again, my lovely girl," he says with a bright smile.

I remind myself of all his sins as I lift the mace.

"Hey, have you guys ever played mace-ball?" Hermes

asked. "It'd be a great way to kill time—er learn about torture and stuff—"

Whatever else he was going to say is lost. I bring the mace down in a violent arc, obliterating his right hand into a pulpy mess.

Sick rises in my throat and I quickly swallow it back down. The mace falls from my hands, clattering to the floor.

"AAAAaaaaaa!" Hermes screams, leaping to his feet. But he doesn't get far because his legs are tangled in the desk. He falls forward, tipping the desk over and crawling away from me. Students in the back stand to get a better look.

"Tell me Stymphalian birds smell amazing," I say to Hermes, my voice calm and low. "And please do not again refer to me as your lovely, pretty, gorgeous, or any other kind of girl."

He stares at me wide-eyed and confused, like I've suddenly started speaking another language.

Turning, I gesture to Tina that it's her turn. She smiles as she steps forward. This time Hermes knows it's coming.

"No, no, Tina. Don't do this, it will upset your bird—"

Hermes's ankle explodes, shards of bone flying out towards our fellow classmates.

"Hey," Nico says, brushing some of the bone from his shirt as he stands. "This does not seem like the sort of thing Kratos—"

"Sit down, Nico," I say, my voice hard.

My eyes meet his. Cocking his head, he stares at me for a long moment. Then he grins. "You wanna prove a point? Okay. Go ahead."

He says it like he's indulging me. If it wasn't for Hermes moaning behind me, I'd be tempted to pick up that mace and go after Nico this time.

I really need to set that boy straight soon and let him know that we are never ever ever getting together.

But first—I need to get through this lesson.

Hermes yells, again, frantically trying to heal himself. His hand was already mostly restructured, but now he's got to redirect his energy to his foot, so his hand hangs in the manacle, muscle and sinew regrown, but not yet covered with skin.

"They smell like roses!" I yell at Hermes.

"But they don't," he responds, as behind my back I gesture to the red-faced healer from before.

Being a healer and not even a student in this class, I'd expected her to balk. But she grabbed onto a spear without hesitation and has been holding it tightly, waiting her turn.

Now, squeezing her eyes shut, she launches her spear. Lucky shot—it pierces Hermes's midsection and pins him to the classroom floor. Unfortunately, the poor girl doesn't have any experience at not vomiting in front of one's peers. She runs out of the classroom with both hands pressed against her face.

Everyone is on their feet now, some students egging me on, some with pained expressions. It's possible someone might have stepped in to stop this, except I've got the two alphas of the classroom on my side—Nico and Val.

And now it's the latter's turn.

Val steps forward with a sword in hand. He holds it with casual authority.

"They smell like ambrosia!" I say.

Val eyes Hermes and then with one clean move, slices Hermes's leg right at the knee. Hermes screams and writhes, his hand now recovered, but his foot still a bloody mess. He tries to crawl away, but the spear has him pinioned to the floor. He pulls it out, inching back on his palms as a little owl shifter steps forward, a throwing star clutched in her hand.

"Like a Hawaiian luau!" I scream, and nod at the girl to send her throwing star.

She hesitates and it looks like she's gonna bail entirely, but then a screech comes out of her that sounds like, "It smells like a pumpkin spice latte!"

The throwing star goes straight into his forehead.

"Oh gods, it's true," Hermes sobs, holding up his manacled hands in clear surrender. "Yes, like Athena's robes, and Metis's bedroom, and a moonlit garden of orchids and the strands of a maiden's hair and all of the honey of all the bees in the world. Stymphalian scent should be captured and bottled and sold and I'll buy every bottle. Please, please stop making them hurt me, Edie."

As he listed the best smells he could think of, Hermes's severed leg caught up to him and reattached itself, his ankle re-knitted together, as well as his forehead—though the throwing star is still jammed in there.

"There we have it," I say, turning to the class as Hermes pulls the star from his head. "Torture *does* work. If you want to get someone to admit to just about anything."

A lot of students applaud me, though others give me a wide berth as they exit the classroom. Val carefully cleans his sword before putting it back into place.

Our eyes meet again and I expect a wink or even a nod of approval. But instead he looks...concerned.

A part of me wants to run over and defend myself. The other knows that there is no defense. I am not the sweet little Edie he first met. Maybe he's not the only one wondering what his crush is capable of.

Or maybe not. Nico's hand lands on my shoulder and he gives it a tight squeeze. "Damn, Edie. I love seeing that side of you. Let's see more of the dragon in the girl and the girl in the dragon," he growls, low close to my ear in a way that's supposed to be sexy. I think.

Before I can finish shuddering, he gives me another squeeze and then bounds out of the room, saying something about rib sandwiches being on the lunch menu and he doesn't want them to run out.

Honestly, a sudden buzzing in my ears made it difficult to hear. And now there's spots in my vision too. I remember feeling this way after the Spring Fling. There was the euphoria of battle and then...the crash, as adrenaline receded and my battered conscience took its place.

"Edie!" Cassie comes running to my side. "That was... well, I don't...I can't decide if I'm proud of you or scared of you."

"You don't have to be either," I say, pushing my hair out of my eyes with a shaky hand. "I didn't do it to prove a point."

"You didn't?" Fern asks. "Because it felt very pointed. Well, the parts I was able to watch, anyway." The same concern that was on Val's face is in Fern's too.

"No," I say, eyeing a moaning Hermes as he pulls himself up off the floor. Stepping forward, I offer him my hand. He startles then scuttles away.

He looks at me like I'm a monster.

Maybe I am.

My dragon has killed, but I never have. I wondered if I was even capable of it.

I guess now I know.

"Edie." Fern and Cassie lean into me on either side. "Are you okay?"

"Sometimes we have to do things," I hear myself say. The

room is empty now except for us, so I don't try to stop the tears as they begin to flow.

I want to tell them more, but not in an open classroom. It could put us all in danger if I explained that I need Zee to believe he can die. And to do that, I need to create a convincing narrative of his death. Part of that is knowing exactly how fast a god can heal. If I was Mr. Zee hearing that, I'd be very afraid.

As my legs give way, Cassie's and Fern's arms fold around me.

*I did this for Mavis*, I add silently. *And for Bella Demopoulous*.

*And my Grandma.*

**15**

———

**M**ore than a few people from class give me a wide berth as we head to the cafeteria. The only ones that seem to be impressed by my violent side are—of course—members of Nico'sshifters-only war party. One of them claps me on the shoulder as we're filling our trays.

"I knew you had it in you," he says. "Even if we haven't seen any real fire since the Spring Fling. Once a killer, always a killer."

I smile wanly and give him a fist bump, nodding noncommittally when he tells me there's a stalk and kill practice session planned after classes today, on the green.

"See you there," he says, giving me an appraising once-over. He's about to touch my shoulder, but rethinks it, settling for a wink instead. No doubt Nico has informed his entire army that I'm his intended—at least in his own mind. So hands off.

I've lost my appetite.

I'm dumping my full tray in the trash when I feel a hand

on my elbow. Either Nico's shifter friend just found his courage or—no wait, this is a cold touch.

I turn to find Val, his face a mask of worry.

"Not eating?"

I shake my head. "Not hungry."

There's a lot of things I'm not lately. Not hungry. Not brave. Not sure. Not confident.

But the one thing I know that I *am*, is perhaps maybe slightly possibly—a little bit in love with Val.

And I just tortured someone in front of him. Which might be a turn off.

His hand tightens on my elbow. "Walk with me," he says.

Quite a few heads turn as we leave the cafeteria together; it probably doesn't help that Val's wearing a T-shirt that reads "FOUNDING MEMBER: STYMPHALIAN BIRD LOVERS CLUB."

"Tina made you another T-shirt," I say, with a nod toward Val's chest. "I like the ambiguity there. Do you love Kevin or is Kevin your..." I stop, realizing that I don't really want to make a sex joke with Val.

But it's too late. "My lover?" Val fills in, his face serious while his eyes laugh at me. "There is definitely chemistry between Kevin and me, but since we're roommates, we both felt it was best to keep things platonic."

I can't help but laugh as we step outside, amazed at how just being with Val can lift my spirits. Kevin launches off Val's shoulder, spreading his wings to catch the fresh air. He takes a lazy loop above us, before landing on Val's shoulder once more. Meanwhile, Val's hand trails down my arm until it closes around mine.

"You might want to be a little more subtle," I tell him, although I don't pull away. "There's a werewolf with an anger control problem who wants to marry me."

"I can handle Nico," Val says, so casually that I can't decide if I'm irritated by his confidence or turned on. "But I don't want to talk to you about him. How is Mavis doing?"

We settle in beneath the branches of a willow, its long trailing fingers hiding us from the outside world. I tell him about my trip to the dungeons, how badly my sister is being treated, and how she believes the only way she can be saved is if Mr. Zee dies.

"And" —I take a deep breath, going all in— "She wants me to do it."

Val nods, unsurprised. "And you could, because you're Zeus's daughter."

I pull back, my thunder stolen. "How did you know that?"

"Let's see." He pretends to think hard, ticking reasons off on his fingers. "You're the first dragon shifter to ever exist, your parents smuggled you off campus after you were born and raised you in secret—"

"Wait," I stop him, and ask again. "How did you know *that*?"

He drops his hand, and levels his gaze at me. "Because I'm working with the monsters."

"Val!" I instinctively reach for him, clutching his hands. "That's incredibly dangerous! Nico has an entire army of students on the lookout for spies and traitors. If he suspected you, it would be the perfect excuse for him to come after you."

"I know," Val agrees. "And I'm being very careful."

I narrow my eyes at him. "I wouldn't say that, exactly. I know there was another Moggy out after curfew the other night. Your bird gave you away."

"This guy has more than one use," Val says, reaching into his pocket for some granola, which the bird gently pecks from his fingers. "Kevin may mark me as a Moggy, but I've trained him to run messages as well. There's a drop not far from here, in the swamp. And a centaur waiting there every evening with treats. Isn't that right, buddy?"

Amazingly, Kevin rests his forehead against Val's for second, and emits something like a low coo. It's sweet, and almost cute—except now I'm worried that Kevin is going to get Val killed.

"Val, if anyone catches you..."

"What about you?" he asks. "You marched straight into the dungeons."

"To see my sister!" I counter. "It was worth the risk."

"Worth killing Zee?" Val asks, and I drop my gaze.

"I don't want to kill anyone, ever again."

Val laughs, a short sharp sound. "Does that mean Tina can stop telling me her plan for how she'll kill you if you win the 'Most Murderous' prize at graduation instead of her?"

I frown at Val, because I'm pretty sure this isn't a joke. "In this scenario is Tina murdering me because I won instead of her, or to prove that she deserves the 'Most Murderous' title?"

"I think it's kind of a two birds, one stone type thing." At this, Kevin squawks in protest at this and Val reassuringly pets his head. "Look, Edie, I think it's great you want to be a pacifist dragon shifter, although it's kinda weird to hear that after what you did to Hermes in class today."

I can't help but stiffen. "You disapprove?"

"Disapprove? No. But..." Val makes a humming sound low in his throat, then he tilts his head to study me for a minute. "Do you know what makes a vampire a vampire? Beyond needing special sunscreen and our hemoglobin heavy diet?"

"Vampires don't sleep, they're cold to the touch, and can sometimes levitate. Remember I've been Tina's roommate for a while now. I know more than you think." I shrug, not liking the turn this conversation has taken. "But what does that have to do with anything?"

"It matters because you need to understand how you're different," Val answers. He turns to me, his eyes intense. "Vampires that are made, the ones turned from humans, are animals. They can't think or feel anything beyond their hunger. We kill those vampires, because they give us, the born vamps, a bad name. The only difference between them and us is that we can control our hunger, but we are all killers at heart."

"You're not like that," I can't help but protest.

"I am exactly like that." Val's mouth twists into one of its half smiles. "I watched the life fade from Maddox's eyes. She died at my hands, Edie. And I took pleasure in it."

"No." I turn away from him, not wanting to hear anymore.

Of course, I'm not an idiot. I know what Val is. I know he's dangerous. And I've been fairly certain he was responsible for Maddox's death. But when I'm with him, none of those things seem true.

"Why are you telling me this?" I ask.

"Because I can't make my heart start beating, any more than you can make yours stop. You're not like most of the students here and that's a good thing. But the way you were with Hermes today...it scared me."

I scoff. "You—the big bad vampire—were scared?"

Val's hand closes around my chin, forcing me to look at him as he tells me, "I was scared *for you*. Of what this place is doing to you. You should leave Mount Olympus and never look back."

Val makes it sound so simple. But this has become my home. I don't know where else I would go. Also there's the small matter of, "Mavis." I say her name aloud, reminding Val of why I can't leave even if I wanted to.

"I know." Releasing me, he sits back. "The monsters are putting together a rescue mission. They haven't forgotten everything Mavis did for them—or you, Edie. The family of the monster baby you saved has vowed to return the favor by freeing Mavis."

"That's..." I feel tears pricking my eyes. "That's so sweet."

But Val shakes his head. "It's not sweet. It's war, and this is an alliance." Suddenly, he's not the Val who never takes anything seriously. Instead, he's all business. "I need to know everything you can remember about the dungeons. Where is Mavis being held? How many guards are there? What kind of protective spells are on the bars?"

"She's in the—" I begin, but Val stops me.

"Tell it to the bird," he says.

"Um... what?"

Val reaches into his pocket, retrieves a little bit of pink powder, and gently blows it into the bird's face. Its eyes go wide and staring, and its beak falls open.

"Tell him," Val says.

Feeling awkward, I turn to the bird and reveal everything I know about the dungeons, adding that Mavis is wearing a collar that prevents her from shifting, and that Kratos is now personally guarding her cell.

I nod to Val when I'm finished, and he reaches into his other pocket, this time producing a blue powder. One whiff of it and the bird cocks its head the other direction, beak still open as my voice comes out of its throat, repeating everything I'd just said, word for word.

"Oh gods, make it stop," I say, burying my face in Val's shoulder.

"I know, it's a little bizarre," he says, tapping the bird between the eyes. It stops talking, then looks to Val for a treat. He hands over the granola, and the bird happily chomps away.

"But wait," I say. "When I told you about Mavis getting a trial, you basically said it was hopeless."

"I know, and I shouldn't have said that. Ever since Larissa died, optimism has not been my first response." Val shakes his head. "And I won't lie to you—it is a long shot. Maddox's last attack on the monsters was a brutal one. They weren't wiped out, exactly, but a lot of them lost the will to fight. You were there, Edie, you saw it. Maddox didn't fight with honor; she was killing non-combatants. The monsters are just like us. They have families and children, and people that they love. A lot of them don't want to risk the lives of their loved ones against an enemy that will stoop that low."

"I used to have a family, too," I say, my chin raised high. "And now all I have is Mavis. You're right, I'm not a stone cold killer. But I will fight for those I love. So what can I do to help the monsters?"

Val hesitates and I wonder if he's not going to answer. But then with a shake of his head, he says, "We're still gathering information, trying to see if there's even a way to get her out of there. Anything you know, any possible weakness could be used to our advantage. But Edie...right now everyone believes that you're a patriot, a true supporter of Mr. Zee. I've been outed as a Moggy and the entire campus knows vampires killed Nico's mom. I'm not risking anything more by spying for the monsters." He pauses before adding, "But you are."

"I accept that," I say. "Now put this bird on record again, I've got a lot to say."

I tell Val—well, his bird—everything. I spill the beans about the weapon in three pieces, how I believe there's a piece at each Academy, and how I've already located the one at MOA. I don't say where I found it, though. I would trust Val with the information, but I still can't forget that a monster killed my father. Each side has its share of good and bad guys.

"And," I add, finishing up, "I'm pretty sure Themis is poisoning Mr. Zee."

"What do you mean?" Val asks, eyebrows raised.

"Haven't you notice that Mr. Zee has been a little...off?"

"He's been like that for a while now."

"That's because of Themis," I tell him. "Although she's not doing it directly. Hepa helps by delivering the poisoned ambrosia to him every evening. By itself it won't kill him—"

"No," he says, understanding, "but it can wither his powers. Possibly to the point where he can be killed. And there's a sword out there strong enough to do that, along with a prophecy saying you must be the one to swing it."

"But I'm not going to," I assure him. "I meant what I said about no more killing. I've done enough."

I think back to the night of the Spring Fling, and the monsters I slaughtered, including Ocypete, my harpy flying instructor who'd tried to bring me over to their side. I ended up allied with the monsters after all, but not before I charred her to ash.

I shake my head again. "I won't kill anyone. Not even if they deserve it. But I need the sword as leverage against Mr. Zee."

Val stands and then holds out a hand to me. I take it and he pulls me up...and then into his arms. I lay my head against his chest, no longer minding the silence that would normally be filled with the beating of his heart.

"Edie, I can get us into Underworld Academy. And I'll do everything I can to help you find another piece of that sword," he says softly. "But this is not a place where weapons are used as bluffs. If you put that sword together, you best be prepared to use it."

He kisses the top of my head. Gently. And then releases me and leaves.

Alone beneath the tree, I hug myself, chilled more by Val's words than his touch.

## 16

That night, I can't sleep. I feel like I'm being torn in half with conflicting advice.

Themis and Metis want me to get the sword and use it to threaten Mr. Zee.

Mavis wants me to kill him.

And Val just thinks I should leave this place and never look back. I wonder if he wants me to leave him too...or if he'd offer to come along with me.

Not that it matters. I'm not going anywhere.

Not without Mavis at my side.

But I don't want her in a body bag.

And I don't want blood on my hands.

Which leaves me...where?

"Stop sighing," Tina snaps at me on her way to the bathroom in the morning. Even though she doesn't use the toilet, Tina spends at least an hour in the bathroom. I think it's time spent primping, applying sunscreen, and just standing around in order to make me wait longer.

Normally, it drives me crazy. But since I'm not yet ready

to face the day. As I snuggle deeper into my bed. I can't help but wish my dad was here. Or mom.

Not my biological parents, but the ones who raised me. They always listened when I had problems. And even when they didn't have answers, it helped to have them there, knowing they'd back me up.

But they're both gone now.

Instead I have...Mr. Zee.

I can't really see him as the heart-to-heart type. Also, it would be awkward having a chat with him about how I should probably kill him, but I really don't want to.

That leaves Adrianna. I could, I suppose, go to the Hall of the Dead and pour out my sorrows to her portrait. But she wouldn't answer back.

Flinging my covers off, I jump out of bed, suddenly remembering the letter I got from Metis. I put it in my desk drawer intending to read it when I was ready. Some part of me imagined lit candles and soft classical music playing, as I finally opened the scroll. Like it was a scene in a movie.

But all that is forgotten now as I grab the letter and crawl back beneath my covers to stay warm.

"Okay, Adrianna," I say while untying the ribbon holding the scroll closed. "I know we never got a chance to have any mother/daughter moments, and I'm kinda putting a lot of pressure on a letter that wasn't even written to me, but please give me sort of direction here."

"Stop talking to yourself, weirdo," Tina yells from the bathroom.

Ignoring her, I slowly unroll the letter and start to read.

*Dear Metis,*

*I am writing to ask for your help. In approximately five months' time I will be giving birth. As the child's father is a god, your help will be necessary if I want any chance of surviving the baby's birthday. I know that I am not the first student to come to you with such a request.*

*I hope you will not withhold your help on account of my waiting three months before sharing this news with you. I feared you would encourage me to abort the child. In truth, when I first realized my condition, this option was my own preference. However, as you know, I am close friends with a seer of no small talent. She sensed what I had brewing in my belly and after laying hands on me, told me the child would be a girl. A girl with the power to destroy the world as we know it. I'm aware that carrying such a fearsome creature within me should have frightened me. But I actually believe the world could do with a bit of destroying. And why shouldn't a girl get to try her hand at it?*

*So I held this secret and the child has grown. The woman in my family carry small, and my magic uniform has adjusted to the few pounds I have put on. I meant her to be my own little seed of rebellion, even if I never lived to see it. You see, I was willing to risk dying in childbirth to bring her into the world. Perhaps I even wished to bring an end to my own existence. It is a foolish mortal who tangles with gods. Though at the start it was exciting, over time it's become clear I am not special in any way. That this god has an endless thirst and I was but a cup of water pressed into his hand.*

*He swallowed me up and pissed me out.*

*Ah, sorry to be crude. The bitterness bubbles up, although less so these days. You see, in the last few weeks something has changed. My little Edie—for that is what I have come to call her—moves within me. I imagine her face and her laugh and...her life.*

*I no longer wish to bring a destroyer into the world. And I no longer wish to push her out into a cold world without her mother at her side. I want to live, Metis. I need to live. I will teach my little girl that not all gods can be trusted. I will teach her to see the foolishness of this endless unwinnable war. I will teach her that there is a difference between justice and vengeance.*

*But mostly, I will teach her love. For I love her already, almost more than I can bear. I will endure anything to bring her safely into this world and to keep her in it.*

*Please help me and my little Edie.*

*With the greatest of hopes,*
    *Adrianna Aspostolos*

Tears course down my cheeks as I press the letter to my chest. I didn't find the answers I wanted here. Instead I found something better.

My mother loved me. She wanted to live. Tried to live. For me.

Carefully, I roll the letter up once more and place it at the back of my wardrobe. I get dressed for the day and by the time I'm ready, I've made up my mind.

I will ask Val to help me get the next piece of the sword. My mother trusted in me, even while knowing the destruction I might be capable of. Maybe I need to trust myself a little more too.

Tina finally comes out of the bathroom and must immediately sense the change in me, because she sighs and says, "Awww, no more gloom and doom face? And I was just about to lend you my black nail polish."

"You're all heart, Tina," I respond, just as there's a knock on the door.

"That's probably Val," she says. "Kevin likes playing with Bowie." Before reaching to open the door, Tina removes

Bowie from the box she keeps him in at night. Popping him on her shoulder, she flings the door open.

My back is turned as I gather my books for the day, but there's no mistaking Tina's hiss. I spin around to see her in full fangs out mode as Nico stands in the hallway.

"Go away," she says, pushing the door closed once more.

With a growl, Nico shoulders his way in. "I'm not here to see you, Moggy."

Normally Tina lets my friends come and go, but well...Nico isn't exactly a friend. And there's so much tension between him and the vamps that I can see why she doesn't want him in her personal space.

It's no surprise when she moves in front of him, blocking his way. "You take another step into this room and we're gonna have a problem."

Nico puffs up as hair sprouts all over his body. He purposely pushes forward, leading with his shoulder. Tina leans forward too.

Hiss.

Growl.

Thunk.

Somehow poor Bowie gets in the middle and falls to the ground.

We all stare down at him. He looks dead. Very very dead.

"What the..." Nico starts to say as he leans down toward the bird. Before he can get any closer, Vee attaches herself to his face.

It happens so quick that I didn't even see her growing a long tendril until she was stretched across the room trying to devour Nico's nose.

"Gah!" He grabs hold of Vee's "throat" and squeezes. I swear Vee moans.

"Nico, no!" I rush forward just as Tina's hands close

around Nico's ruined face.

I shove her away with one talon and Nico with the other. Then I reach down toward Vee.

"Don't!" Tina exclaims, nudging me aside. "You'll hurt her more, you big clumsy dragon."

I didn't even realize I'd shifted. It's the first time that's happened. Usually there's a moment where I give way, but this time—it was seamless. Maybe someday I'll actually reach a point that most shifters begin at: being at one with my other half. For Nico, Jordan, and Greg—they are their animal and their animal is them. It all fits under the big "me" umbrella. I'm not quite there yet.

With the tip of a wing, I scoop up Vee's now crushed tendril and drape it over Tina's shoulder. She glances up at me in surprise, as I shift back, having proven my point. Although, as usual, she doesn't seem to care.

Tina gathers up Vee and her pot, then stalks toward the door. She pauses in front of Nico and leans in close, "If you ever invade my room again, I will kill you."

He starts his growling nonsense again, but this time I've had enough.

"Nico, we've got the whole campus. Do you really need to be here?"

He turns to me wide-eyed and almost hurt. "I can't come to my girlfriend's room then?"

"Girlfriend?" Tina laughs. "Okay then." She glances back at me. "I'm gonna go meet Val. He doesn't need to start his morning being part of this mess." With that she sweeps out into the hallway. "Bowie, c'mon," she calls as an afterthought.

Somewhere in all the chaos Bowie found his feet again, and he totters out the door.

Nico frowns, watching it, then turns to me. "I could've

sworn that bird was dead."

I shrug and force a smile. "Tina taught it to play dead. Convincing, right?" Nico doesn't look convinced, but I'm not really in the mood to appease him right now, so I cut to the chase. "Nico, what are you doing here?"

"Sorry. Next time I want to surprise you with a gift, I guess I'll schedule it with Tina first." With angry, jerky movements, Nico takes off his pack and unzips it. Just barely I keep myself from rolling my eyes at this passive aggressive display. "Here," he says, shoving a bouquet of red roses in my face. "These are for you."

My eyes widen in surprise. Nico never really struck me as the giving flowers type. "Okay," I say, taking the crushed roses. "Thank you?"

Nico nods as if whatever this is has gotten back on track. I'm still confused when he takes my hand in both of his and places it over his heart.

"When my father first met my mother, he wanted to prove he could be useful to her. So he killed a satyr, cut it into pieces, and gifted her different parts for five days— ending on the last day with the head." Nico has a dreamy look in his eyes, like this is what happens in epic romances or something. "My mom always said she was pretty sure she I was conceived on that fifth night."

"Ew." I don't mean to say it out loud, but it's hard to keep that level of disgust bottled inside.

"I know," Nico says, nodding like we're on the same wavelength. "Parents having sex is gross, but it's important because it's where my life began and...it's where I want to begin with you."

Releasing my hand, Nico gets down on one knee. The way a person does when they're getting ready to propose marriage.

Since I'm at the point where I don't even want to share a turkey sandwich with Nico, I really hope he's not gonna suggest we pledge to share the rest of our lives together.

He pulls something out of his pocket. I breathe a sigh of relief when it's only a piece of paper and not a ring box.

"Edie, I've noticed you've been a little distant lately. And I realized it's because I haven't proven myself to you the way my father did with my mom. So I want you to have this." He stretches his arm up to me.

After a moment of hesitation, I take it from his hand.

"Read it," he urges.

Slowly, I unfold the piece of paper and then read the words written upon it.

Leviathan. Bay of Biscay.

Nico stands, a grin on his face. "I've got a portal key, so we can leave right away. Mr. Zee gave us permission to miss classes."

My head is pounding and my mouth has gone dry. Leviathan killed my father. I came to Mount Olympus Academy with the goal of killing him. But that seems like a million years ago.

"I..." No words come to me, until finally, "How did you even know about Levi and what he did?"

"Your sister told me."

"*What*?" My hands clench, crushing that paper. "Is this when you were torturing her?"

"No, of course not!" I'm slightly mollified when he seems offended by the very thought. But then he adds, "It was when I was threatening to torture her. She told me you loved red roses and then when I told her that I needed more than that, she gave me the whole ugly story of your parents' love triangle with Levi."

"It wasn't a love triangle!" I respond angrily. "Levi fell for my mom and she wanted nothing to do with him."

Nico shakes his head, "That's not what Hermes told me. I went to him for the key and he said your mom was a bit of a tease. Hermes says she flirted with Levi, encouraged him—"

I am so mad that I can't see straight. "What does Hermes know about it?"

Nico responds with something about my mom coming on to Hermes too...but it's lost behind a buzzing in my ears as the pieces fall into place.

"Is Hermes the one who gave you Leviathan's current location?" I ask, interrupting Nico mid-sentence.

"Yes. As a personal favor to me," Nico says, as if making sure he gets the credit instead of Hermes is the important thing here.

But that really couldn't matter less to me, because suddenly I'm seeing the big picture.

Hermes killed my grandma. He was there that day at the same time as Leviathan—almost like he knew the monster was coming. Hermes is the one who first focused my attention on Levi too. Using him as proof that the monsters are bad. And that I needed to come with him to Mount Olympus Academy.

But I have a strong suspicion that Levi was just as much a pawn as I was.

I can easily imagine Hermes, pushing him to go after my mom, encouraging him, even. Telling Levi she was a sure thing. And then after mom rejected him, Hermes would be in his ear again, this time with an idea for revenge.

Of course, that's no excuse for Levi killing my dad.

"How would we kill Leviathan?" I ask Nico. My voice is soft and seems to come from a long distance away.

Nico grins. "Don't worry, it'll be easy. He's big and strong, but also kind of an idiot. Between the two of us, we should be able to take him down with no problems." Nico hesitates, concern clouding his face, "Unless you want to do it alone and just have me there as backup. But you know I like to be there in the middle of the action."

"And you don't mind getting blood on your hands," I add.

Nico nods, although less enthusiastically. It's possible he's finally understanding that I'm not feeling the same way as he is about this.

"Look, Edie—" he starts to say.

I cut him off. "Why would I kill someone if he only acted because my mother was toying with his affections?"

"Well, that doesn't excuse what he—"

"So did she flirt with him? Or was it more?" I demand. "Did Hermes say she and Levi were having an affair?"

Nico frowns. "He might've implied it... But, Edie, that's all in the past. And we both know that sometimes our parents—"

"It doesn't matter if my mother slept with a thousand guys, that doesn't excuse what Levi did," I break in again as my anger reaches a boiling point. "And did you ever think that Hermes might be lying to you?"

Both my biological mother and adopted mom were used by the gods. I'm starting to understand why Adrianna was excited at the idea of giving birth to a daughter who could destroy everything. The gods see all humans as lesser, but women are especially vulnerable. Gods messed with both of my mothers' lives.

Nico isn't a god, of course. But he certainly seems to share their philosophy of see it, want it, take it.

He's not having me, though. Not today. And not ever.

"Do you ever think at all? 'Cause if you did, maybe you'd

realize that I will never marry you or even date you. You imprisoned and tortured my sister."

Confusion sparks in Nico's eyes too. "I told you before, we'd have to work past that."

"No, we don't. Because that's only *one* problem. The other is that I. Don't. Like. You. Maybe you could've been a decent guy, but your mother twisted you, she wanted so bad to make you into her little mini me."

"Don't you bring my mother into his," he growls, angry now.

"So you can slut-shame my mom, but you can't hear the truth about your own mother? She was a *monster*, Nico. Worse than any monster she ever hunted. I think it's terrible the vampires killed her the way they did, but honestly, I'm glad she's dead. The world is better without her in it. And if you keep on going with the idea that you're gonna be just like her, then maybe it would be better off without you too."

Nico gapes at me. Shock, hurt, and rage are all evident on his face.

Normally this is the point where I'd feel bad for him.

But not anymore. I pick up the roses and shove them into his arms.

"Get out, Nico. We're not killing Levi or anyone else. Because, thank the gods, I am not a blood-thirsty alphahole who wants to hurt everyone to cover up my own hurt."

I push his chest and he stumbles backward out into the hallway.

Right before I slam the door, I watch as Nico's face contorts, fangs pushing his lips grotesquely outwards. "You'll regret this."

"No, I won't." I sit on my bed and let out a shaky laugh.

For the first time in a long time, I am absolutely sure that I have done the right thing.

## 17

I feel strangely free as I walk the campus, on my way to *Advanced History of the Gods.*

Fern jogs up behind me with Greg at her side. "Edie, you look...happy?"

I grin. "I just told Nico that we are not and will never be a thing." We spot Marguerite with a bunch of vampires, including Val and Tina, and change course to meet them.

"Good for you!" she tells me. Then frowns.

"Bummer," Greg unexpectedly adds.

"What?" Fern and I both exclaim at once.

"Well, if it's between Vedie or Nedie, I think Nedie sounds more interesting," Greg explains with a twinkle in his eye.

I laugh and nudge him. "What about Grassie? Is that a thing?"

"Oooh, oooh," Fern jumps in. "Marguerite and I can be Ferguerite. Fergie for short."

It feels good to laugh and be silly after the tension of this morning. It helps cool some of the lingering anger still simmering in my belly.

We're still giggling over Fergie as we reach the group of vamps.

"What's so funny?" Marguerite asks.

Fern hurries to Marguerite's side and gives her a sweet kiss. "We're Fergie," she announces.

"Gross. Boring," Tina says dismissively. "Let's talk about something more interesting...like how the whole campus is buzzing with the news that Edie kicked Nico's doggy ass to the curb."

I glance at Val, who looks majorly amused.

"He wasn't the one for me," I say, meeting his eyes.

"Blood traitor!" someone yells and I whirl in time to receive an apple to the forehead.

"What the Hades?" Did someone just throw fruit at me?

There are a group of shifters—Nico's crew, standing with their breakfast trays. They look beyond pissed.

"Nico told us what you've become, traitor," one of them yells.

"Because I don't want to marry that psycho?" I ask. How did me dumping Nico turn into treason?

"She doesn't owe him anything," Fern agrees.

"Yeah, it looks like you both prefer necrophilia," another shifter says. The same one that slapped me on the back when I'd tortured Hermes. Clearly, they're itching for a fight.

Marguerite puts a hand on Fern's elbow and tries to pull her away.

Val steps forward. "You'd better quit while you're ahead," he says, his voice soft, but threatening nonetheless.

"Or what, Moggy?"

"Or you're gonna get a bat up your ass." Greg flies in, darting at the boy's face, before zipping back toward Val and hovering over his shoulder. Leaning close to Val's ear, he says softly, "I think that might've come out wrong..."

"You're a traitor, little shifter," Nico's friend replies. "I would care, if you weren't so useless."

"What's going on here?" Nico's voice rings out. He elbows his way through the crowd of shifters and stops when he spots me with Val and the other vampires.

"Oh," he says, his voice deadly serious. "I see now." He focuses on me. "I know you have a kind heart, Edie. I know you pity the Moggies but you don't have to screw a vampire just so you don't feel bad about their pathetic little lives."

There's a change in the air. A strong breeze comes through, ruffling everyone's hair. And then a slight drizzle begins to fall.

I look to Val. His mother was a magical mutt. Somewhere in his genes is a water nymph, just like Tina received the tree nymph powers. This isn't the first time I've seen him change the weather.

Beside me Tina hisses. Bowie, sitting on her shoulder, imitates this sound. I feel fire bloom in my belly.

But I know repeating my feelings will only embarrass him in front of his friends and make things worse. "Nico," I say, keeping my voice steady. "It doesn't have to be this way."

"Oh, right," Nico sneers. "Should we just be friends then? Like you are with Val and Jordan and Greg, and I don't know who else. Everyone on campus already knows, Edie's the friendliest girl around."

Thunder rumbles in the distance as Val steps forward until he's only inches away from Nico.

So quick, I can't even see the movement, Val slaps Nico. There's the sound of his hand connecting and then Nico's head snaps back. Kevin swoops down, but Val waves him away.

With a snarl, Nico half-shifts, canines once again

erupting from his mouth. "Or maybe I should make your little dead boyfriend dead for real."

"Like we did to your mom?" Tina asks, stepping up to Val's side.

The moment that follows feels like it lasts a million years. Nico's face changes from anger to pure hatred. He and his friends all shift into a variety of animals, mostly werewolves.

Val, Tina, Marguerite, and all the other vamps bare their fangs, ready for battle. Tina sets Bowie on the ground and Kevin lands beside him, guiding him away to safety. Greg flutters above it all, shouting about how he's going to tear Nico to pieces.

"Edie," Fern grabs hold of my arm. "People are going to get killed here."

I'd been fighting the urge to shift and jump into the action as well. I could easily make Nico pay for smearing my reputation on campus. But with Fern's words, my fire extinguishes.

Why did I let this get so out of hand? It felt so good to have my friends line up in front of me, ready to fight. I know it's not all about me, either; this fight has been coming for a long time.

"Guys, let's just calm down," I say.

But it's way too little. Way too late.

Nico launches himself at Tina, with a howl that raises every hair on my body. The other werewolves howl back at him.

Val stops Nico mid-leap and they tumble to the ground. Another werewolf joins them, but Tina isn't going to stand by and allow the werewolves to gang up on her twin. She snags the wolf by the scruff of her neck, dragging her away from Val. Tina gets both of her hands around the wolf's head and guessing what comes next, I run forward.

"Tina, no!"

There is a sickening crunch. Tina releases the wolf who falls to the ground—dead. I watch as the wolf shifts back into a girl who I sometimes said hi to in the library.

"Sorry," Tina says to me. "Did you want that one?"

"No," I shout, but it comes out as more like a whisper.

Vampires and shifters are at each other's throats.

Val and Nico are fighting faster than I can even see. They're both trained assassins, top of their class, and neither of them gains the upper hand on the other.

Meanwhile, Tina has backed a werewolf into a bush. She uses her tree nymph powers to make the branches snake around the wolf's chest and neck. As it hangs there help-lessly she steps forward and in one smooth motion, punches through his chest and pulls out his heart. In triumph, she squeezes it, letting the blood drip down her arm as she raises it overhead. With an outraged howl a werewolf leaps at her. Laughing, Tina meets him mid-air.

She's having fun, I realize.

To my left Marguerite is fighting off two cat shifters, a lion and a tiger, who are trying to surround her. Her expres-sion is also one of intense concentration mixed with enjoyment.

What was it Val said about vampires? "We are all killers at heart." I don't think I quite believed him. But I do now. I see Fern on her knees trying to help a werewolf whose arm has been ripped off. Blood spurts from his shoulder and Fern frantically ties a tourniquet with her school tie.

Everywhere I look, I want to jump into the fight to help my friends. But these aren't like the monsters that attacked us during the Spring Fling. Or the ones who kidnapped

Cassie. There are students I've had classes with. I could shift and reduce them all to ashes. Being the destroyer my mother's seer friend foresaw.

Suddenly Fern cries out, as she gets trampled beneath the feet of a werewolf fighting one of the vamps.

With a giant roar I change into my dragon form. Taking to the air, I stay low so I can easily pluck Fern out of the action. I set her down outside the circle of carnage.

"Edie, don't—" Fern starts to say as I rise once more. I realize that she thinks I'm joining the fight.

"I'm stopping this," I call back to her.

Fern's expression turns to one of horror and I realize that she only heard my dragon screech. Only shifters understand other shifters when we're not in our human form. Clearly, she's expecting me to char everyone.

There's no time to shift back and explain to her that I'm understanding something new about my power. It doesn't have to be used to fight. Or to kill. Or to maim.

I can end the fighting.

I start by separating the vamps from the werewolves, tossing the vampires onto the green and the werewolves on top of the dining hall building. I hope it will take them a second to find their way down.

Finally, I spot Val and Nico. I know to stop this, I must first stop them.

I land next to them and try to get in between them. Nico bites me on the arm, but my thick dragonhide barely feels the pressure. Val backs off, so as not to place me in the middle, which Nico uses as a chance to press his attack. He grabs Val by the ankle and crunches it between his teeth.

Greg swoops down from out of nowhere and in sync, both Val and Nico shoo him away.

"I'm helping," he squeaks.

"No," I tell Greg plucking him out of the air with one of my talons. "You're getting in the way."

I launch him, the same way I would a paper airplane, toward a bank of trees, hoping he has the sense to steer around them.

I turn back to Val and Nico in time to see Val shove a thumb in Nico's remaining good eye. Nico whimpers but refuses to release Val. Val takes a deep breath and suddenly the water from a nearby fountain surrounds Nico's head in a great roiling ball.

Val is going to drown him.

"ENOUGH!" a voice booms through the fight.

For a moment, I am powerless.

Me, and everyone else who has shifted, return to their human forms. The bubble of water that surrounds Nico splashes to the ground. He gasps for air, glaring at Val.

Suddenly I lose feeling in my whole body. I crash to the ground, barely managing to keep myself from falling right on my face. Other students are not as lucky. All around me, the whole field of fighters are on the ground, flopping around like fish plucked from the water.

In the air above us is Mr. Zee. Except right now he seems more like what he's always been—the mighty Zeus, king of the gods, strong and tall and shining. As he looks down at us the sky lights up with a bolt of electricity.

"By gods, I love a fight, but there is a place and time for such things!" As he speaks, he seems to deflate a bit, looking more like his withered Mr. Zee self.

I flex my fingers and curl my toes as I regain power over my extremities.

Mr. Zee floats back down to the ground, landing between Themis and Kratos.

"Nico," Kratos barks. "You gotta do a better job of

watching the whole field. And Val, you're not fully guarding your left flank."

Themis whirls toward Kratos. "This isn't a lesson! Students aren't allowed to rumble in the middle of the afternoon like they're the Sharks and Jets." She scans the field. Everyone able to has gotten up once Mr. Zee released us. But that only makes the people who aren't able to get up more obvious. "There are dead students here. Which means I will need to call their parents and deliver the shameful news that their child died, not fighting monsters, but rather, fighting each other."

"I'll make the calls," Mr. Zee announces. "I'll tell them their children were taken down by murdering Moggies."

"You will do no such thing," Themis snaps. "This"—she gestures to all of us— "is the result of your Moggy discrimination nonsense. Your experiment has failed, Zee. And now it's over."

"Woman! Thou shalt not—cough. Cough!" Zee starts strong, his voice booming in his proclamation voice that in the past seems binding in a way that Themis is unable to overrule. But this time before he can lay down his law, he's overtaken by a coughing fit.

"Oh dear, Zee," Themis says, and I could swear she's holding back a gleeful smirk. "You aren't well." She looks to Kratos. "Get him to his rooms." She pats Zee's arm. "And I'll have Hepa bring you some warm ambrosia just the way you like it later this evening."

He looks like an old man as he nods and shuffles off beside Kratos.

Themis turns back to survey us students. "Now for the rest of you..." Her gaze lands on me. "Edie. I am mistaken or are you somehow at the center of all this?"

Nico barks out a sharp laugh and coughs up some water. Val seethes.

"That bitch started this all," Nico sputters, getting to his feet. "She's as bad as her slut mom."

"Edie wasn't involved," Val says and all eyes are on him. "She was trying to stop us."

"We'll see," Themis says. "Every student here will come to my office and be judged. Moggy or pureblood, the scales will decide your fate. You will tell me all you know. If you are found lacking, you will be expelled." She surveys the scene. "There has never been a darker moment at Mount Olympus Academy than right now."

"Anyone who needs the infirmary, go. Otherwise wait in your rooms. Kratos will come and fetch you to receive your judgement. If you can't be found, Artemis will hunt you down and drag you back." Kratos returns and she turns to him with a nod.

"Let's start with Mr. Tralano, shall we?"

"This is unfair!" Nico yells. "Where is Mr. Zee?" Nico backs away but Kratos grabs him and carries him away.

"I am nothing if not fair, Mr. Tralano," Themis tells him. She turns to address us again. "Disperse," she commands, and we rush to obey.

## 18

I rush to Val and slip under his arm, helping him walk on his ruined ankle. I know he's hurting, but right now my heart is breaking too. Val was a ringleader. He is definitely getting expelled.

"You're going to have to leave MOA."

"Don't worry, Edie. It'll be fine," he assures me. Grabbing onto my arm, he steers me toward the infirmary.

We pass Tina who looks more cheerful than I've ever seen her before. So cheerful that she's whistling, despite the jagged slash on her arm and puncture in her cheek.

"I'm so sorry," I tell her...and Val too.

"I'm not," Tina says. "This place has sucked since we were outed. I'm fine with getting kicked out."

"Yeah," Val says. "There's always UWA."

I take a deep shuddering breath, fighting tears. Val doesn't even seem to care that we'll be at different schools with no way to communicate. That we might in fact never see each other again.

"We're going to the infirmary," I tell Tina. "You should probably come with."

"Nope," she says, veering off in the other direction. "I want to gloat over their dead and make sure our own are treated with the respect they deserve."

I have no idea how to respond to this, and luckily I don't have to as Val tugs me away. As we walk along one of the beautifully landscaped paths, I can't help but think how every part of being on campus will be less enjoyable without Val. I never left my room without hoping I might run into him. And those times when I did and we had a few moments alone together...

Even when he was engaged to Larissa, I couldn't fight the spark between us.

But on Val's side it seems to have gone out.

I'm so lost in my own feelings, that I don't even notice we're not anywhere near the infirmary until Val comes to a stop. Blinking, I look around.

"Why are we at the lagoon?"

Without answering Val pulls his shirt over his head and drops it onto the sand at our feet.

I swallow audibly and he looks at me with a smile and then reaches for the waistband of his pants. Without any warning, I find out that Val is definitely a boxer briefs guy. And they look good on him.

Turning, he hops toward the water on his good foot. He should look ridiculous, but I'm not anywhere near laughing. We're in the middle of a beautiful lush lagoon and yet my mouth is dry like we just trekked into the desert.

At the edge of the water, Val uses his injured leg to squat low and then leaps, flipping in the air before diving beneath the water.

I laugh as he comes up for air. "Show off."

Wading in the deep end, he gestures. "Come on in, the water's warm."

"No thanks." I hug my arms around myself. "I'm a little chilled from that unexpected rainstorm we had earlier."

With long strokes Val swims toward me. "Come closer."

"Are you going to pull me in?"

"Nope. I'm going to convince you to get in of your own free will."

I walk nearer to the water's edge. It feels like something bigger is at play right now between us, but I can't quite figure out what it is. "All right. Convince me."

Flipping onto his back, Val puts his hands behind his head and floats. "There's an old story," he begins. "About a bet between the wind and the sun. They saw a man walking along a beach much like this one, wearing a long coat. The sun boasted that she could get him to remove it first. The wind, not to be outdone, said he could do it much quicker than the sun. The sun, confident of her abilities, allowed the wind to get first.

"So, the wind, as expected, blew against the man. Tugging and pulling at his coat. The man, of course, pulled his coat tighter against his body. The wind blew again, even harder. The coat flapped against the man's legs, but he did up every button and huddled deeper inside it. Finally, the wind blew as hard as it could. The man was pushed backwards and then even flew up into the air, but his coat stayed on. Defeated, the wind grumbled to the sun, 'Fine, you try, but that man must love that coat more than he loves his life.' With a silvery little laugh, the sun beamed down on the man. Softly at first. He relaxed, no longer holding his coat tight. She blazed brighter, warming him further."

Suddenly, sweat drips down my face and realize the sun in real life is imitating the one in Val's story. Toeing off my shoes and socks, I let the water lap over my feet.

Meanwhile, Val continues, "The man unbuttoned his

coat, letting it fly open. Encouraged, the sun covered with her rays. She was burning him, blistering his skin the man no longer cared. He threw off his coat and all the rest of his clothes, then jumped into the water."

As Val says this, I follow suit, pulling off my uniform and tossing it over my shoulder. No longer floating, Val stands in the water. Wearing only my bra and underwear, I run into the water and then into his arms.

We fall into the water together. Our limbs tangle as the water covers our heads. Every inch of my skin feels alive. The water is like a warm caress. But it's Val's cold skin that I crave. Even here in the warm water, beneath the hot sun, he remains icy to the touch.

We come up for air and then descend again, becoming otters. We play tag, taking turns chasing each other. His cold hand slides the length of my leg before closing around my ankle in capture. Then it's my turn. My hands travel the length of his muscled back before locking around his middle.

The unspoken words with each capture: I got you. I got you. I got you.

Finally we collapse on a small island of soft grass at the far corner of the lagoon. It's just barely big enough for the two of us to lie side by side. But we don't need much space as we grab hold of one another, our mouths meeting hungry and hot. We help each other shed the last bit of clothing separating us from each other, and then—

Well, maybe Val's Moggy past means he has a witch in his family too.

Because what happens next is magical.

I curl into Val when it's over, wishing we could stay here forever.

"So in that story," I say with a yawn. "Am I the sun, or are you?"

Val chuckles softly. "We're both the sun and the world revolves around us both."

"You should get Tina to put that on a T-shirt," I laugh. But the mention of Tina pulls me back into the real world. "Oh gods, I hope Artemis doesn't show up to drag you away!"

"I already know I'm getting expelled. Let them work for it." Val stretches lazily, obviously no longer concerned with what Themis wants now that he's on his way out.

"I'll miss you," I say in a small voice, trying not to feel pathetic. And naked. Although I am in every way.

Reaching over, Val pulls me close again. "No, you won't. Because there are ways around the rules and I will find all of them. It seems like Tina and I are probably going to end up at UWA. So you sneak into the underworld and I'll sneak back here. And when we can't get away, we'll use Kevin." Val holds up a hand and almost immediately Kevin lands on it. "I'll send him here. Tomorrow night. And you can return him when you come visit me at UWA."

"*When* I come visit?"

Val gives me a lopsided smile. "I'll tell them you're thinking about joining the non-living so we can be together. They'll give you a day pass. Then we can find the next piece of your sword."

I frown, studying Val. "I thought you didn't want me to put the sword together?"

"No, I wanted you to be fully aware of what having that sword means." He shakes his head. "I was being an ass. I've been at your side in several battles. You do what needs to be done. You're a merciful killer." Running a hand through his hair, Val sighs. "We both saw Mr. Zee this afternoon. He's looking more and more like a dog that needs to be put down. If it comes down to it, you're the one I trust to do it."

His belief in me feels like an almost physical thing that I can carry around with me and call on when I'm uncertain. But I also think it's misplaced.

"Val, I don't think I can—"

He jumps up and as I struggle not to ogle his below the waist parts, he pulls me up beside him. "One last swim," he demands, tugging me toward the water once more.

The clouds, that Val had formed above, shielding us from the sun, part, and it beams down once more.

"What about Themis?" I ask.

Val throws me over his shoulder and jumps high into the air. Right before we hit the water and go under, he answers, "Let Themis wait."

## 19

Missing Tina is weird. Missing David Bowie is even weirder.

Every time I walk into our dorm room I'm ready for an insult or an attack about something I did wrong (or forgot to do), or even just Tina being in a pissy mood for no reason whatsoever.

I never thought I would miss my bitchy vampire roommate. But her bare mattress, and the empty spot on the windowsill where Vee sat, makes me super depressed when I come home. Even the dirty spot on the wall where David Bowie kept knocking himself senseless bums me out.

It's not just my dorm room that's different. The whole campus has changed.

Themis ended up expelling Nico and two of his friends, and seven vampires—including Val, Tina, and Marguerite.

The rest of the vamps on campus saw it as pure bias...although to be fair, most of the deaths were from them. But the vampires argued that by pissing them off, the shifters got what was coming to them. In the week after the expulsions, more and more vampires left MOA for UWA.

Since all the vampires were in the Assassination class, the sudden drop in the vampire population was immediately obvious for me. In a way, it was kinda good, because it forced me to look around and realize I didn't belong there anymore either.

Themis was right from the very start. I never should've been in the assassination class. I transferred that same day to the spy class. It seemed like the best choice for the moment, and I figured I might also pick up some tips that could help me work with the monsters to free Mavis.

Cassie was devastated by my switch, even while she admitted it was a good choice. She tried to switch with me, but none of the other classes would let her in. So now she mostly just cuts classes, hanging out in the quad or with her mom in the archives. Because Merilee carries all the details of MOA in her head, and has a magic spell to transfer everything to Cassie upon her death, no one here is gonna flunk her out.

Now most of my classes are with Jordan, who is always entertaining. And I've gotten to know Nico's old roommate, the little chicken shifter, better too. He is, of course, thrilled with Nico's expulsion and no longer having to share a room with someone who regularly terrified him. For some reason I keep finding myself telling him stories of when I first met Nico. Even after everything, I can't stop a small part of myself from hoping that he'll one day figure out how to be a better man.

Now two weeks later, as I prepare to visit Val at Underworld Academy on a visitation pass just like he'd promised, Fern is at my side once more. She came straight to my room after checking on Mavis. With the trial now only one week away, we're all growing increasingly anxious about how it will all shake out.

Seeing my agitation, Fern changes the subject.

"If you see Marguerite, tell her I miss her. Tell her I'm doing great. Better than great." Fern paces. "Okay, wait. Don't lie. Tell her I'm having a hard time, but don't mention the crying or that day I couldn't get out of bed."

"Fern." I give her a big hug. "If I see Marguerite, I will tell her you miss her."

This sets off a fresh round of tears. But she gets past them relatively quickly and walks with me to the portal fountain.

Metis is waiting there when we arrive.

The majority of the portals have been sealed off due to Mr. Zee's growing paranoia about one of his bastard children coming to kill him. Metis, though, talked to Hades and arranged for me to take a "campus visit day" to Underworld Academy, something Hades had been more than willing to accommodate.

"He thinks he's on a roll now that he's taken most of our vampires," Metis explains, rolling her eyes as she hands me a day pass. "Convincing the only dragon shifter ever to die for a place at UWA would be quite a feather in his cap."

"Yeah, that's not going to happen," I say.

"I'm sure Themis has big plans for you once you graduate," Metis replies crisply. "With you at the helm of our intimidation team, I think we could make the monsters sign a peace agreement giving in to all our demands. Gods, it must've been at least seventy centuries past or more since we last got them so fully under our boots. And then we made the monsters lick them." She smiles at me, her eyes cold. "Edie, would you like to have a monster lick your boots clean every day? Their spit adds a special sort of polish. They positively gleam."

She says this so seriously, like this is the plan. I try to

swallow, but my mouth has gone dry. "I don't really wear boots," I finally say.

Totally lame, I know. But I don't want to cross swords with Metis right now about the gods' treatment of monsters. Still, not setting her straight right here on the spot makes me nervous. Like I'm agreeing to that future for myself.

Or maybe it's just because I've been thinking about what I'm going to do after Mount Olympus Academy, and drawing a big blank.

Even though I believe in the monsters' cause, I don't want to be drawn into their never-ending war with the gods. On either side.

But what else is there for a dragon shifter to do?

I'm still pondering this question as I step into the freezing cold of the black nothing that magically takes me from one place to another.

One more step and I'm standing in the middle of a dry fountain with yet another naked Hermes statue. My teeth chatter from the cold of the portal and now from the snow swirling down around me.

I put a shivering hand out to catch a flake. Mid-October seems a little early for snow.

"I thought it would be romantic," says a low voice in my ear. "Snow. New York City." He holds a hot cocoa up beneath my nose. "Warm drinks in mittened hands."

I take the cocoa. "Have you been reading my diary or watching too much of the Hallmark Channel?"

Val keeps a straight face but his eyes twinkle at me. "The second one, actually. I never knew such a thing existed, but last week I was one of the losers of the school-wide limbo contest—"

"School-wide?" I echo.

"Uh-huh. Apparently, they're held regularly and there

are some intense rivalries to see how low can you go. The losers have to watch twelve hours of television of Hades's choosing." He leans in close, his breath colder than the chilly New York air. "Don't tell anyone, but I sorta liked it."

I laugh, ignoring the pang in my heart at the realization that Val is happy at his new school. Quickly, I push that feeling down. I want Val to be happy. Of course I do. It's just difficult when I feel less and less certain about where I belong.

But I refuse to spend this brief time with Val worried and moping.

Giving him a kiss on the cheek, I slip my hand into his.

"I assume you know where you're going?" I ask Val.

"Of course. Right now we're in a quiet section of Central Park, but around the corner is a lovely subway station. And that's our destination."

We chat as we talk. I catch him up on all the Mount Olympus news. Val tells me that the monsters found all my inside information about the prison helpful and the plan to save Mavis is coming along. Abruptly we stop.

"Where now?" I ask.

Val points at steps leading to the underground subway station. "Down."

We head into the subway tunnels, where Val confidently unlocks a keypad-protected door by swiping his Underworld Academy student pass. Seeing that in his hand, even more so than the limbo story, reminds me that he now belongs to this other place.

The light on the door turns green and Val wrenches the door—four inches of solid steel—open. It clicks shut behind us, and we're left standing on a metal staircase that leads down into darkness.

"Don't we have a tour guide, or something?" I ask Val. "Where's the welcoming committee?"

"Do you really want to meet the welcoming committee at a school where the first requirement for enrollment is that you are dead?" Val asks, and I huff.

"No, I just..." The truth is, going to Hades is a little scary.

"Remember the lotus stream?" Val asks me, and I nod.

In order to gain admission to Mount Olympus Academy, I'd been dropped—literally—by Hermes into a swamp, where I'd had to find a stream of lotus flowers which led me to the entrance of MOA. It was a test to see if I had what it took to be admitted.

"So it's like that?" I ask. "Except..." I look at the rust on the stairs, the darkness welling at our feet. "More depressing?"

"Well, my test for actual enrollment was a bit different than whatever this is. Right here is actually the visitors' entrance, which is usually easier...but in this instance..." Val shrugs. "Maybe not."

I glare at him knowing there's something he's not telling me. "Just spill it, Val. Ignorance won't make it easier."

He sighs. "I don't know anything for certain. I was just told that having parents on campus puts on the damper on the fun-loving atmosphere and so Hades might've made the visitors' entrance a little more intimidating than the actual student entrance exam."

"And what was the entrance test?"

"You don't want to know."

"Oh gods. Did you have to kiss another girl or even—"

"Edie, no!" Val puts his arms around me and pulls me close. "It was nothing like that. We had to play beer pong with ambrosia."

"Beer pong!" I explode, unable to believe that can be a test to get into a supernatural academy.

"Well the ambrosia was barely watered down and we all had horrible hangovers the next day, so..."

"Whatever," I say, more annoyed than I should be, though I can't pin down why. Actually, I know why. It's because Val is having all these adventures without me. When I first arrived at MOA it all felt a bit like a game, too—not a game of beer pong—but still, it was all shiny and new and full of possibility.

But the bloom is way off that rose now. And I'm still stuck with it.

For now.

Soon though, Mavis will be free. And then I too can find new adventures beyond Mount Olympus Academy. I need to stop thinking about the possibilities my dragon shifting has closed off for me and think about the ones it will open up.

Feeling better about the future just for having decided that it's my own to make, I put my chin up and head down the steps, while Val's footsteps sound on the stairs behind me.

We lose the light entirely after we've descended to the third platform. Val bumps into my back, then grabs my waist to keep me from falling.

"Sorry," he says, his cold breath in my ear. He doesn't drop his hands from my waist.

It's distracting. And it's dark. The sort of dark that feels like you're drowning in black ink. And while I certainly don't mind our situation, I am not entirely sure there isn't a fatal fall waiting for me in the next few steps. It kind of takes the heat out of my blood.

Speaking of heat...

"Val, how confident are you in Fern's fireproofing spell?"

"Pretty confident. Why?"

I don't explain, just raise his hand next to my face and expel a stream of dragon's fire at it. He jumps, but doesn't react otherwise. My fire burns, endlessly looking for something to devour, while his skin refuses to catch, providing us with an unending light source.

"Does it hurt?" I ask.

"It's not exactly comfortable," Val says. "But I'll manage. Onward."

We descend, continually edging forward. I test each step with one foot before trusting it to hold my weight. Val hovers behind me—literally—his lit hand raised to light the way, the other clutching my arm in case the stairs give out. I wish I could unfurl my wings and fly, but there's not enough room.

We finally reach the bottom, a layer of concrete with something fuzzy growing about an inch thick on top of it. There's also a bundle of rags resting at the bottom of the steps, a stench emanating from it that I also choose to let remain a mystery. Val lifts his lit arm, glancing both ways down the passage.

"Password?" The bundle of rags says, and I scream. Val spins, ready to set the thing on fire, when he spots a pair of eyes looking out.

"Password?" It says again, and I lean in closer, covering my mouth and nose. It's human, I'm pretty sure.

"Sir?" I ask, then to decide to cover all my bases. "Ma'am? Do you need help? Are you in need of medical attention?"

"I need the godsdamned password," it says.

"Saturday night dance fever," Val says, and I give him a solid smack.

"This isn't funny," I say. "A demented homeless person has found their way down here, and we need to get them out. Who knows how long—"

"Saturday night dance fever," Val says again, and the bundle of rags raises an arm, pointing to the left.

"Proceed."

Val leads the way, fire held aloft.

Wanting to stay close, I clutch the back of his shirt. "They really take the whole party school thing seriously," I can't help but observe.

"Yeah, it's pretty much the only thing they take seriously," Val replies. "Tina's going crazy. Nothing here challenges her. She might transfer to a vamp school."

"And what about you?" I can't help but ask. "You seem to like it."

"Do I?" Val voice is laced with amusement. "Honestly, I refuse to take any of these academies seriously. We act like they're different, but really they're just variations on the same bullshit."

I knew Val wasn't into the whole school thing, but there's a bitterness in his voice that I've never heard before. "You don't believe in education."

He makes a scoffing noise. "This isn't education, it's propaganda."

Before I can ask more about that, I see something glowing up ahead. "Look." I point a finger over Val's shoulder. "Is that the entrance?"

"I don't think so," Val answers as we get closer.

It turns out to be graffitti, the letters taller than us and spelling out EXISTENCE IS FLAWED.

A flickering light ahead catches our attention and we aim for it, the hall growing thinner as we go. It's squeezing my shoulders by the time we reach the light. I slip out of the passageway into a circular room, where Val stands before an elevator door.

It only has one button—down. He pushes it, and the doors slide open, a Muzak version of "Stairway to Heaven" playing for our benefit.

"Charming," Val says, shaking out the fire on his hand, since the elevator has lighting.

On the inside of the car, there is just a single button, pointing down.

"How far below do you think we already are?" I ask with a shiver.

"Not at the bottom yet," Val says. "But at least it's all downhill from here."

"Great dad joke," I tell him, humorlessly.

He shrugs and pushes the button. We begin to sink.

It feels like it takes forever. I hold Val's hand. It's the one that had been on fire, so it's still slightly warm. I don't usually give much thought to the fact that he's a vampire, and his cold touch sometimes takes me by surprise. To feel his hand warm in mine is even more weird, but I don't mind it.

Finally, the elevator rumbles to a halt, and the doors slide open to reveal a large, attractive man in a toga, a puff of very dark hair erupting from the folds at his chest. "Edie," he says, holding his arms out wide, to reveal that he's hairy everywhere.

"I am Hades, and welcome to Underworld Academy."

**20**

----

ades's gaze drops to Val's and my entwined fingers, and I immediately let go of Val's hand. "Don't be shy on account of me," Hades says, pulling us both forward, out of the elevator car. "Down here, we don't believe in the interspecies dating ban. In fact, down here..." He nudges Val like they're best buddies. "Anything goes." He winks at me.

"Sounds like MOA, circa my mother's time," I say under my breath, and Hades shoots me a glance.

"What's that?"

"I said it sounds like a circus, and a good time," I say, raising my voice.

"Definitely, definitely," Hades agrees, rubbing his hands together as he leads us out onto what looks like a subway platform decorated in rotting high-end Victorian style.

"What is this place?" I ask, taking in the length of the vaulted ceiling, where cherubs and satyrs are carved into filth covered marble.

"This is the Vanderbilt station," Hades says. "At the turn of the century the old money families wanted all the best of the modern amenities...but not if they came with the unpleasantness of rubbing shoulders with anyone who could buy a subway ticket. So, they built their own subway below the public one. Lavishly decorated, of course. Everything down here is the best of the best," Hades says, slapping a marble pillar. A rat scurries out from under his feet, somewhat detracting from his point.

"This extends how far?" I ask, wowed by what I'm seeing.

"Oh, all the original stops are included," Hermes says. "But the trains don't run anymore. All the rich folks bought automobiles and left this to rot. Which is where I came in. Underworld Academy is the newest of the supernatural academies, and if I may say so myself, the most legendary. We have quite a reputation."

"As a party school," I said.

"What's that?" Hades asks.

"I said that's cool," I repeat.

Val gives me a little nudge with his elbow. I can't tell if it's meant as a warning or a secret sorta high-five.

Hades leads us to a shredded velvet curtain that pulls back to reveal yet another door. We walk through in front of him and descend down a last set of stairs. Beneath us, everything glows, and there's a constant thrumming under our feet.

"It's Black Light Friday Night," Hades says, raising his voice to be heard as we get closer to the music.

"But it's one in the afternoon!" I yell back.

"They don't know that," he says. "We don't have any windows."

We get to the bottom of the steps and someone hands me a cup full of ambrosia. I can see the room—a mass of young shifters, vampires, and witches—all vibrating along with the music, their bodies outlined in glow paint. Dozens of bats flit above their heads, which seems like a nice atmospheric touch, until I see a few of them dip into the crowd and shift into human form.

Greg once told me he was the first of his family to attend Mount Olympus Academy. He said it like this was a big deal and I assumed it was the first academy anyone in his family had gone to at all. But now I suspect that what he really meant was that the rest of his family chose UWA.

Hades clamps a meaty hand onto my shoulder.

"Bar is over there," he says, waving toward the corner. "Your pass will get you two free drinks. Don't get pregnant, and don't get killed, okay? Those are my only two rules for visitors from the other campuses. I'm sure the pleasures of our school will be more than enough to tempt you to the dark side. Have fun, kids."

And with that, he's gone, slipping away to bump and grind along with his students.

Val steers me over to what at first I think is a punch bowl. Upon closer inspection, though, it's filled with condoms. Reaching in, Val hands me one.

"I'm here on important business," I tell him with a grin.

"So, no fun?" he asks me.

"Maybe..." I look into his dark eyes and all thoughts of my "important business" are gone. I shake my head. Between the flashing blacklights and the booming music and Val's closeness I'm finding it hard to focus.

"Can we go somewhere else?" I shout.

"What?" he asks.

"IT'S SO LOUD," I say.

"What?" he repeats.

I put my hand over my ears and give him a pouty face. I swear he says, "Adorable," as he takes my hand and leads me out of the rave into a dark, brick hallway.

As we walk and the party sounds lessen behind us, I lean into his shoulder. "Is there any actual learning at this school?"

"Sure, if that's what you're here for. My father was not happy about my expulsion from MOA, but when we came here to visit, Hades was all 'best place for the undead' and 'state of the art lecture hall.' He didn't tell my dad that attendance was optional. Like I said, Tina is thinking of transferring to a vamp school. Somewhere they don't know we're Moggies."

"And Marguerite?" I ask.

"She's been really mopey."

"Fern too! Anyone who would break those two up is a terrible person. They belong together."

"Yeah, I'm going to let Marguerite use Kevin to send messages." We take a right, then a left. I'm lost but Val seems to know where we're going.

"They should both just drop out...I mean, MOA is going to shit and UWA seems pointless," I say.

"Well, it's not that easy. Marguerite has her vampire family obligations and Fern has..." he looks around, "other concerns."

I nod. Fern is working for the monsters and so is Val. "Speaking of which...did you get the information on the sword?"

"Yes, I'm taking you to—" He stops abruptly and pulls me close, kissing me as a drunk student stumbles behind us.

"Niiiiice," the student says to Val.

I pull away. "Was that kiss just a cover?" I ask in a teasingly upset voice.

"That one was. This one is for me," he says as he leans in again. This time the kiss leaves my legs shaky.

I put my head on his chest. I wish we could stay this way

forever, but I have to finish what I came here for. Regretfully, I take a full step back.

"Time to get down to business?" he asks.

I nod and sigh. "Unfortunately."

"Okay," he continues down the hall while he explains. "In the underworld there are six rivers, each dealing with a different aspect of the afterlife. Hatred, Pain, Forgetfulness, Fire, Wailing.

"That's...unpleasant," I say. "And only five."

"The last one is a river that encircles the world...but that's not important. The one we need, according to my contacts, is the Phlegothon. The river of fire. The blade is hidden in the middle of the river where it crosses paths with the mortal realm."

"Well, that's perfect!" I say. "I'm a dragon and you're fire-proof! So, we're going there now?"

"No," he admits. "The problem is, I can't get us there. Only a few gods know the way."

"Okay, so...?"

"While here I've made friends with the goddess Hecate."

"You've made friends with a goddess?" I ask. All the deities I know are super attractive and extra horny. "Should I be jealous?"

"Always," he says. "But no, not really. Hecate is different. Misunderstood, really. She's the goddess of many things, including the moon, witchcraft, dogs and...and crossroads and entrance ways."

"Hecate can get us to the crossroads where the sword blade is hidden!" I say.

"Exactly, and I've been leading us to her office, though it's more like a cave. I just want to warn you about her appearance."

"Too hot for words?" I ask.

"Not exactly. Just don't make a big deal." He pushes open the door and we enter an office like none at Mount Olympus Academy. The place is covered in books and scrolls and potion bottles and random trinkets. It's a sharp contrast to Metis's tidy room.

"Hecate," Val calls out and an old woman appears, shuffling toward us. I gasp but try to cover it up with a cough. She's not tall or fit or gorgeous. She looks like a withered old woman. I'm surprised she's at UWA; it's not what I would expect from a party school. She also appears as homeless as the lump of rags we gave the password to, but she has a sparkle in her eyes.

"Val, my boy!" she calls.

She looks me up and down with her wizened face. "You're the one. huh?" There's a squawk and a Stymphalian bird lands on her shoulder.

"Is that...Bowie?" I ask. He's looking good. "Did you resurrect him?"

Val shakes his head. "Hecate is adept at necromancy," he explains. "Bowie isn't living but neither is he dead."

"Just like his vampire mistress. She left him here, but comes to visit. That one pretends not to care, but she's a good girl at heart."

I nod, missing Tina even more.

"Hecate, we've come for the blade. We need to reach the river of fire."

"Phlegethon. Yes. I will send you there now." She puts a clawed, bony hand on each of our shoulders. "Children, be careful. You are on a noble quest, but even the most worthy actions can have dire consequences. And remember the living cannot enter any river in the underworld." She turns to me.

"If you play with fire, you will get burned."

One moment we are standing in front of her and the next we are standing on the banks of a river of pure fire. The heat blasts my face and I stumble back.

"Holy Hades," Val says as he stares at the river of molten liquid fire. Flames dance on the surface.

"Do you see the blade?" I ask, my eyes watering.

He walks forward, stripping off his clothes.

"Wait," I cry out, but he ignores me and puts a foot into the river. I rush toward him, but can't stand the heat and have to walk away.

"Hecate said the living can't enter the river," he calls back to me. "I am neither living nor dead."

My heart jumps but amazingly, the fire doesn't burn him. He is completely unfazed as he makes his way to the middle of the river, the lava up to his chest.

"I see it!" he shouts. Trudging back, he carries the blade in his hands, careful not to cut himself. He holds it out to me and when I take it, it is cold to the touch. It weighs next to nothing.

"One step closer," he tells me.

"I thought it would be bigger," I admit. It's more like a long knife. It fits easily in my backpack.

"The words every man fears," Val observes wryly.

I nudge him. "If you're fishing for a compliment, Val, then let me say I found you completely satisfactory in size."

He clutches at his stomach as if I just stabbed him with the blade. Then he straightens and takes a step closer. "There was a lot going on that day, maybe you're not recalling—"

"Some of the smaller details?" I ask, making my eyes wide and innocent.

"I walked into that one. I'll admit it." Laughing, Val playfully nips at my shoulder before adding, "Hecate said that if we leave through the doorway we'll be back in New York. Do you have to rush off?".

"Hmm..." I pretend to consider the question as I carefully set the blade down on the ground. When I straighten back up, Val stands before me, naked, perfect, and definitely more than satisfactory in size.

"I can stay a while longer," I tell him with a wicked grin.

## 21

I 'm waiting to see Metis in her office when I notice that all my arm hair is singed off.

It's the side of my body that was closest to the Phlegothon, so I'm not entirely surprised. I mean, I had sex next to a river of fire in literal hell. I guess I can't expect to climb out of the Underworld completely unscathed.

I'm thinking about this, thinking about how seeing Val wade into flames up to his chest made my own body burn with something close to utter panic, when Metis's door opens.

"Oh, Edie," she says, feigning surprise. "Did you want to see me about your..." She eyes the healer who had been ensconced with her, dropping her voice to a whisper. "Condition?"

"Yes, my...condition," I dutifully repeat, making the healer give me the side-eye as she slips past me to her next class. "Great, thanks," I tell Metis, once her door closes behind us. "Nico called me a slut and now half the campus will think I have an STD."

"But you can't have, can you?" Metis asks slyly. "Not

when you're a shifter, your lover is a vampire, and there's been a ban on interspecies dating."

My cheeks are as hot as the Phlegothon had been. "Val and I are...it's complicated. Didn't Themis lift the ban?" I ask.

She only shrugs. "It's not official. Once Zeus is gone this silly ban will be just a bad memory, anyway. Now...did you get the second piece?"

"Yes," I say, taking the seat opposite her desk. She remains standing, leaning in toward me. She reminds me of a scavenger, about to peck to see if its meal is still alive, or if it just needs to wait a little longer.

"Well?" She leans closer, her hair swinging down from one shoulder to brush the top of her desk. "Where is it?"

"Somewhere safe," I say.

Metis seems to accept that. She pulls back, resettles her skirts before taking her seat. When she looks back up at me, her eyes are soft again, the little feral curl gone from her lips. "We're almost there, Edie," she says. "The last piece should be simple enough."

"The one at Amazon Academy?" I ask. "What is it?"

I already have a blade, and a hilt. One is heavy, the other sharp. What else do I need?

"It's a gemstone," Metis says. "But not an ordinary one. I drew ichor from Zeus while he slept off a drunken rout and infused it into the stone."

"Ichor. Blood of the gods," I automatically translate. "Mr. Zee's blood."

"Precisely," Metis nods. "Once it's fitted into the hilt, the blade will click into place, and you'll wield a weapon capable of slaying the king of the gods."

"*If* I wanted to kill him," I remind her. "Which I don't. I'm just going to Amazon Academy to retrieve the last piece so that we have the bargaining power to encourage him to step down."

"Forcefully encourage," Metis prompts. But I only narrow my eyes.

"Yes," Metis says after a beat, continuing on lightly. "Athena runs Amazon Academy, and Zeus trusts her to keep the gemstone safe. I always did say he spoiled her a little, but I wasn't much involved with her rearing. I mean, I didn't even give birth to her—she's that much her father's child. She popped right out of his head, instead of coming out of my womb. How do you like that?"

"I...don't?" This seems to be the best response. I don't like the idea of a baby popping out of me anywhere, top or bottom. "But wait—Athena is your daughter? With Zeus?"

"Yes, yes," Metis waves a hand. "Don't you know our family trees by now?"

"Does anyone?"

"Well, I have to admit, even we get confused sometimes. Which is why so many of us end up sleeping with our cousins."

"Right," I say, but I try not to sound too judgmental.

"Regardless," Metis continues. "That was thousands of years ago. Water under the bridge. But whether I gave birth to her or not, I know my daughter. And she does have her weaknesses."

"Such as?" I ask.

Metis smiles at me, slowly. "Heroes. The prettier the better."

"I'm not giving her Val!" I stand up suddenly, my knees hitting her desk, the chair smacking into the wall behind me.

"Oh, sweetheart." Metis chuckles, coming around the desk to reach out, cupping my chin in one hand. "It's not your vampire she's interested in. Athena wants to meet *you*."

———

Traveling through another portal when I haven't fully gotten the chill from the last one out of my veins leaves me colder than ever.

I'm shivering, running my hands up and down my arms to try to create some friction in the heavy mist that surrounds me the second I come out of the other end of the portal—on Maiden Sky Island—where Amazon Academy is hidden from the outside world.

Athena was supposed to meet me here. But I don't see anyone...and yet, I don't feel precisely alone, either.

There's a feeling in the air around me, something heavier than the mist. It clings to me, almost like fingertips fluttering over my skin. There's a breath in my ear, and I jump, spinning to face whoever is behind me. But there's no one.

A strand of my hair lifts, as if being inspected, and I snatch it back from mid-air, popping my dragon wings out. They're a bright magenta at the moment—a warning. I'm not ready to incinerate...whatever this might be. But I'm letting it know that I'm willing to.

"Hippolyta, she is not for you!" a voice cuts through the mist, and the feeling of a presence immediately vanishes, though the fog surrounds me still.

A woman emerges—more accurately a goddess, and easily identifiable as one. Athena is tall, gorgeous, gray-eyed with light hair, a sword strapped across her back. Her face is serious as she approaches me, and I leave my wings out, letting her know I have my own weapons, too.

"Edie," she says. "Welcome to Amazon Academy." At her words, the mists lift, and I see that we are standing on a green, next to a white marble building, very Grecian in style.

"So the mist is like your gate?" I ask, remembering the iron bars that stand in the swamp, guarding the entrance to Mount Olympus Academy.

"In a way," Athena says, leading me to walk with her around the campus. "We're on an island, and so putting a gate around the campus seems unnecessary. The mist keeps any uninvited—or uninitiated—guests away until they have been approved."

"Approved by who?" I ask, thinking of the light fingers that grazed my skin.

"Hippolyta, the first Amazon, mother of all Amazons," Athena answers. "I run this academy, but she chooses who may enter. Applicants come to our island hoping to be trained in our ways. But to truly be an Amazon you must have an inner spirit, a spark, that cannot be taught. Hippolyta recognizes that in all who are allowed to enter, dubbing them Amazons the moment they receive her approval."

"And if they don't?" I ask.

Athena shrugs. "They leave. Some choose Underworld Academy as an appropriate alternative."

I remember the raging party, the black lights, the loose atmosphere in the Underworld. That's nothing like this campus, with its pristine white marble buildings, and the carefully manicured greens.

"It might be an alternative," I tell Athena. "But *appropriate* is definitely stretching it. Nothing about Underworld Academy is appropriate. Anyone who aimed for this, and found themselves there..."

I let my words trail off, sad for the girls who come here, only to be rejected.

But Athena shrugs. "My Amazons are my world. My only interest is in the girls who remain."

"And me," I remind her. "Metis said that you wanted to meet me."

"Yes." She pauses on the green, turning to face me and run one long, white finger over my wings, which are a calmer shade of pink now. "I'm interested in you, Edie. A dragon shifter. A warrior, by all accounts."

"A reluctant one," I tell her. "I do not enjoy killing."

"Not enjoy killing?" she asks. "Why not?"

"I..." There's no good way for me to answer that question. I guess killing is kind of like pistachio ice cream. You either like it, or you don't.

"Never mind," Athena says, waving her hand in the air, no longer interested in me. "Metis sent you here to gather something?"

"Yes," I say carefully.

I'm not sure how much I'm supposed to trust Athena. Metis only said that gathering the gemstone from Amazon Academy would be easy, but I'm realizing now that she never actually told me where it was. And I don't know if Athena is going to be totally open to the idea of me dethroning her father. Metis did say Athena was always Zee's favorite daughter. That makes this woman, this goddess, my sister.

The thought makes me falter. "It's uh...like a gemstone, I think?"

"When will my father learn?" Athena says, her temper suddenly flaring. "I've told him over and over that I'm never going to be into accessories! I'm just not that kind of girl."

"No, of course not," I say quickly, because it's true.

Athena is wearing some type of leather skirt, and body armor across her chest. Her hair is braided close to her head, showing off her unpierced ears.

"Again and again, I've told him—no, I won't wear the necklace. Do you know how easy it is for someone to choke you with your own jewelry? Just come up behind you and—"

She grabs my collar to illustrate and my oxygen is immediately cut off. I try to nod as enthusiastically as possible before I die, hoping that just being agreeable is all it takes to make her stop throttling me.

"But oh no," she goes on, releasing me. I gasp for air as her tirade against Zeus continues. "It will set off your eyes so well," she mimics him, in a weirdly high-pitched voice. "A pretty girl needs pretty things. Ugh...I could just..."

She shakes her fist at the sky, then turns back to me. "Men!" she huffs, and spits on the ground.

I spit too, then stamp on it, grinding my foot into the ground like she is. She nods her approval.

"So Metis wants the necklace now?" Athena asks. "Trying to crawl back into his bed? Get into his good graces? Does she think a pretty bauble will make him forget what a lying, two-faced manipulator she is?"

"Um," is all I manage to squeak out, but it's pretty obvious that Athena really doesn't need me to answer her anyway. Seems like most of her questions are rhetorical.

"Well she's welcome to it," she announces.

"Great." I smile, relieved. "Where can I find it?"

"No idea," Athena says, and my spirits plummet. "I gave it to some pretty little thing that was trying to impress one of the warriors. I don't know where it got to after that. Taylor!"

She says this last in a shout, and a woman comes

running across the green, a clipboard clutched to her chest. "Yes, Athena?"

"Edie is here to retrieve that hideous necklace my father sent a while back. Any idea where it might be?"

Taylor consults her clipboard, but I know she's only buying time. There was a flicker of panic on her face at the word *necklace*. Athena saw it too.

"Who was that girl? The one who had a thing for Rada last semester?"

"One of the kitchen workers, Athena. Your kindness to her was—"

Clearly irritated, Athena waves away this compliment. "Yes, yes, she introduced me to avocado toast and I quite enjoyed it. I was grateful. Now, what do you know?"

Taylor swallows. "I don't believe she had much luck gaining Rada's attention. And, uh, she didn't end up coming back this semester."

"Rada may know something then," Athena says, her eyes roaming the campus as classes let out, girls streaming out of the buildings. "Rada!" she shouts, her voice booming over the green.

A tall girl with red, curly hair breaks free from a group, jogging over to where we stand. She's well-muscled, with a freckled face and a serious expression.

"Yes, Athena?" she asks, and the goddess merely points at me to redirect Rada's attention, then stalks off across the campus, all interest in me gone. It's pretty obvious that once I made my pacifist stance clear any interest Athena might've had in me vanished. Taylor scurries after her, clutching the clipboard.

"Um, hi?" I say, and the Amazon raises her eyebrows at me quizzically.

"Yes?" She's not being rude, exactly, but it's clear she was on her way somewhere else. And while running an errand for Athena has captured her attention, she's now stuck with an outsider.

"Metis sent me to get a gemstone, or well..." I retrace my steps, trying to remember what Athena had said. "I guess it was set into a necklace."

"Oh." Rada's voice remains clear, but her skin goes a shade more pale under the freckles.

"Athena thought you might know something about it?" I ask.

"Was this necklace...important? To...anyone important?"

Now it's my turn to raise my eyebrows. This is not sounding good. Metis had it in her head that his would be the easiest retrieval of the three pieces, but it's not looking that way, at all. Rada is positively white now.

"Yes. No," I say, then trying to sound like I know what I'm talking about, add, "Look, Metis would very much like the gemstone *from the necklace* back."

"Oh, okay," Rada immediately brightens, an audible sigh escaping. "That I can do. C'mon."

I follow the redhead across campus, heading towards a white columned building that appears to be where she lives. We pass Amazons sparring in the fields with swords, staffs, and in simple hand-to-hand combat.

"What class is that?" I ask.

Rada smiles. "That's not a class. Just some girls having a bit of fun." While I'm absorbing this interesting definition of fun—one that's so very different from Underworld Academy —Rada waves to one of the few girls standing alone. Without a partner she still seems well-occupied as she casually twirls a sword with a blade on both ends like it's a parade baton. "Hey, Lilliana, I'll be out in a bit and we'll see how well your new weapon fares against my pole arms."

"No worries, I can wait to kick your ass," Lilliana replies cheerfully.

"In your dreams," Rada retorts and looks back longingly.

I can't help but feel bad. "Sorry I'm taking you away from your fun sparring time."

Rada levels me with a very direct and serious look. "Sparring is not fun time for me. I'm sorry you misunderstood, but Lilliana and I are testing out newly constructed weapons. We have the world's best armorers here at Amazon Academy and take great pride in their work. Although my personal weapon of choice—like that of most Amazons—is the bow and arrow, it's my goal to be proficient in all weapon categories by the time I graduate."

"Oh, wow," I say, wishing that Rada would crack a smile. Her gravity makes me feel like I'm on the verge of being scolded. Trying to find a topic of mutual interest, I turn to the dorms.

"So, this is your dorm?" I ask. "Is it co-ed?"

Rada wrinkles her nose and I immediately realize my mistake. At MOA, the dorms are determined by your course of study—assassin, tracker, healer, spy—and the floors separated by gender. But here, it's even simpler. They're all Amazons. And they're all female.

"Sorry, dumb question," I say, as I trail Rada down the hall.

"No problem. Some girls struggle to get used to it. But a world without men? I don't want to ever leave."

We come to a stop next to the communal bathroom, where the door is propped open.

"I guess there's not a huge need for privacy without any boys," I say.

"Nope," Rada agrees. "And this door is so noisy. If you

had to pee in the night, you woke up half the hallway. So we propped it."

A blush creeps up her cheek at the mention of propping open the door, and when I look down, I see why. There, jammed under the dented corner of the bathroom door and the faded marble tile, is a blood red ruby about the size of a tennis ball.

"Oh my gods!" I cry, dropping to my knees, and trying to wedge it out from under the door.

"Please don't tell Metis!" Rada says, pushing against the door as I pull on the ruby. "We didn't know it was of any real value."

"Any real value?" I repeat. "It's a huge gemstone!"

"Right, but...well, that doesn't matter much here. When you live on the island long enough, your values change."

"I bet if it was a weapon it wouldn't be used as a doorstop," I say, falling backwards as the jewel comes loose.

"Sorry," Rada says, letting go of the door to pull me to my feet. "We just thought the necklace was pointless. No one here wants anything like that. And the stone was the perfect size so we just..."

"Put it to use," I tell her, slipping the ruby into my pocket. "It's okay. I won't tell Metis."

Rada lets out a breath, visibly relieved. "Thanks. I mean, I'd hate to see Athena get in trouble with her mom because of something we did."

It's touching, how much she cares about Athena. I wonder what that's like, to have someone running your school who you actually look up to. Someone you respect.

Must be nice.

## 22

I t's sad when the highlight of my day is listening to my boyfriend's voice come out of an ugly bird's mouth.

At least Kevin was delivering good news. An entire army's worth of volunteers will be coming on the day of Mavis's trial. If they can free her...

I stop that thought. If the monsters come through, I will cheer them on. But the only person I can truly count on saving Mavis is myself.

With the sword.

If only I could get it into one piece.

"This sword is killing me," I cry out in frustration.

"At least it's not literally killing you," Cassie replies.

It just doesn't make sense. It doesn't even look like if *should* fit together, the teeny blade and the massive gem.

"I don't know, Edie," Cassie says, her eyes roving over the three pieces—hilt, blade and jewel. "It just won't... stay."

She's right. Cassie's wearing a pair of heavy duty gloves, borrowed from Fern and the healing ward. Apparently they use them to work on porcupine shifters. Cassie is holding the blade cautiously, trying not to get sliced while pushing the other end into the hilt, me pushing back, both of us red in the face. It falls out when we let go, both of us jumping back for fear of getting cut when the blade slips.

"Any ideas?" I ask Cassie.

"Maybe try putting the gem in the hilt first?" she says. "Like there's an order of operations. If the gem is in the hilt maybe it'll hold the blade in place?"

"Worth a try," I shrug, pulling the gem from my pocket. It's impressive, large and blood red in my palm. It should be beautiful. It should take my breath away. It doesn't. There's no sparkle inside of it, even though it's infused with ichor, the blood of the gods. And not just any god—Zeus himself.

Even so, it doesn't catch the light. Doesn't shine with any life at all.

Still, it does fit inside the hilt perfectly, falling into place with a click. The blade then slides in easily, catching under the ruby and staying solidly mounted when Cassie takes her hands away.

"Got it!" Cassie says, relief in her voice, but nothing like the victorious tones that should be there. We just reconstructed a blade that can kill a god. But I don't feel anything other than tired as I lift the weapon.

It's small but heavy, the weight of it difficult to wield. How is a person supposed to fight with something like this? It would take both my arms and all my strength just to take a single swing.

Something is wrong. Something isn't working. I just don't know what.

Cassie feels it too, her brows coming together as she watches me take an experimental stab at an invisible foe. The weight throws my balance off and I stumble forward, falling to the floor with a thud. The sword flies from my hands, stabbing the wooden floor where it sticks for a second before slowly falling over.

Cassie pulls me up, and I retrieve the sword. Holding it up again, it feels awkward, heavy and oddly...dead. Or like a willful toddler playing dead.

The summer after eighth grade I ended up babysitting a monstrous two-year-old neighbor who had a constant runny nose, liked to bite, and threw temper tantrums loud enough to make his whole house shake. But the worst part was his parents' insistence that all naughty behavior be followed by a trip to the thinking chair. Most of the time I had to carry him there. And every time he would go limp, letting his weight sag in my arms. It was a relief when I got fired after accidentally dropping him on his head.

I can see my own misgivings on Cassie's face.

"Well..." she says, eyeing the sword dubiously. "It might look nice hanging on the wall."

———

"Nonsense," Metis says, eyeing me over her desk with something close to disgust on her face. "What do you mean it's not working? It's a sword. It doesn't have to work, only the hand that holds it does."

"See for yourself," I say, pulling the blade out of my bag.

I put the sword on her desk where it rests, heavy and cold as it was yesterday in my room. Metis takes one glance, her confidence slipping when her instinct tells her the same thing mine does; this is no weapon. It's only ornamental. But her face changes as she looks down at it, a flicker of understanding lighting up her eyes.

"Watch this, girl," she says, and closes her hand over the hilt.

Everything changes.

The gem sparks, a fiery light taking hold deep inside of it that continues to grow, its life spreading out into the metal of the blade and hilt, suffusing it with a warmth I can feel even from where I stand. The blade grows, lengthening into a broadsword. Metis lifts it deftly, and I somehow know it's not her goddess's strength that lets her do it. With the ruby alight, the blade is lighter, easier to wield.

Almost like it wants to kill.

Metis swirls the sword around her, slicing the air with practiced moves that whip too close for comfort. I back away, stumbling into my chair as she lowers the weapon, her eyes as bright as the ruby.

"What happened?" I ask. "What changed?"

Metis lays the sword back down on her desk, where it falls dead again, light diffused, once more a piece of heavy, unwieldy metal.

"It's like I said," Metis answers me. "It's not the sword that has a job, it's the hand that holds it. Zeus was a horrible husband, and Hephaestus forged this sword for vengeance. It comes alive to my touch because I have a grudge, the will to see Zeus struck down. You..."

Her eyes go to mine, clearly disappointed.

"You do not."

"I told you that from the beginning," I say. "I don't want to kill anyone, ever again. I got all the pieces, just as you asked. I put them together. It's not my fault I'm not a cold-blooded murderer."

Metis shrugs. "Then it was pointless. Where there's a will, there's a way. You lack the first."

"It's not pointless," I insist, reaching for the sword. It falls heavy in my hand, dragging down my shoulder as I pull it off her desk. It shortens back to its stubby knife form. "I wanted to have this blade so that we could use it as a tool, not a weapon. I can still take it to Mr. Zee, tell him that I am his Moggy child, and convince him to leave the school."

Metis's gaze goes to my hand, where the sword hangs, its ruby dead and dull.

"Of course, you may *try*," she says, emphasis on the last word. "But remember, though these days Zee comes off as a doddering old fool, he still remains the king of the gods. You might want to let a sleeping bear lie, unless you know exactly what you're going to do with him once he wakes up, and how you're going to protect yourself."

"It's not me who needs protection," I tell Metis, my hand on the door. "It's Mavis. Everything I've done, I've done for my sister."

"Oh yes," she says. "The trial starts tomorrow, doesn't it?" Her eyes go to the sword once again, a barely concealed glint of mocking humor in them. "Best of luck."

———

I didn't need the reminder from Metis that my sister's trial starts tomorrow. I haven't seen her since I wore Fern's face, and Mavis told me that I'd have to choose between killing Zee or letting her die.

She'd been down then, and I can't imagine what she feels like now.

My own optimism is flagging; can the ragtag remnant of the monsters' resistance army really help my sister? Can I?

Even though I lack the resolve to kill Zee, I've tried to stick with the plan of showing him the sword and telling the truth about my bloodline. I wasn't even going to ask him to leave MOA anymore, just to give me my sister and let us leave quietly.

But fear has a deep grip on Mr. Zee now; he never leaves his office and won't allow anyone to see him—other than Themis and Hepa, who is continuing to bring him his tainted ambrosia.

Themis managed to convince Zee that the trial must have some semblance of seriousness, given the seriousness of Mavis's crimes, and that she could be sentenced to death. Apparently Themis had bargained with Zee—he could have his Hawaiian luau theme, but only if the jury was comprised of Mavis's peers. If students filled the benches instead of gods, it might at least appear to be something less than the celebration of murdering a teenage girl, traitor or not.

Zee agreed.

And that, unfortunately, puts Cassie on the spot. As in, the stand.

"I want to help," Cassie tells me now, as we sit huddled together on my bed, an extra blanket across our legs for warmth. "But if I lie, I don't think I could hold up to Zee's questioning."

"No one is asking you to lie," I say. "Besides, I don't even know if you can, if Themis has her scales of justice."

The first time I'd seen the scales on Themis's desk, she'd been using them to track the progress of the gods' war against the monsters. When they make their appearance tomorrow at the trial, they'll be doing something altogether different—deciding the fate of my sister, along with the students selected for the jury.

As Mavis's former roommate, Cassie is coming forward both as a character witness, and to be examined by the prosecutor—Zee himself, of course. And Cassie's right; she won't be able to lie. While she might not have outright known that Mavis had been spying for the monsters, she'd had her suspicions. And those will all come out into the light tomorrow.

"Try not to worry," I say, wrapping an arm around Cassie's shoulders. "Remember we're not going to be able to prove her innocent; everyone knows what Mavis did, and I hear that Nico is even returning to testify. With that empty eye socket, he'll make a compelling witness. She doesn't stand a chance of not being convicted; we're just trying to get the jury to agree not to kill her."

"Fire or flood," Cassie whispers, her voice thick with tears.

My own eyes fill as well. If the jury decides against her, Zee will kill Mavis on the spot. I press my palms over my eyes, knowing I'd rather rip them out than watch Mavis die. "By the end of the day tomorrow, it will be all over," I say. "No matter what happens, nothing will be the same."

Cassie grabs hold of both my hands. "Edie! Ever since touching the Seer Stone my visions have been stronger and more focused. Do you want me to try and see some of tomorrow? Nothing is set in stone—if we know it will go badly—"

"Then we can maybe change it," I finish for her. "Yes, if you think you can handle it."

I grab the Seer Stone from where I stashed it in my underwear drawer. Getting down on the floor, Cassie sits in lotus position. Her chin sinks to her chest as she takes deep breaths and then slowly releases them. I hand her the stone.

I wait, quietly, watching her and resisting the urge to ask her "Anything yet?"

Suddenly she gasps. Her eyes pop open and meet mine. She looks...horrified.

"Cassie, is it Mavis—?" I ask, as she shoots to her feet.

She shakes her head wildly, like she's trying to get something out of it. "No, no, no."

I put a hand on her arm. "What is it? Please, tell me!" She jerks away from me so hard that she stumbles into the wall. It seems to knock some sense back into her, because she looks at me this time as if she actually remembers who I am. The stone drops from her hands and shatters on the floor.

"It wasn't Mavis. Or it had to do with her, but I'm not sure. I think she'll survive. Maybe. I don't know." She is weeping now, but when I again try to reach for her she scuttles sideways until the door is at her back. "There's nothing you can change. You wouldn't want to anyway. It's all how it has to be." The door flies open and Cassie slips out in the hallway. "I'll see you tomorrow!"

And with that she's gone.

I sink onto the floor, not bothering to hold back my sobs.

Whatever's gonna happen tomorrow—it's definitely gonna be bad.

## 23

When I wake up the next morning, I feel like even the weather is being contrary.

It's a beautiful day. The smell of roasting pork filters across the campus, slipping into the window while I get dressed. The day when my sister's fate is sealed should be gloomy.

Normally my magical uniform makes getting ready easy, but today I have to figure out the best way to hide the small, dense sword. Under my skirt, it hangs at my thigh, so heavy that I have to practice walking, adjusting my gait to allow for its weight.

It reminds me of Mavis trying to teach me how to walk in heels when I was fourteen, me fumbling and falling all over the place, Mavis laughing from her bed, ducking when I finally gave up and threw the shoes at her.

The memory pierces me like a knife.

I shake my head, trying to clear it, just as the sounds of a steel drum band warming up joins the scent of the pork.

"Utter bullshit," I say under my breath, slamming the window shut.

If it looks like things are going badly for Mavis at the trial, I will announce myself from the crowd, claim my bloodline, and let Zeus know that I've got the sword that can bring him down. Hopefully he'll overlook the fact that without the burn of vengeance in my blood, the sword couldn't slice an apple, much less a god.

Students are streaming out across the green and I join them, Cassie and Greg at my side, as we all make our way to the amphitheater.

I try to get a moment alone with Cassie to ask if she's okay, but she deliberately deflects, turning away each time.

"Something's up with her," Greg whispers to me. "She came to my room last night all freaked out. And then..." His words trail off, as he blushes bright red.

"And then what?" I demand.

He pulls me in closes and lowers his voice even further. Straining to hear, I lean in more, his lips nearly at my ear as he tells me, "She asked if I was a virgin. And I told her sort of yes, and well, long story short, this morning I am definitely *not* a virgin anymore."

I jerk back my eyes wide. Of course, I knew that Cassie and Greg had a thing going on, but what did she see that made her decide to go and jump his bones?

My hands go cold as the only possible answer occurs to me. Cassie's going to get hurt. Maybe even die today. Oh gods.

Pulling Greg close again, I quickly explain about Cassie's vision and then my suspicions about what she saw.

He frowns at me when I finish. "You're kinda guessing a lot there, Edie. Maybe she saw bloodshed in general. You know she still has PTSD from when you and Nico broke her out of prison last summer; it might've triggered her."

"Maybe," I say doubtfully. I glance over my shoulder

where Cassie has fallen behind us. "It felt more specific than that, though. I'm afraid for her."

Greg nods. "Don't worry, I'll watch her."

"Good." I squeeze his arm. "And if anything happens, get her to me. I'll make sure she's protected."

"Gods!" Greg glares at me. "She's my girlfriend. I'll protect her!"

"This is Cassie's life we're talking about. Don't be stupid," I shout whisper at him.

"I know you think I'm totally useless, Edie. But I'm not." And with that, Greg turns on his heel and stalks off in the other direction.

Which means that I enter my sister's trial alone.

The benches are all full—Mr. Zee has made attendance at the trial mandatory.

Whole pigs are roasting on spits, and we're all handed leis as we filter into our seats. I pull the flower necklace over my head, wishing this were just one of those trippy dreams I used to have as a kid when my fever got too high. It seems that way. The atmosphere here feels like a carnival mixed with a funeral mixed with...bacon.

I'm already sweating under the cloak, and am glad to sit down. Cassie goes to the front to be seated with the other witnesses, Greg finding a seat in the row behind her. I take a seat next to Jordan and Hepa, who both look at me solemnly. They're holding hands and Hepa gives me a "I gave in" shrug.

"It will be okay, Edie," Jordan assures me, but he doesn't sound like he actually believes it. Not even light-hearted Jordan can find the silver lining in this cloud.

Zeus sits on a throne in the middle of the stage, presiding as judge at a trial he cannot be impartial to. He wants Mavis dead, and has made that clear from the beginning. Hades is there and I try not to make eye contact. I don't want to deal with his party bro shit right now. Themis, Metis, Hermes, and a handful of other gods are on the left side of the stage, and I see the glint of Themis's scales under her chair when she arranges her robes.

She catches my eye and gives me a nod. Her scales are divinely inspired to weigh the truth. If the monsters don't make it, we can always ask that the scales decide Mavis's fate. The downside is that Mavis is a spy; that's the truth. And she's done some pretty horrible things in the service of the monsters...like gouging out Nico's eye.

He's here, despite being expelled from campus. I expected it, but my stomach still gives a lurch when I see him in the front row, with the other witnesses who will be called. He's alongside Cassie, and a few other students, most of whom I recognize as shifters from his little army, ones who weren't expelled. Somehow I doubt they're going to be called as character witnesses.

On the right-hand side of the stage sits the jury, a gathering of Mavis's peers. They're all students, a good mix of shifters, healers, and vampires. I don't know any of them personally, so I have no idea which way the wind is blowing...other than not at all.

Fern joins us, pushing past Jordan and Hepa to squeeze in beside me.

"Watch it," Hepa says as she scoots down a seat.

Fern ignores her and leans in to whisper, "I've had a message from Marguerite." Jealousy, then fear flares in me. Val hadn't sent Kevin to me this morning. Why?

"The rescue is on," she tells me. "Unless—"

"Fern!" Kratos calls. "Come attend to the prisoner!"

Oh Gods. Unless what!? But I can't ask with Kratos's eyes

on Fern. She shoots me a look then scrambles back past Jordan and Hepa.

I wipe a sheen of sweat from my brow as Themis rises, clearing her throat. "Students of Mount Olympus Academy, we are gathered here today to hear testimony regarding the actions of Mavis Evans, a.k.a. Emmie Jenkins, former student, shifter, and spy."

"And traitor," Mr. Zee says, rising to his feet to grip both sides of his throne, his face already flush with ambrosia.

"That's for the jury to decide," Themis says easily, waving for Kratos to bring Mavis in.

I haven't seen her since my visit to the dungeons, and my sister hasn't improved in the meantime. She holds her head up when she walks onto the stage, but I can tell it takes real effort. She's tired and underfed, the manacles on her ankles and wrists dragging with every step. The magical collar to prevent her from shifting has worn sore spots on the skin of her neck, some of which ooze blood. Her clothes are a tattered mess, and—judging by the reaction from the front row—she doesn't smell very good.

But she keeps her head high as she is led to her chair; a plain wooden one next to Zee's golden throne. Fern stands behind her, ready to attend her if the strain of the trial becomes too much. Fern's eyes keep flitting to the sky and I can't help looking up as well, wondering what she's seeing. But there's nothing there except a brilliant blue dotted with fluffy white clouds.

Once Mavis is seated Themis explains that she is expected to sit quietly and listen to all the witnesses before being given a chance to speak. Themis doesn't add "if we get that far," but I can see her thinking it as she slants a narrow look in Zee's direction.

He's already had one outburst. It wouldn't be surprising

at all if he decided to forgo any semblance of a fair trial and simply incinerate my sister with a lightning bolt on the spot. He could. And no one could stop him.

The idea makes my skin prickle, goosebumps breaking out under the sweat. I rub the sword strapped to my leg. *I could stop him.*

The first person called to testify is Nico.

It's painful seeing his smug smile as he watches Mavis, while she strains to stay upright in her chair. But it's even worse when he starts to tell his story of how she took his eye. The worst part is that even though the story is horribly one-sided, painting him as ceaselessly loyal to the gods and Mavis as the conniving backstabber, it's also clear that Nico believes all of it.

Jordan leans over. "You should have let him die in the desert." I nod my agreement.

There's only one moment where I'm reminded of why I once considered Nico a friend.

It's when Themis asks him, "I believe you once had a romantic relationship with Mavis as well. What did you see in her?"

"Nothing!" Nico insists, his single eye narrowed to a slit. "She tricked me."

"Yes, that's well established," Themis says, her voice lightly mocking. "So she simply played you for the entirety of your relationship as well."

"No..." Nico pauses, obviously thrown off. Again his eyes go to Mavis, but this time there's no glee. He stares for a long moment with something almost like heartbreak. "She was smart," he says at last. "We talked about our families. Although most of what she said was lies—"

"It wasn't," Mavis softly protests. She turns to meet

Nico's eyes. "I lied about the details of their lives. But how I felt about them, that was all true."

The moment stretches out and it feels for a moment like Nico might flip and ask for leniency. But then he jerks his gaze away from Mavis. "Look, it doesn't matter how I felt about Mavis then. The facts are the facts. Even if she'd given me steak and BJs every day, I would still say she's a traitor and there's no need for this trial. Because that's the truth and it's all that matters."

As Nico leans back in his chair, there's a lot of agreement and whispers from the jury and my stomach drops.

Themis stands then. "Nico, we appreciate your testimony and require no further comments." She addresses the jury. "I think that the focus of this trial should not be on Mavis's guilt or innocence. She betrayed the Academy. That is a fact."

"Then let's kill her," Zee yells.

"Yes, kill her!" Hades calls out. "I could use her at UWA!" He takes a big bite of pork.

"No, brother," Zee wags a finger. "This one gets eternal torture. No further schooling parties, or boyfriends. No afterlife."

"Oooh, torture." Hades rubs his hands together. "You know I'm up for that, brother."

Themis closes her eyes, takes a deep breath. "Let's focus on what an acceptable punishment would be. Does Mavis deserve to have her soul extinguished for her crimes?"

"An eye for an eye!" someone shouts.

"That's not a bad idea," Hepa says, her tone thoughtful.

I look at her aghast. Jordan pipes up, "What? Hepa's right. If she gets off with only having to give up her eye!? That's, like, best case scenario right now."

"It's sad when losing an eye seems like the best option," I tell them.

Themis calls Cassie to the stand. Cassie looks terrified as she goes up the stairs of the stage, her eyes on Mavis. Mavis gives her a nod.

She's asked to relay her time as Mavis's roommate and what her suspicions were. "She was always out late, and hardly ever in bed at night. I thought she was...you know... with Nico or Derrick. It can't be easy juggling two boys like that. Especially werewolves, who are totally the jealous type."

"Did you know she was a spy?" Zee asks.

"Well yeah. She was in the spy class," Cassie says and I hand it to her for her sass.

"For. The. Monsters," Zee clarifies.

"Did I know that Mavis was a femme fatale double agent? No. I can honestly say I didn't."

"Thank you for your testimony," Themis tells her. "You can leave."

"No."

"No?" Zee booms.

"This is quite good fun," Hades says, chugging another cup of ambrosia.

"I'm not done saying what I have to say," Cassie explains.

"Then by all means, continue," Themis allows.

"I don't think that Mavis should be put to death." There's an outraged response, including boos from Hades and a thunderclap from Zee. "No, listen. Maddox Tralano killed a student, murdered her in cold blood, and was banished. Why should Mavis have a harsher treatment? She didn't even kill Nico. Just took his eye. If anything, she should be stripped of her powers and banished. That's what makes the most sense."

My heart is full to bursting as Cassie stands and retakes her seat in the front row.

Zee seems to be considering this, his chin resting in his palm, eyes on Mavis. The mood of the court has shifted; earlier he could have smote her where she stood and even asked for a drumroll without much pushback from the crowd.

But after hearing Cassie's testimony, it's clear that the pendulum has swung in the other direction. The jury might not vote for death, even though Zee has made it no secret it's what he wants.

The suggestion that Mavis be given the same punishment as Maddox is a good one. Mavis will never be seen again, an embarrassment that will fade with time. Being stripped of the ability to shift is a horrible thought for most shifters...almost worse than death. It means living life as a human, which to many of them is inconceivable. Any holdouts among Nico's friends would definitely think Mavis had suffered enough, and those who take her side won't be enraged by her death.

It's a master stroke. Everyone wins. For once.

"Please," I say under my breath, fingers clenched on my sword hilt at my thigh, eyes locked on Zeus. "Please do the smart thing."

A shadow passes over the amphitheater, and the rush of wings fills the air as a Stymphalian bird swoops low, landing on an arm of Mr. Zee's throne. He gives it an inquisitive look, and it cocks its head back at him, in perfect mimicry. The bird opens its mouth and Val's voice comes out.

"Narcissistic asshole says what?" Kevin asks.

"What?" Mr. Zee says.

And then all hell breaks loose.

## 24

V al promised me an army, and it's here.

Monsters descend upon the amphitheater in a rush, minotaurs, satyrs, harpies, and centaurs all charging toward the stage. Students are on their feet in a moment, ready to fight.

Nico is already in werewolf form, claws out, teeth bared. All around me vampires are flashing their fangs, ready to fight. My own wings erupt, and I take to the sky along with other winged shifters for a better view.

But this isn't the Spring Fling, and these monsters aren't here for blood. I see Jordan take a running leap at a minotaur, who bounces him off his shield, sending the panther rolling. But the minotaur doesn't follow through with a killing swing; instead he keeps his distance while Jordan gains his feet, prowling around the monster in a confused circle. His teeth are bared, and a deep growl emanates from his chest, but he's not advancing. He knows that the minotaur could have killed him while he was down, and chose not to.

Similar things are happening all around me. Vampires

are hissing, showing their fangs and lunging at monsters who refuse to fight back. A few blood-minded shifters are going all out, elbow deep in brawls that are drawing blood, but even when monsters gain the upper hand, they won't kill. They are on defense only, and that approach has thrown off the entire student body.

I'm glad to see it, but also worried. The no-kill approach isn't helping them gain ground on where Mavis sits huddled in her chair. Even worse, after the gods initially did their typical duck and cover move, they seemed to quickly realize this wasn't an attack. Even as I watch, Kratos comes out from where he was hiding behind the witness stand to take position beside Mavis, arms crossed over his chest.

I want to scream with frustration. The longer this fight goes on, the more likely it is that people will get hurt—on both sides. You can only fight defensively for so long. Plus Mr. Zee could postpone the trial and lock Mavis away once more. Or worse—he could cancel the trial and execute her without any further discussion.

I look his way and am relieved to see that right now he looks...delighted. There's a large glass of ambrosia in his hand and he's watching the fight like a little kid sitting in the stands of a three-ring circus. He can't seem to decide where to focus his attention, because delightful sights are everywhere.

With a sigh, I settle back to the ground, finding a quiet spot away from the action.

There's a cool breeze next to me, lifting the edges of my skirt, and bringing relief from the oppressive heat with it.

I turn to find Val at my elbow.

"Hi," he says, casual as all get out.

I can't help it. I weakly smile back. "Hi."

"Nice weather we're having," Val adds, as a vampire

charges one of the pig roasting fires. The vamp tears the pig off the spit, then launches it toward a minotaur, who blocks the improvised spear with his shield...yet still refuses to hit back.

"Works great with the luau theme," Val adds, and I give him a shove.

"What in all Hades is going on?" I demand, but Val only shrugs.

"I decided to crash the party," he says, as clouds start to form all around us, a spray of rain beginning to fall. I look up into the steadily increasing downpour.

"This sudden change of weather is you, right?" I ask, but Val's already headed toward the stage, where Zeus and the other gods are now surrounded by a phalanx of loyal MOA students, taking orders from Nico.

There's a mix of shifters and vamps, and a few healers too. They're all ready to die for the gods, like they've been taught. But not everyone has joined them.

Fern stands by Mavis, trying to keep her out of harm. Marguerite appears and she and Fern embrace. "I told you to stay away," Fern tells her. "I didn't want you in danger."

"I had to come," Marguerite tells her. "I never want to leave your side again." They kiss deeply, but quickly, and Marguerite crouches and hisses at the gods. Kratos picks her up and throws her off the stage.

Mavis says quietly but sternly, "Go to her." And Fern leaves my sister's side.

Jordan, Greg, Cassie, Hepa, and quite a few others have reached a cautious impasse with the monsters, both sides on high alert, but no one making any threatening moves. There are similar face-offs scattered throughout the amphitheater, small bands of monsters and students eyeing each other carefully while slipping glances toward the stage.

Kratos remains near Mavis's chair, guarding her and looking like he's itching for a fight. I honestly don't think Kratos has ever been too into the whole 'hide behind the students' thing.

Val jumps up on the stage and holds out his arm. Kevin comes to him immediately, pulling a treat from his fingers.

"Vile traitor!" Mr. Zee shrieks, pointing over the shoulders of two students who stand in front of him. I'm not sure if it's Kevin or Val or both of them together, but Mr. Zee's no longer entertained. His moods have always changed quickly, but they seem more intense these days. From the highest of highs to the lowest of lows.

Right now his rage actually comes off of him in waves, making the entire stage tremble.

Not wanting to leave Val alone up there, taking the full brunt of it—especially when this is my fight—I take to the air.

"A traitor?" Val is nodding as I land softly beside him. "Yes. Vile...that depends. Should we ask the jury?"

He turns to them, still sitting in their box, hunched tightly together. "Is it vile to revolt against a tyrant?" They look at one another, stealing glances at Zee as well. Even now, they don't want to speak against him. But Val doesn't really need an answer.

"That's what she did," he points at Mavis, who raises her head a little higher, looking down her nose at the jury. "She did what she thought was right."

"And took my eye!" Nico, back in human form, leaps onto the stage, anger turning his handsome face into something horrible. "She is a traitor, a spy, a deceiver! In my mother's time she would've been put to death immediately. There wouldn't even be a trial!"

"Yes," Val says, his voice suddenly cold. "And look what happened to your mother."

Nico growls low in his throat, his back arching as he shifts again, his rage forcing him into werewolf form. Monsters pour on to the stage, more coming to flank Val, facing down Nico. I stand in between them, soaked to the skin as rain continues to fall around us.

"Stop," I say, my hands out to both sides, imploring. "Just...stop."

My voice breaks, a sob coming from deep inside me to crack open on the last word. My hands are shaking, my heart hammering in my chest. Cassie climbs onto the stage, running to my side.

"Edie," she says, wrapping her arm around my waist. It brushes against the sword, and she looks at me, questioning.

I shake my head. I don't want to swing it. Don't even know if I have the strength. All of my time at Mount Olympus Academy, all of the friends gained and lives lost have come down to this—me standing in between Val and Nico in the middle of a stage, my sister in chains.

I've fought so hard, and so much. I've killed. I've broken bones and spilled blood and turned living things into ash.

And none of it got me anywhere.

It just brought more violence, more questions, and I'm just as lost and scared now as I was the first day I came here, the day Cassie greeted me at the gates and welcomed me to this school.

I don't want to be at MOA anymore. Val is expelled, Tina is gone. And half the people here want to kill my sister. After everything I've been through, it comes down to something incredibly simple.

I just want to go home. And Mavis is my home.

"Please," I spin, turning to Zeus, my hands clasped. "Please," I beg. "Let my sister go. Let *us* go. She's my family."

The amphitheater is utterly silent, everyone watching the drama unfold on stage.

Zeus steps out from behind the students guarding him.

His gait is ragged; he's favoring one knee like a linebacker who played five seasons too long. His bulk, while all muscle, teeters as he comes toward me, the smell of ambrosia following him.

And yet, despite all that, the power he carries within his withered frame is undeniable. There's a charge in the air; static electricity rolls off him, leaving everyone's hair standing on end.

"Your sister?" Zee sneers. "Do you really think that appealing to familial bonds is the best way to win me over?"

From the corner of my eye I see Themis give a quick shake of her head, which might've been a helpful hint if she'd given it before I opened my mouth.

"Do you know what my sister did to me?" Zeus asks, his voice rising. "She sent snakes to kill my son Hercules in his crib when he was only an infant. She turned my lovers into animals—a cow, and a bear—so that I could not touch them!"

"But you did anyway." Val interrupts. "You also married your sister so that's kind of on you."

"SILENCE," Zeus roars, and Val goes quiet. Eerily quiet. I turn to see him touching his lips, a concerned expression on his face. His eyes go to mine, stunned.

"What?" I ask, concern rising in me like a balloon, filling my throat.

He shakes his head and I realize he can't answer me. Zeus has taken his voice.

"Edie..." Themis steps forward, as if to come to my side but Zeus spins on her.

"Stop!" he commands, and Themis does, faltering in her steps. "Have you all forgotten who I am?" Zeus asks, turning to direct his question to everyone on stage, sweeping me, Val, the jury, Mavis, the monsters, and his fellow gods.

All of us, without exception, are terrified.

Because we did. We did forget.

The bumbling, doddering, vaguely creepy guy I thought of as Mr. Zee is gone.

This is Zeus, king of the gods. And we have royally pissed him off.

He chuckles again, enjoying himself as he paces the stage.

"You know better," he says, almost quietly, as he approaches his fellow gods. Themis falls back, and the students form ranks again, but they're confused now. Are they protecting the gods from the monsters, or the gods from Zeus?

"You know me," Zeus sneers at Themis. "You know what I can do. And you." He turns to Metis, who holds his gaze, her own burning just as intently. "You know more than most what I'm capable of." He spins on his heel to take in us, the students, staring at him. "But they don't know. And they should. So who wants to tell them?"

Hades takes a step forward, "Brother, I'd be happy to deliver a history lesson on your behalf."

Zee chuckles jovially, though the sound is still full of menace. Walking over to Hades's side, he puts an arm around his brother's shoulders. "It was a rhetorical question. Maybe you didn't notice, but I'm having a moment here. If you step on it again, I'll rip your head from your shoulders, lock it in a box, and hide it at the furthest reaches of this world so you'll never be reunited with your body again."

Hades smiles tremulously and then silently pulls away from Zee.

With a satisfied nod, Zee turns back to his audience, spreading his arms out wide, encompassing the rest of us, students and monsters alike. "Who wants to tell the youngsters what I can do?"

No one says anything. Beside me, Cassie grips my wrist, squeezing hard.

"Nobody?" Zeus asks, scanning the crowd as if for a volunteer. "Well, then, I guess I'll just show them."

He lifts an arm, and points it at my sister.

"No," I screech, the word angry and guttural from my dragon mouth.

My heart catches in my throat as I leap forward.

Time seems to slow.

My wings are spread wide, my talons outstretched, but the air around me might as well be made of molasses. I cannot move fast enough.

Kratos dives out of the way as a bolt of lightning flies from Zeus's outstretched hand.

Mavis's mouth is a wide O of surprise as the bolt catches her directly in the chest. She flies upward and back, cracking into the arched marble that spans the top of the amphitheater.

It shatters like glass with the force and Mavis falls, her limp body hitting the stage floor as a mountain of rubble lands on top of her.

Everyone is screaming. Fights have broken out anew in the aisles, students attacking monsters, who look to Val for the order to fight back. He can't give it, his hands are on his throat, the muscles working madly as he tries to find a way to speak. Cassie shoves me to the side as more of the ceiling collapses and we skid to a halt together, at Zeus's feet. A bat flutters over our heads, darting this way and that in agitation. Greg, of course.

With a casual backhand, Mr. Zee bats Greg away. Then he bends down, inspecting me as if I were a bug.

"You just want to take your sister and go?" he asks. "Go ahead. She's all yours."

## 25

There's blood pooling out from under the rubble where Mavis fell. I scramble to it, Cassie grabbing my ankle as I go.

"Wait, Edie," she calls. "There's nothing you can do."

I know that. My sister was dead the moment the lightning bolt hit her. But I don't care. My father disappeared after his death, swept out to sea., My mother I could speak to, but not make her recognize me. I'm going to say goodbye to my sister, even if I have to crawl through her blood to do it.

I start shifting rocks, Cassie at my side. She's joined by Greg, Jordan, Fern, and Hepa, but Val and Marguerite's freakish vampire strength is needed to move some of the larger boulders. Zeus has taken command of the students, instructing them to attack at all costs, but confusion still reigns. Most of the monsters have fled, now that the goal—getting Mavis out alive—is impossible.

The first thing I see is her hand, still manacled, fingers broken and wrist bent at an awkward angle. I cry out at the sight, digging more frantically until only last piece of stone covers her.

I reach for it, but someone else beats me to it.

Nico.

He lifts it away and then stares down at Mavis, now fully visible...and utterly broken.

"I'm sorry," he says, his voice hoarse. There is a look of confusion on his face as he continues to stare, all while hugging that final stone in his arms. "I thought this would be different. Feel different." Shaking his head, he stumbles back a few steps and then wanders away, all the anger and passion gone from him.

I watch him until he's out of sight, his back slumped in regret. It's easier to look at him than what's left of my sister.

It's cowardly and I know were it me, Mavis would do better. So I force myself to look at her once more, my beautiful bossy older sister.

I pull her into my arms and she sags oddly, all of her bones reduced to dust inside of her skin.

She's like a rag doll in my arms; there is nothing left here of my sister.

Unlike Val, I still have my voice. But there are no words. Nothing to say that can fix it. Nothing that will bring back chasing fireflies in the backyard or splashing in the baby pool. Nothing that can retrieve the good moments or make the bad ones go away...

Like the last time we spoke.

When she told me it was either her, or Zeus.

"You were right," I say, cradling her head in my arms, her bloodied hair leaving streaks on my skin. "I should have listened to you."

Hepa and Fern are moving their hands over Mavis's skin

but I already know what's in their eyes before they tell me—there's no hope here. My sister has gone to the Underworld.

"You were right," I say again, a heat rising in my gut. "I should have killed him when I had the chance."

"Edie," Greg settles on my shoulder. "Let me do something. Cassie told me about the sword. Let me distract Zee while you get stabby—"

"Shut up," I answer softly, furious with him for reasons too complicated to sort out at the moment. Or maybe it's not that complicated. Maybe it's the same as when Nico was bullying his little rooster roommate out of jealousy over his big loving family while Nico had no one.

Or maybe it's even more simple. Greg always wants to be at the center of the action, but the only thing that ever seems at stake for him—is his pride.

He's not in the middle of a prophecy.

He doesn't lose sleep at night because of all the lives he's taken.

He hasn't woken up every morning for weeks on end, fearing the last of his family would die that day.

Nothing in his life is deep and dark and complicated. For him this all might as well be a godsdamned game.

"Go away, Greg," I snap. "Unless you want to get yourself killed, which is pretty much the only thing you can do at this point."

Cassie clutches my arm. "Edie," she says softly. "Oh, you said it. You really said it."

I shake her off too. Distantly, I hear her calling for Greg, begging him to stay.

All my attention is on Zee as his shadow casts me in his darkness. He stands over me, a smile on his face. "I see you've found her. My, my, my. She doesn't look well, does she?" A chuckle that seems to start from deep within him, rolls out of his mouth.

My blood boils hot, as I realize something—I can kill this bastard.

It won't bring my sister back. It won't save her.

I know that.

And yes, I was done with killing. Because I was sick of destruction. And violence that only leads to more violence.

But killing Zee would mean an end to violence. An end to *his* destruction.

In many ways it would be a kindness. A righting of so many wrongs.

I am his daughter, the one able to wield the sword. The one prophesied to kill him with it.

Not doing it isn't courage. It's encouragement. To Mr. Zee. For him to continue on as he's done all these centuries past. Without remorse. Without any check on his power. Without ever having to answer for what he's done.

I let Mavis's broken body fall to the ground.

He is a cancer. Letting it continue to grow would kill more than simply cutting it out.

I stand tall in the pool of my sister's blood, wrath and justice mixed, one giving strength to the other.

And still, the chuckle continues to rumble from him.

"You killed my sister," I say, my voice hollow and dark.

"Edie..." Fern, still on her knees, looks up at me. "There's something on your leg..."

I glance down to see the sword has lengthened. I pull it from its binding at my leg. The ruby in the hilt glows blood-red, my righteous vengeance infusing it with the ability to kill.

It's not a toy anymore, not a weight to be swung with great effort. This is a weapon, a blade that wants to kill.

And so do I.

My voice rises to fill the entire theater. "We did forget who you are," I yell at Mr. Zee. "King of the gods, wielder of lightning. But you're also a liar and a deceiver, a tyrant and a bully, a lascivious old fornicator."

There are some nods of agreement from the students. While Metis smiles slightly, her eyes alight with vicious glee.

"We forgot," I repeat as Zeus eyes me, his gaze dropping to the sword. "But you never figured out who *I* was. Who I am. All this time under your nose. The only dragon shifter ever in existence. How odd. How strange. How could such a thing happen?"

"Edie," Themis says, a warning in her voice.

Ignoring her, I draw the sword, the entire theater gasping as it dazzles brightly, the god's blood at the heart of the ruby pulsing with light as my rage infuses it.

"I'm your Moggy bastard child," I say to Zeus. "And I'm here to kill you, Father."

All confidence falls from Zee's face and he backpedals, pulling students in front of him as a shield. "Where did you get that?" he screams.

"From Amazon Academy. And from the Underworld," I tell him, stalking his steps. The students part, making a path. "And from behind my mother's portrait. Adrianna Aspostolos."

"What? I..." Mr. Zee is confused, looking from Hermes to Themis, and back again. "Who?" he finally asks, turning to me.

I bring the sword up and it sings through the air, landing with it's tip at Zee's throat like it was made to fit there. "Think hard," I growl. "It wasn't too long ago."

"Yes, yes! I remember!" he cries out, his desperation clear. "Of course, I do. Dear Adrianna, I loved her. I did!"

I shift my hand slightly, so the sword nicks the soft skin of his throat and blood begins to flow. "Describe her to me."

"Uhh..." His chin trembles. "She had eyes, two of them. Lovely, lovely eyes. Like yours I believe. And she was a buxom girl. I mean a man has a type so it stands to reason...and uh, blonde! She was a true blonde, the curtains matched the drapes—"

His description ends in a shriek as I pull the blade back and then tilt it down, preparing to drive it into his heart.

Zee dives out of the way as a strong arm stops me. I whirl, expecting to find Kratos, or Hermes, loyal to the end. But it's Themis who holds me by the shoulder.

"Let me go!" I yell at her. "Let me take my revenge."

"I cannot," Themis shakes her head. "If we kill Zeus the world will be thrown into chaos."

"You don't know that!" Metis yells, stepping out from behind the healers who had crowded around her. "It's only what you fear; you don't know what will happen. All we know for sure is that Zeus deserves to die, and here stands one capable of doing it."

Themis scowls, her gaze moving between me and Metis. "You did this? You gathered these pieces?"

"Yes, you told me to..." My words die off as I watch Themis's brow cloud, her eyes darken as she looks at Metis. "You didn't know, did you?" I ask. "You didn't know I went after the sword?"

Themis shakes her head. "No, I would never sanction a weapon so powerful in the hands of anyone, let alone a student. We wish for Zee to step down, that is all. His death would be catastrophic."

"That's right," Zee yells from behind Hermes and Kratos. "My death would suck big time."

I look down at the blade in my hands, and the bloodied footprints—my own—trailing after me, leading back to Mavis's broken body. "No," I shake my head. I'm past believing that Zeus can simply be sent off to early retirement.

"Edie..." Themis leans in, dropping her voice. "Think."

It's what Ocypete said to me, right before I incinerated her. She begged me to rethink my loyalty to the gods. To question everything they had been telling me.

Now I know she was right. She was the one I should have trusted.

None of the gods at Mount Olympus Academy have had anything but their own best interest at heart. Zeus wants only blood and women, Metis revenge on an errant husband, Kratos to spread violence, Hermes to live his never-ending life to the utmost pleasure.

We're their pawns, and I'm done with that.

I don't know what Themis's agenda is, but I doubt the suffering of humankind keeps her up at night. This is about some ongoing power struggle she has with Mr. Zee. Mavis. Me. Maybe even all the way back to when she raised my father. We were nothing but pawns in her endless game of chess with an overpowered idiot who beat her every time.

"All your gallons of drugged ambrosia and he is still capable of destruction. You have no idea how to keep him on his leash. Though my guess is you've been trying for millennia. Your way didn't work and now it's time to try it my way," I say, drawing myself up under her gaze, my wings unfurling into a deep, dark red to match the stains on my feet. "Let me kill him."

There's a rumble of agreement from the students aligning with me. Cassie comes to my side, shaken, but still with me. One by one, my other friends join her. Jordan. Hepa. Val. Fern. Marguerite. All of them staring down Zeus, Hermes, and Kratos. No sign of Greg; he must have flown off to lick his wounds. Regret for my harsh words flickers through me and is then gone. I simply don't have the bandwidth to deal with that right now.

Metis turns to Themis. "Let your scales decide."

Themis immediately brightens. Her scales are never wrong and it is impossible to argue with any verdict they deliver.

Themis goes to her chair, bringing out the scales as a light rain continues to fall. Kneeling, she sets them on an uncracked portion of the stage, where it's perfectly level. She kicks aside some rubble, finally deciding on two smaller pieces of cracked marble.

"Edie," she proclaims, raising one piece. "Is it your wish to fight Zeus, king of the gods, in combat until one of you is dead?"

"Yes," I say, without hesitation. Metis places the stone on one side of her scales, which remain balanced despite the lack of a counterweight. She holds the second piece of marble aloft.

"Zeus," she calls. "Is it your desire to fight Edie, the first dragon-shifter, your Moggy-born bastard child in combat until one of you is dead?"

"No," Mr. Zee says. He slips out from behind Hermes and Kratos, coming toward me with outstretched hands. "Who would want to kill such a beautiful young thing? Daughter!" He cries, warily eyeing my blade as he approaches. "Of course I remember your mother, Adrianna Poopadoopalous."

"You disgusting snake," I seethe.

Themis puts Zee's rock onto the scale, which holds a

perfect balance for a few seconds. The amphitheater is utterly still, everyone's eyes locked on the scales, as the side with my rock comes crashing down, resonating throughout the hall.

"Very well," Themis sighs. "It is just. You shall fight."

## 26

Once it's decided, Themis is all business.

"This is a death match," she announces. "There will be no interference." She casts a dark look at Hermes and Hades, but I'm more worried about Val. He doesn't have a voice, but he doesn't need one; his emotions are plain on his face. He would happily kill Zee for me...if he could.

But only I can do this.

"Contestants." Themis beckons to us, bringing me and Mr. Zee within reaching distance of one another. We face off, my cheeks still hot with rage, his red with ambrosia. "Acknowledge each other," Themis commands.

I spit at Zeus, and he flicks me off. Apparently, this is enough to cover the bare minimum of "acknowledging" each other. Themis backs away, edging to the side of the stage.

"To prevent any aid being given to either opponent, the fighting arena will be sealed off," Themis announces, and a thin line of fire creeps from her fingertip. She points at the stage floor, and the fire runs in a perfect circle around me and Zee, meeting itself with a *snap*. Smoke rises, thick and oily, creating a dome around us.

"Good luck, Edie," Themis says, and then the smoke rises past her face, blotting out everyone.

There are no onlookers. No well-wishers. No one to cheer or jeer. No one to help or hinder. It's just me and Zeus, staring each other down in this encapsulated world that only one of us will leave alive.

"I don't remember your mother," Mr. Zee says, all pretense at civility dropped. "How could I? There have been so many."

He's trying to rile me, trying to get me to make a foolish lunge like I did before. Only this time he's ready.

I don't fall for it.

Instead I circle him, the sword light and lithe in my grip, ready to perform its duty. Hopeful for a kill. I don't rise to his bait, instead watching, waiting for Zee to make a move.

"Although it's a good thing you unmasked yourself, in the end," Zeus continues, turning with me as I make my circle. "You're a pretty little thing, and I do have my weaknesses. What's one more relative, anyway?"

He feints to the left and I fall for it, side-stepping in the wrong direction. I recover quickly, but he laughs, the sound rolling across the little arena we have to fight in. "Oh, little Edie," he sighs. "We could've had some fun."

He makes another grab, this one not a fake, and I take to the air, wings snapping out. There's a split second when I'm above him, his massive shoulders turned away that I see the chance to drop like a rock and bury the sword between his shoulder blades. I lunge downward, but too late. Zeus senses my movement and spins, one arm up defensively.

The sword slides through his arm like butter and blood sprays, catching the light as it flows down his wounded arm.

It takes me by surprise and I don't adjust my trajectory well, bouncing off Zee's arm and hitting the side of the dome.

It looks like smoke but feels like stone, and I hit hard, my arm going numb with the impact. The sword clatters to the ground and I fall after it, a crumpled heap.

"Oh please," Zeus says, striding toward me. "Don't tell me it's that easy. Or maybe you are just like your mother, after all."

"You bastard," I spit, grabbing the sword and coming back to my feet. Something caves in my side and I'm pretty sure a rib is broken. I switch sword hands, clutching my side with the free one.

"No, you're the bastard," Zeus says, conversationally. "In the true sense of the word. You and your trash Moggy boyfriend."

I rush him, sword out, blind rage sending me at a run.

Zeus grabs my arm at the elbow, almost casually, and sends me flying through the air, headed for another bone-crushing impact with the smokescreen.

I pump my wings, gain some altitude and spin away from the wall, putting some distance between us as well. I've got to do what Ocypete told me so long ago—THINK! I've got to get his smug voice out of my head and come up with a plan other than blind rage.

"Can't shift, can you? No, no, no," Zeus wags a finger at me. "Shift into a dragon and you won't be able to hold the sword. Damndest things, talons. Good for slashing, bad for fine motor skills."

"Shut up," I say, landing a few feet away from him, trying to get my bearings.

"What?" Zeus shrugs. "I'm just trying to help you out,

save some time. Think about it, Edie. Shift into a dragon and you can burn me, tear me, bite me…it's an attractive option."

It is. Just looking at the drops of his blood on the stage floor has my dragon-self salivating, wanting to know the taste of ichor.

"But…" Zeus forehead crinkles, like he's actually thinking this out. "It won't do you much good will it? I mean, I'm the king of the gods. You've seen my healing powers, right, Edie? *Right*?"

His voice shifts on the last word, anger getting into his tone. Mr. Zee twists to show me his arm, open to the bone. It morphs and twists as I watch, muscles knitting themselves back together, tendons reconnecting as the skin seals over it, bright and new as a baby's.

"See?" Zeus asks, running a hand over the healed arm, and I take a step back, alarmed at how quickly he can rejuvenate when he turns his attention to it. That was nothing like Hermes, who would barely have one wound begun before I struck the next. Even with this sword, I don't stand a chance of striking a killing blow, not when his wounds close so fast.

I'm still backing away, and my heel slips in a splash of ichor. I go down on one knee, the sword heavy again in my hand as my rage weakens into doubt.

"What's the point, really?" Zeus asks, still advancing on me. "You shift, you try to burn me, you try to slice me, you try to kill me, and I just keep healing, over and over again. You'll get tired, and you *will* get tired, Edie, so you'll shift back into a human girl, try the sword again, but you're worn out. You're exhausted. You don't have any strength left…and do you know why?"

I'm shrinking away from his leer as he bends over me,

pressed against the barrier, tears streaming down my face as the broken rib grinds against my lungs.

"Because you are just a human girl," Zee whispers in my ear, his mouth pressed against it. "And *I am a god*. Turn into a dragon, and you drop the sword. It'll be mine, and you can't kill me without it."

He pulls back, smirking. "You're either a dragon, or you're a girl, Edie. You can't be both. So, all that's left is for you to decide which form you want to die in. I'll give you ten seconds."

Zeus walks to the middle of the arena, and cracks his knuckles, ready to use his lightning again. Ready to send me to the underworld with my Mavis.

"Ten... Nine..."

*You can't be both.*

It rings in my head, Zeus accidentally giving a voice to everything that has plagued me during my time at Mount Olympus Academy. I've been struggling with my dragon self, trying to separate it from Edie, the nice girl who never knew she was anything else. Anything different. Anything more. I'd pushed back against my rage, scared of what it could do. And now, here I am, paying for drawing that line.

"Eight... Seven...Six..."

Zeus is right. I can't hold the sword while I'm a dragon, and I can't strike fast enough to counteract his healing powers as a human. But there is one thing a selfish coward like Zeus would never think of, a trick up my sleeve that would never occur to someone who uses students as human shields in order to avoid any harm to himself.

"Five... Four... Three..."

I zip into the air, Zeus's eyes tracking my movement as he prepares to throw a bolt. "So you want to die as a human with wings? Weird choice, but okay."

"Two... One."

I do the one thing Zeus doesn't expect, the one thing he would never do himself. I raise the sword, and drive it through my own shoulder. The pain is sharp and immediate, the blade parting flesh and grating over bone. But I don't have time to consider it as I shift in midair, the blade still stuck in my dragon flesh as I ascend, this time with a ball of fire growing in my belly.

Zeus throws lightning, but it meets my fire, causing an enormous explosion that knocks him off his feet. I advance, fire flowing like lava, lighting his robes, his skin crackling black, his hair catching immediately.

He might be able to heal himself, but he feels the pain. His screams say as much. Ichor flows where the skin cracks open, ragged streaks rapidly repairing him as he gets back to his feet, burning and healing at the same time.

I shift back to a human, pull the sword from my own shoulder and drive it home, right through his black and rotten heart.

## 27

I mmediately the smoke disperses.

Everyone is still standing where they had been. There are gasps, and cries, and even a few cheers when everyone sees Zee lying at my feet, his hands wrapped around the blade of the sword as he tries in vain to remove it from his chest.

The earth beneath my feet trembles and a rough wind picks up, strong enough to blow up anything not bolted to the stage.

"It's begun," Themis says.

"Edie, I knew you could do it." The voice in my ear sounds like Mavis. A hallucination brought on by my overwhelmed senses. Except she keeps talking. "You have the sword still, press the gods for concessions. Free the monsters from them once and for all."

Am I truly having a vision of my dead sister bossing me around?

A hand wraps around my uninjured arm. My head turns slowly, afraid of what I'll see.

Mavis. No longer broken. Not even bruised.

Alive. And breathing.

"Mavis..." I can't get out more than that as the tears start to flow.

"Shhh. Edie. Don't fall apart on me now. Don't let your friend's sacrifice be for nothing."

I still can't believe she's beside me. I reach out to touch her. My fingers trail down her cheek, the skin warm against mine. Slowly, slowly, her words penetrate the fog in my brain.

"What friend? What do you mean about a sacrifice?"

"The little bat boy. He flew down to the Underworld. Made some sort of deal with Hecate down there. I didn't get all the details, just that his family were UWA legacies and they owed him a favor. He cashed it in for me."

"Greg," I say, a smile stretching my mouth, as I look around for him. What an idiot I was to underestimate him. "Where is he?"

Mavis frowns. "Edie...he traded his life for mine. It had to be that way."

"No..." I shake my head wildly at the same moment that my eyes meet Cassie's. She doesn't look surprised at all. "You saw it," I say to her. "You knew."

Cassie nods. "It had to be," she says softly.

My own words come back to me. *"Go away unless you want to get yourself killed, which is pretty much the only thing you can do at this point."*

Cassie had known I would say it. And she knew how Greg would react.

Oh gods.

And then Themis is in front of me. "Edie, Zee will draw his last breath if you don't remove that sword immediately. Your sister has been restored to you Now is the time to show the same mercy that was granted to her—"

"Mercy! It was a transaction!" I have to shout over the wind which has picked up once more. "Her life purchased with Greg's." The ground beneath us shakes and then the stage begins to roll as if a huge wave is surging up beneath it. I fall to my knees beside Zee.

But my eyes aren't on him. It's Themis's scales I watch as they spin wildly, like a carnival ride, moving faster and faster. The weighing plates fly out while the chains that connect them rattle ominously. With a crack, the plates fly off, whooshing right over our heads. Abruptly the scales stop spinning and what's left of them crumbles to dust.

Sooo...it's possible maybe Themis wasn't bluffing about that whole end of the world thing.

Grasping the sword with two hands, I look up at the gods arrayed before me. "The war against the monsters is over. They will live freely and never be bothered by any of you again."

"They must vow," Mavis adds in, and then leaning in to me she says in a softer voice, "For gods, vowing to something is magically binding. They'd give up their own immortality if they tried to go back on something they vowed to."

I nod. This is good information to have. And for the first time, instead of seeing Mavis as bossy, I realize what our relationship could be going forward. Sisters, working as a team, together.

Sometimes I'll hold the sword. Sometimes she will. Sometimes I'll know the words and at other times Mavis will supply them.

"You heard her," I say. "Make your vow."

Hermes, Kratos, Themis, Hades—all the gods—they stare back at me dumbly.

"Now!"

Hand to heart, they each make a solemn promise to make peace with the monsters.

I look down at Zee and his watery eyes meet mine. "You too."

He nods and his mouth moves but no words come out.

"Try harder," I tell him.

"I vow," he whispers, his voice hoarse. I make him say the whole thing, then have them vow to not hurt myself, my friends gathered here, or my family. They swear it.

I do the whole thing again, but this time making them all swear.

Satisfied and knowing Zee is running out of time, I grasp the hilt, ready to pull it from his heart, hoping that I am not making the wrong choice.

With a horrible crash, the earth trembles once more and then with a deep groan, it splits open wide. The sword slips from my hands as I fall, deep into an endless darkness. Mavis's scream is at my ear as she falls beside me. My wings pop out and I snatch Mavis with a single talon. A quick glance below shows me the ruby stone, growing smaller as it travels further—Zee presumably still with it.

"Edie," I hear Val yell from above. A moment later Cassie's and then Fern's voice echoes his.

I let Mr. Zee and the sword go, all the way down to Hades if that's where this darkness ends. My heart clenches as I think of Greg down there with him.

"Give him hell, Greg," I screech into the black, wishing and hoping that he somehow hears.

Then, holding my sister tight, I fly up toward the light.

I'm pretty sure it's the end of the world up there.

But I feel fairly certain of something else too.

I've got Mavis. Val. And my friends. So long as we stick together—we'll be fine.

# EPILOGUE

I burst from the bowels of the earth with Mavis clutched in a talon.

Above, on steadier ground, Val and Cassie standby, wearing near identical expressions of concern. They don't wait for me to shift back before throwing their arms around me and Mavis.

Needing to hug them all back, I shift.

Seconds later, I hear Fern say, "Group hug," and then she and Marguerite join us.

We stay that way for a long time, all of our arms wrapped around one another. It's the happiest and saddest moment of my life.

I have Mavis back. But lost Greg.

Zeus is dead. But I *had* to kill him.

And also, we maybe sorta broke the world.

I look at my friends. "Did I do the right thing?" my voice catches on that last word.

Val laces his fingers through mine and tugs me close. "You did what had to be done."

I nod, feeling a little better.

Although...Val is my boyfriend so he has to say that. Also, he's not exactly a softie himself. Plus, he didn't exactly say I did the right thing. But I guess maybe what's true is that I did the hard thing. The thing no one else could do.

I look over at Cassie and Fern, my moral compasses. They meet my eyes, straight on.

"The world isn't ending," Fern assures me. "It's just shaking a bit."

"No, it's definitely the apocalypse," Cassie says.

Fern elbows her and I can't help but let a little moan of despair escape. "Oh gods!"

Realizing her mistake, Cassie quickly backtracks. "It's okay, though. I mean, Zeus would've caused way worse stuff if you hadn't stopped him. Apocalypse now or Apocalypse later, it's sorta like ripping off a band-aid."

"Oh, please," Marguerite scoffs as she loops an arm around Fern's shoulder. "Vampires have caused the end of civilization as we know it, countless times. Everyone gets all upset and then eventually they sort it out and civilization starts itself up again."

I nod, feeling slightly better. "So probably by this time next year things will be back to normal?"

"Next year!" Marguerite laughs. "Not hardly! Maybe next cent—OOF!"

Fern's sharp elbow finds her girlfriend's spleen.

"Ouch, easy baby," Marguerite throws a hurt look at Fern, who gives her a stern one in return. With a sigh, Marguerite turns to me. "Look, the world never had a dragon shifter on its side before. Who knows what you can make happen?"

"Especially with all of us at *your* side," Fern quickly adds.

"Cassie!" Merilee runs toward us, leaping over wreckage

with surprising athleticism. As she reaches Cassie, they fall into each other's arms.

Quickly Cassie fills her mother in on what she missed—with an emphasis on Greg's role.

"Oh, darling," Merilee pulls Cassie closer. "I'm so sorry. If only someone had stopped him." Realizing that Mavis and I are both nearby, Merilee quickly adds, "I mean, there must have been another way."

"There wasn't," Mavis says. Stepping close to Cassie, she holds her hands out, almost as if in supplication. "I would never have accepted if I had a choice, but Greg made the deal with Hecate before I knew anything about it. A life for a life. If I hadn't taken the offer to have mine returned, it would've gone to someone else."

Cassie places both of her hands inside of Mavis's. "I understand. Actually, I understood even before he did. Greg did what had to be done. For him. For you. For Edie. And for the world."

Mavis's eyes fill with tears. "But that because he switched me with me, Greg won't be at Underworld Academy. I was..." She gulps and shudders. "Some giant worm thing ate me and was slowly digest—"

I gasp, and even though I want Cassie and Mavis to have this moment without getting involved, I can't stop myself from pulling Mavis into a strangling hug.

"Greg isn't being eaten by a worm," Cassie assures both of us. "His family has been students at UWA for generations. All the bat shifters would riot if that happened to him."

Mavis wipes her sleeve across her eyes as I release her. "And Hecate is known for having a soft spot for bat boys." She rubs Cassie's back. "You're right. I'm sure he's not getting the giant worm treatment."

We all share watery small and then go in for yet another group hug. It's that kind of night, I guess.

Hepa joins us with Jordan's arm slung over her shoulder. He looks a bit dazed.

"A building fell on my head, but I'm okay," he says.

"He doesn't use it often anyway," Hepa says, though her voice carries a lot of affection. "Can we cut the group cheer short and start tending the wounded?" She demands as the earth trembles once more.

Mavis, having recovered from her tears, takes charge. "We're also in the middle of a major seismic event and below sea level. Let's start evacuating. Val and Marguerite, gather any remaining monsters and return through the same portal that brought you here. Fern and Hepa, identify the wounded, so we can get them out first."

"I'll help them," I say, "In case anyone needs to be airlifted."

"You're among the injured," Mavis counters, hands on her hips. "You need to find a safe spot, sit, and wait."

"Not gonna happen," I say.

Mavis's eyes narrow in her 'how dare you question my older sibling authority' sort of way. Luckily, Themis appears and steps between us before we can get into a full-blown sister-on-sister argument.

"Mavis, I am glad you have returned from Hades. It was not the place for you. Yet."

Even now Themis cannot admit how much she loves us, her onetime daughters. Mavis must know it too, because she throws her arms around the woman. After a moment, Themis extricates herself.

"Mount Olympus Academy is closed for the foreseeable future." She holds out a handful of portal keys. "These should help with your evacuation plans."

Mavis takes them. "What about you?"

"I will, of course, stay here," Themis says as if it's obvious.

"I'm staying with her," Merilee adds. She pats Cassie, "But you will evacuate, daughter. The end of the world probably isn't the best time for you to explore the gates beyond Mount Olympus, but there is nothing left her for you."

"Except for you!" Cassie protests.

Merilee smiles. "You can still visit, darling. And I'll come see you as well. And I'll help you get settled. I'm sure Edie wouldn't mind a roommate…"

"Cassie will have a home wherever I am," I assure her.

"Oh! I forget…" Merilee fumbles through the many pockets of the long drapey sweater, finally extracting a scroll. "Themis came to me when the prophecy about Zee first surfaced. She wanted to be prepared in case the worst actually happened."

"I'm standing right here," I remind Merilee.

"Right! Sorry." Merilee gives me an absent smile. "Sorry, Edie. I'm not saying, what you did was not the worst. Arguably, there are worse things than the end of the world."

"Um, Mom," Cassie interrupts, before this can get more depressing. "What's on that scroll?"

Merilee looks down as if surprised to see it in her hand. "Oh yes. I came across this earlier today, right when I was getting ready to come to the trial. I didn't want to miss your performance, Cassie."

"Testimony," Themis corrects dryly.

"I'm sure it got quite testy," Merilee agrees, only half paying attention to everyone else as she unrolls the scroll. "Unfortunately, once I came across this beauty, all else was forgotten. It explains that when a god dies, their powers don't die with them. Instead, they go out into the world and find a worthy soul. Well, one hopes the soul is worthy. That's a bit worrisome, isn't it?" Merilee's brow furrows, but then she brightens again as she points at a different part of the scroll. "It also says, if a god is very powerful, like Zee, the powers can sometimes be divided among two or even three individuals."

"They will need to be found," Themis says, taking the scroll from Merilee. Or trying to. The pair engage in a brief tug of war before Themis wins. "Zee's powers in the wrong hands, or even the right ones...we will have to find this person and train them, make sure they understand the grave responsibility they've inherited—"

"Wait," I interrupt. "We need to find one, two, or maybe even three people who suddenly inherited Zeus's powers?" Something else occurs to me, and I wonder if this might be the light at the end of the tunnel. "And then they can be the new Zeus and everything will be better?"

"Possibly," Themis says, as she studies the scroll. "In the meantime, Merilee and I will look for more answers and watch over what's left here at MOA. Especially the archives. It holds treasures that Zeus has guarded for centuries, without him here..."

"It'll be open season," I finish for her. "And what of the other gods?"

Themis holds out both hands, indicating the chaotic amphitheater. Students are everywhere, panicked, crying, some cheering and reveling in the chaos. But there are no gods, our teachers, anywhere. "As you can see, they have left. They will all be forming new alliances and rivalries among themselves. Humans will suffer terribly."

Cassie suddenly stumbles and her eyes go cloudy. "Things will be bad, but if closed hearts cannot open, they will be worse still. In time civilization can be set to rights or completely shattered."

"Oh sweetheart," Merilee pulls her daughter close as Cassie blinks her eyes back to normal.

Her prophecy is followed by the worst quake yet. The land rolls in waves. Smoke and dust fills the air as every structure around us crumbles. When the earth settles once more, everything has been flattened. The dorms, the amphitheater, even the archives. It looks like Themis and Merilee will be busy digging out all those precious treasures before they can start guarding them.

Cries of pain and others pleading for help, come from every direction. We jump into action. It takes hours to evacuate but at the end of it Val and I are the last ones left. The tremors have stopped for now.

Val pulls me close. "What now?" he asks.

"Well, you go back to Underworld Academy and keep an eye on Hades. And tell Greg..." I pause as I get choked up once more "Tell him I'm sorry and thank you and..." I shake my head. And look at Val, needing help. "Words seem so inadequate. Should I send him a cookie bouquet or something? How do I tell my friend, 'thank you for trading your life for my sister's?"

Val kisses the top of my head. "He did it for you, Edie. And for Mavis. But I think he did it for himself too. He needed to prove something. In the story of Zeus's death, Greg is almost as legendary as you."

"I don't want to be legendary."

The right side of Val's mouth slides up into its customary smirk. "Too late. Tina's already making you a t-shirt. *Dragon, Slayer of Gods*. And mine will say: *I'm With Her*."

I laugh. "Can we go on a real date together someday and definitely *not* wear those?"

"What does one wear on a real date?"

I brush my hands down Val's chest. "Well, I'd love to see you in a suit and tie. We could have a fancy dinner somewhere. There was this seafood place my parents used to—"

I stop. My parent's loss bubbles up, the pain still surprisingly fresh. And then there's another pain, the realization that the seafood place is probably gone. Along with most of the Florida coastline.

I swallow. "Maybe we should put the dinner plans on hold until I clean up the mess I created."

We've reached the fountain portal and together step through. The icy coldness surrounds us and then we emerge onto a street in the middle of New York City. It's not exactly the best place to be. Alarms sound from every corner. And ocean water surges up the street.

"You're gonna need scuba gear to get down to UWA," I say to Val, feeling overwhelmed by seeing firsthand the evidence of my actions.

Val takes my face in his hands, so I only see him. "You will find the new Zeus. I know it. And in the end, the whole world will be better off."

I smile. "Do you have second sight now too?"

"No," Val kisses my nose. "Just faith in you. Legendary, remember?"

"I love you, Val. Is it too soon to say that?"

He kisses me again, but this time his mouth meets mine. The whole broken world melts away for several long moments. He pulls away too soon. "If I wasn't such a tough guy, I'd tell you that I love you too."

"Maybe Tina can put that on a T-shirt for you too." Val's eyes light up and I groan. "You're totally gonna have her do that, aren't you?"

"I wear my heart on my sleeve," Val says with his trademark smirk.

We share one more long kiss, before pulling apart.

"Time to unbreak the world," I say.

Shifting into dragon mode, I launch into the sky, and then circle the city.

I came to Mount Olympus for revenge. And to find out who I am.

As it turns out, I'm more into rescue than revenge.

I swoop down, ready to fix what I can for now.

And then later, I'll find new Zeus and repair the rest.

It's just what us legendary heroes do.

## THERE'S MORE TO READ IN THE MYTHVERSE...

Enjoying the Mythverse? Please leave us a review and let us know! The more stars we get, the more books we write!

Want to know about all the latest releases? Sign up for the Mythverse Newsletter!

When you sign up you'll receive THREE FREE SHORT STORIES—all set in the Mythverse!

We'd also love to have you join our Facebook group—Myth-verse Fandom!

Here you can yell at us about cliffhangers, chat with other fans about our books, get exclusive early book excerpts, and even snippets from our Slack convos!

**Also available from the Mythverse...**

You can find more of Edie in the next book in the Mythverse - available NOW - **Amazon Academy: Amazon Princess, Mythverse Book 4**

**The events in this book take place immediately AFTER the events in this book. Keep reading to continue the adventures!**

**What shade of nail polish works best for life in a post-apocalyptic hellscape?**

I'm Brandee Jean, just your average Midwestern teenage beauty queen trying to survive the end of the world. If it wasn't for the super strength I picked up after getting struck by lightning, I'd be struggling worse than a pageant girl trying to win the swimsuit competition with a wedgie.

I'm not the only one who got zapped. Turns out some fancy god guy kicked the bucket, and his powers got shuffled and dealt out to ten different teenagers.

Flying. Teleportation. Virility. Wisdom. And more. We all got something.

Now all ten of us are gonna attend Amazon Academy, where we'll take classes and compete in different tasks. At the end of it - winner takes all. The losers give up their powers, while the winner becomes a god and an official Amazon Princess.

Now that's a crown worth competing for.

This young adult magic academy fantasy novel features: non-stop action, lots of cute boys, favorite characters from Mount Olympus Academy, a hero who's a total Darcy, and lots of plot twists to keep the pages turning.

Drop Dead Gorgeous meets The Hunger Games in this fun spin-off series!

**PLUS**, with Amazon Princess you'll get a bonus novella continuing the adventures from Mount Olympus Academy.

Bah Humbug! I'm Nico Tralano and I'm gonna bite the next person to wish me Merry Christmas.

It's the end of the world and life is good for this one-eyed werewolf. I've been making bank as a paid assassin.

But now I've been offered a job to kidnap one of my old Mount Olympus Academy classmates. On Christmas Day too. She was always nice to me, but the money is too good to turn down.

Except before I can do the job, I start seeing ghosts. They show me things from the past, present, and future. They reveal that my lack of holiday spirit might not ruin only this Christmas, but the entire world.

Can I change my heart or will it be too late?

CHAOS & CHRISTMAS is a 15,000 word novella. The events in this book occur after WITHER & WOUND: MOUNT OLYMPUS ACADEMY BOOK 3 and before AMAZON PRINCESS: AMAZON ACADEMY BOOK 1.

This is a reimagined urban fantasy version of The Christmas Carol story we all know and love.

———

**Keep reading for a sneak peak at Chapter 1 of Amazon Princess...**

## CHAPTER ONE

*I am beauty, I am grace. I will punch you in the face.*

This has become my new mantra since the end of the world. My old mantra was, *Miss Teen Wisconsin or Bust*, but sometimes ya gotta adjust your goals.

I get out of my beat-to-crap pick-up truck carefully, making sure not to step on the train of my long sparkling gown. Even though there aren't any more pageants, I still don't wanna ruin it. All the Swarovski crystals on it cost me an arm and a leg.

Cost me an arm and a leg. That's kinda a joke, but also kinda *not*.

Last week, I totally saw Miss Teen Dairy Queen on the side of the road. She was missing her left leg and had clearly bled out. I tried real hard to *not* think about how that might've happened. Years ago she'd had those long legs insured for something like a hundred grand a piece.

Seems unfair the insurance won't be paying out on them suckers. But a lotta things ain't fair these days, and I can't say it was always all that better in the before times either.

I covered what was left of Desirae up with a blanket. And then, even though I'm not much for religion, I had a little chat with God after I got her all tucked in.

"Hey God, sorry I been cursing your name so much

lately. Don't take it personal, okay? I know you get touchy 'bout how folks use your name. But this ain't about me. I'm calling up to you about Desirae here. Dessie was crowned Miss Teen Dairy Queen three years running. Those cow folks loved her legs. Anyway, you treat her like royalty up there, cuz that's what she is."

Who can say whether God was listening? From what I hear 'round town, his response rate isn't what it used to be.

Now, kicking my truck door shut with a combat-booted heel, and clutching my baseball bat, I head into the Piggly Wiggly.

Six months ago, I was Brandee Jean Mason, resident Beauty Queen. Headed for big things and the bright lights... or at least, the state fair circuit.

Then came the earthquakes.

And the floods.

NYC fell into the ocean. California is now an island.

I mean, that's the last I heard.

There hasn't been a news broadcast in months, and the one guy in town who's got a shortwave radio isn't inclined to share info unless I do some sharing of *other* things—and that sure ain't happening. No way, no how.

I think I'd rather not know, anyway.

Now I grab a shopping cart and wipe down the handle with the wet wipes, still in the dispenser. The apocalypse is not a good time to get salmonella.

Wisconsin weathered the storms better than most states. We've got our own farms and fields, and enough people got solar panels and even their own wind turbines, that some folks even still have electric. But unless you know how to hunt, raise, or grow your own food, you're still stuck shopping.

Which can be a real pain in my ass—my very nice, award-winning ass.

Carl looks up from the year-old magazine he's reading behind the check-out line. "Hi, Brandee Jean."

There's a machine gun next to him on the counter. Bandits killed his dad a few months back and he's not about to let them get him too.

I relax a little. Carl's a good guy, always polite. I've known him since middle school.

I push the cart over to him, putting a little swing into my hips. "What we got today?"

"Corn. And more corn." He peeks at me over the magazine. "Nice dress."

"It's my armor." I tell him, doing a twirl, then a little curtsy.

"The baseball bat really makes the outfit. I give it ten out of ten."

My bat is spangled and painted bright red. I found it at the back of my closet, leftover from a "Damn Yankees" dance routine I did years ago. Weaponry is the to-die-for accessory this season, and I do like to stay on trend.

I smile with a wide-open mouth, showing all my teeth, just like I would on the pageant stage. I put a hand to my chest. "Why thank you. I'm just so very honored to be here today."

He laughs. "We did get in a fresh batch of Quik Powder..."

"Well, why didn't you start with that?" I ask.

Quik Powder is a refined food source. You can make bread or pancakes, or just mix it with water and drink it. It tastes like glue, but it also sticks to your ribs in about the same way, which means that you can eat a little and stay full for a whole day.

I load up my cart with five canisters of powder, then with dairy products and beef (God bless the great state of Wisconsin). I push the cart to the front and Carl surveys my take.

"That will be two hundred and fifty dollars."

Damned inflation. There goes my college fund. Not that I'm going to college anymore. The end of the world really put a pin in my five-year success plan.

I sigh. "Will you take a check?"

"You know I won't," he tells me with a kind smile.

I smile back, showing the teeth, then leaning forward and pressing my elbows together just enough to make it clear that my cleavage is very serious about needing some protein.

He looks. Of course he looks. Beautiful girls in gowns aren't sashaying down these aisles every day. But he also blushes, which is damn decent of him.

"Look, if you pay for the powder and beef, I'll give you the dairy for free."

"Deal!"

"So that will be…two hundred even. Cash or trade only."

"Thanks, Carl!" I throw the bills down on the counter. Before I wheel my cart on out, I ask him the same question I always do. "Hey, uh, any outsiders come through town lately?"

He looks at me with something like pity in his eyes. "Ya know I woulda told you, if I did."

"Right, I know," I lie. The truth is, I'm pretty sure Carl would lie. He thinks my plan to get myself kidnapped in order to save my best friend is suicidal.

"I'll see you next week," I promise him with one last smile and wave.

I keep an eye on the lot as I move out toward my truck.

The group I'm looking to have steal me aren't the only villains roaming these streets. These are desperate times. It's best to assume somebody's watching me, wanting to find out what I bought and how hard it would be to take it from me. And if that somebody decides I'm an easy target, they'll attack now—while I'm moving stuff over to my vehicle, no hands free to wield my bat.

I saw a movie once where a secret agent infiltrates a beauty pageant. Her talent is self- defense. I wish I'd made that my talent instead of tap. What, am I going to dance an attacker to death? Although I did take kickboxing down at the Y twice a week, so I know a few moves. Kickboxing burns some damn calories, let me tell you. Also, you could bounce a quarter off my ass after only two months.

"Brandee Jean?" someone says, and I spin around, baseball bat raised, heart pounding with fear.

It's a girl about my age. She's beautiful, with long legs and a heart shaped face. With a little refinement, she could kill it on the pageant circuit. She's also wearing some kind of school girl outfit, from a private school or something. Or a porn film shoot. I hear *that* business is still doing just fine.

"What do you want?" I ask, brandishing the bat.

She smiles, not at all afraid. "My name is Edie and I'm here to take you to Amazon Academy."

I spit out a laugh. "Guuurl, I'm not into that line of work."

I look around to make sure there's no one else lurking nearby. Sometimes they work in groups. One will distract you while someone else steals your stuff.

"I don't want your food," she tells me. "I just need you to listen for a moment..."

I don't let her finish. I get into the truck and hit the gas, giving her a pageant wave as I speed away. The world is crazy enough. I don't need a rando girl talking about academies—whatever that's code for. And given her getup, I'm assuming something slightly south of acceptable.

I watch her grow smaller in the rearview mirror. It looks like she doesn't have a vehicle either, which means she won't be giving chase. That's a relief. My old truck starts to rattle something awful anytime I get over 40mph.

Usually, I can relax a little once I turn onto my street. But as I make the left onto Colby Court, I spot something flying overhead. I immediately pull the truck over, scanning the perfectly blue slice of sky in the rearview mirror.

Is it a helicopter? Is someone coming to restore order and make everything go back to the way it used to be?

I get out, shading my eyes.

Dammit. No, of course not.

It's a stupid dragon up there.

I give the dragon the finger. The world is a messed-up place now. Six months ago, I would've thought I was taking too many diet pills. Or that I just needed a Lunesta and a good long nap.

Now, though, a dragon doesn't even count as the weirdest thing I've seen lately. Before the news went out, there were reports that vampires are real. And I swear, last month I saw a girl change into a cat and run off.

When I get home, the same girl from the Piggly Wiggly parking lot is waiting on my doorstep. I get out of the truck, bat in hand and ready to swing. I'm not playing right now. This is my property. My safe place. But her being here makes it a lot less safe.

And I hate that.

"How do you know where I live?" I ask, tightening the grip on my bat.

"I Googled you," she tells me with a smirk.

"How did you get here so fast?"

"I flew. And you really didn't need to flip me off," she adds.

I'm about to ask her what in the seven pageant hells she's talking about (circle two is the swimsuit competition), when purple wings sprout out of her back. Crap.

I keep my bat up as I approach her. "*You're* the dragon?"

"Are you ready to listen now?"

I hesitate, weighing the risks and rewards. If this dragon wanted to hurt me, she would've done it already. Unless she's a psychopath dragon who likes to play with her victims first. Either way, she seems determined. I'd rather invite her into my home, than have her go all dragon again and come crashing down through the roof.

"Sure," I say, trying not to look impressed. "If you help me get the groceries inside." My mama taught me that whatever else is going on, keep your priorities on track. Dragon-girl shrugs and grabs a box of Quik Powder.

"And no shoes in the house," I call over my shoulder. I put the food in the icebox and motion for her to sit at the kitchen table. I also make two glasses of Quik Powder as a snack. When I place it in front of her she stares at the mixture like it's roadkill.

"Drink up," I tell her. "That stuff's precious."

"Yes, of course." She takes a hesitant sip.

"So," I eye her. "What do you want with me?"

"Well, here's the thing—god is dead."

"Oh no, are you one of those end-of-the-worlders?" I shake my head. "I'm not joining your dragon cult and sacrificing myself to the flames, or whatever it is you weirdos do. Sorry, but I already got plans to join this 'we keep girls in cages' group next time they come through town recruiting."

She frowns at me. "You want to join a group that plans to put you in a cage?"

"Long story, I'd rather not get into it right now." It's actually not that long of a story, but I don't feel like sharing it with a stranger. "So if your group is looking for some sucker to feed one of their organs to a warlock who promises to roll back time, well sorry, but I'm not voluntarily giving any of them up."

One year, Miss North County Bee Hive Queen donated a kidney, faked appendicitis, and had her uterus removed, all in an effort to lose a few pounds. Her scars totally showed during the bikini competition though. Not worth it.

"There are no warlocks who can turn back time. Probably. Not that I know of. And—" She stops and takes another sip of Quik Powder. "We've gotten off course. Let me start again. A god is dead. Zeus, to be exact."

"The lightning bolt guy?"

"Yes. Exactly." She looks relieved. "You know who Mr. Zee, er, Zeus is. At least that's one less thing I have to explain."

"No...I think you still got a lot to explain. But let's start with Zeus. You're telling me he's real and also that he's now dead. And I'm...what? His long-lost daughter set to inherit everything he left behind?"

"Actually..." She hesitates and I see laughter in her eyes. Like she knows this is absurd. "*I'm* his long-lost daughter."

I take a moment to wonder if I got a batch of bad powder and am hallucinating. But, if people accept that vampires are real, and I witnessed this girl—as a dragon—follow me home from the Piggly Wiggly, how much larger a leap is required to accept that the Greek gods are real?

She gives me a sugar-free candy smile. Sweet, but definitely not the real thing. She'd never make it on the beauty queen circuit. "Anyway, after Zeus died, things went to Hades overnight. A bunch of the minor gods went haywire without anybody in charge. There were crazy storms. Earthquakes. Hurricanes. Tornadoes."

"I noticed," I tell her. "Here in Wisconsin we had a blizzard in August. Also, you know, vampires. And"—I give her the side eye just so she knows not to make fun of me when I finish my sentence—"I totally saw a girl turn into a housecat."

"Oh," Edie lights up. "That was my sister, Mavis. With all the chaos in the world, many of us supernatural creatures have been doing what we can to restore the balance. Mavis has been keeping an eye on you for a while."

My side eye still stands. "*Because?*"

"We're pretty sure some of Zeus's powers went to you when he died." She studies me, almost like she's trying to see beneath my skin. "Notice anything weird lately?"

"Oh, I don't know, like maybe that time I got struck by lightning and it didn't kill me?"

Edie leans back in her chair. "Can you walk me through exactly what happened?"

"I was out looking for Bethany Ully—she's Miss All-Midwest Body Butter. I had a bone to pick with her, on account of I found out she'd been using body wraps to shed some pounds."

"Is that illegal in a pageant?" Edie asks, and I shake my head.

"No, but we'd all made a pact that we were playing it straight for the summer. Strictly self-starving. But I spotted Bethany's name on the sign-in sheet at the Skinned and Tanned—that's a local business that does real well around here. The husband is a taxidermist and the wife is a cosmetologist."

"So they're both into preservation," Edie says, with a wry smile.

"Anyway," I say, waving my hand, "I went in for my bi-weekly tanning bed bake and that's when I saw her big loopy handwriting three slots above mine. She'd been in for a wrap appointment earlier that day." I shake my head, still peeved about it. "Beth didn't even bother covering her tracks. You can be shady or you can be sloppy, but not both. At least that's what my mama taught me. As a friend, I decided to deliver that message to her in person."

"Just a friendly chat?" she asks, raising her eyebrows.

"Not hardly. I was gonna rip out every single one of her new extensions."

"Seriously?" Edie looks disgusted and I wonder if she's some sort of pacifist dragon, but then she adds, "Hair pulling. Slapping. Spitting. That sort of fighting almost seems quaint."

I narrow my eyes at her. "Quaint my ass. She would've had bald patches when I was done with her."

Edie gives a slight nod that almost looks like approval. Not a peace-lover after all, then, I guess.

"So what happened?" Edie asks.

"I stopped home before paying her a visit. I wanted to wear my crown from the Miss Street & Sanitation competition, just to remind her what's what. I was cutting across the high school soccer fields when the first storm whipped up."

"Let me guess," Edie interrupts. "The sky went from bright blue to darkest black in an instant?"

"Out. Of. Nowhere," I confirm. "I made a run for it, but I might as well have had a lightning rod on my head. Took all of three steps before—*WHAM!*"

I smack the table with both hands and Edie jumps.

"Just like that I was on my ass, smelling like a Pop Tart that's been in the toaster too long."

"And...?" Edie prompts me. "Did you notice anything after the lightning strike? Anything unusual?" She's leaning forward, practically salivating.

"Like the fact that I can deadlift three hundred times my own body weight?" I ask, chugging down my Quik Powder and wiping my mouth.

It took me a few weeks to figure that out. At first I was just happy to have survived that lightning strike. Then all the social fabric busted wide open—kinda like when Jenny May Malone dropped her baton at the third annual Miss Midwest Pure Pork Princess and the seams on her dress couldn't continue hiding her five months along baby belly. It wasn't pretty.

I can't remember much of the dark days right after that. Mama was real low and I didn't see the point of pulling her out of it. But then one night she woke me at 3 a.m., all hopped up on something that made the smile on her face look all painful and stretched out. Mama said she'd had a vision that mani-pedis would help pull us through the apocalypse. By the time I pulled on the dress Mama insisted I wear, she was passed out cold. But I figured I'd go and get the nail polishes Mama wanted anyway. Figured it might keep Mama from sinking back down in the darkness...and taking me with her.

I was picking my way across Main Street when an abandoned car rolled onto my evening gown hem. That's when I noticed the not-so-nice guy eyeing me from the alley. Instead of ripping my dress (Dolce & Gabbana, secondhand, $4,500), I tried to lift the car...and succeeded.

I thought it was just the adrenaline, you know, like when a woman goes all mama bear because her baby is in danger?

But then when I got back home I did an experiment and flipped the neighbor's RV. So...

"That's not normal," Edie says, grinning.

"I do know that," I tell her. "So fine, if you say I got a bit of Zeus's power or whatever, I believe you."

"Good!" She sits back. "You're honestly way ahead of where I was when I started."

"You still haven't said what you want with me."

"If you want to keep your new power, you have to come with me to Amazon Academy. Once you're there, they'll find out if you can fill the void that was created when Zeus died. A bunch of different people got different pieces of him. We need all of you to compete. One winner will end up with all of Zeus's powers, and he or she can then restore order to the world." She sits back with an 'easy peasy' look on her face.

But I feel like she left out a big piece of the puzzle. "Okay and what about the losers?"

"Oh, um," Edie clears her throat. "If you lose, you lose your powers."

"But you just said I gotta go to this Amazon Academy if I want to *keep* my power!" The words explode out of me, because truth to tell, even though my super strength is still new, it's already become a part of me. Sorta like when you get a new lipstick and immediately realize it's gonna be your new signature color.

Edie holds her hands out in a calm down gesture. "Okay, look. Anyone who doesn't arrive at Amazon Academy by the evening of the opening ceremony will lose their powers. And that's tomorrow."

"Tomorrow!" I take a deep breath, fighting back the growing panic. "So let me get this straight. If I want to stay super strong, I gotta follow you to this Wonder Woman

Academy, Hunger Games it out with a bunch of other suddenly supers, and eventually rise to the top?"

"Don't freak out, but"—she reaches across the table and takes my hand—"the other contestants aren't all people. Some are vampires or shifters, like me, and yes, some are humans like you. And there are quite a few royals in the mix."

A sharp laugh escapes me. "Like another pageant queen?"

"Well...no. Royalty by blood," Edie admits.

"So you got stuck with me, a beauty queen? Are they punishing you?"

"No, actually. I chose you."

I bark out a laugh. "You had the option of picking an actual princess or queen or whatever, and you chose me? Aren't I a longshot?" What's wrong with this girl? Mama always said you gotta back a winner, even if you like the loser.

"I'm not going to lie to you. The general consensus is that you're the underdog. But I was once like you. I thought I was normal and then discovered I had incredible power. With my help, I think you can do this. You can be crowned the new Zeus." She pauses. "I'm not explaining this very well, am I?"

"Nah, you're doing just fine. You want me to compete for a crown. If I win, I'll be in charge of the gods."

My heart pounds loud in my chest as I look around the house. Mama wasn't much into decorating, but she always made sure to frame and hang my pageant pictures. From ages five and up, I'm there on the wall, competing for sashes and scepters.

Usually winning meant a crown, a sash, and a cash prize. Most of the money would go to paying for my dresses, the

dance choreographer, and dental work. Shiny chompers
don't come cheap. Any money left over, Mama would hide
in a Ziploc at the back of the freezer. Her not believing in
banking institutions is why I still got money to spend.

Some of the bigger pageants cost so much up front that
—even though Mama never said it aloud—losing wasn't an
option. I always at least placed at those times. Mama always
said, "You're a diamond, Brandee Jean. You shine brightest
when you're pressed the hardest."

She also said, "Only losers worry about what happens
when they lose."

Finally, I turn to Edie, and push my chair back with a
screech.

"Girl, I understand perfectly." I stand. "Let me grab my
tiara, then we'll go show them what a real queen looks like."


BUY IT NOW!

memories. Memories of a reckless, desperate wish . . . a bloody razor . . . and the faces of other girls who disappeared.

Piece by piece, Annaliese's fractured memories come together to reveal a violent, endless cycle that she will never escape—unless she can unlock the twisted secrets of her past.

**CLICK NOW to buy or borrow with KU!**

———

**THE SHOW MUST GO ON by Kate Karyus Quinn**

*While You Were Sleeping* meets *Pitch Perfect* in this hilarious romantic comedy that will have you laughing—and singing along too.

Jenna is certain of three things:

1. No way is she already thirty years old.

   (Except...she is.)

2. *Annie* the musical should never be crossed with *Fifty Shades of*

*Grey.*

(But this perfectly describes the show she's currently starring in.)

and

3. She can never return home—even if after twelve years her ex-boyfriend, Danny, wakes up from his coma and asks for her by name.

(Which he does.)

Okay, so sometimes Jenna gets a few things wrong. But she's definitely sticking with her never going home plan. (At least until Danny's younger brother, Will, arrives on Jenna's doorstep and insists on escorting her back to Buffalo, NY—and Danny's bedside.)

Fine. Maybe Jenna can go home again. But she's not staying.

And she's definitely not falling in love.

(Right?)

For fans of Sally Thorne, Penny Reid, and Lucy Parker, this standalone chick lit novel will give you all the feels.

**FREE with KindleUnlimited!**

————

**IN THE AFTER by Demitria Lunetta**

Perfect for fans of *The 5th Wave* and *A Quiet Place*.

Amy Harris's life changed forever when They took over. Her parents—vanished. The government—obsolete. Societal structure —nonexistent. No one knows where They came from, but these vicious creatures have been rapidly devouring mankind since They appeared.

With fierce survivor instincts, Amy manages to stay alive—and even rescues "Baby," a toddler who was left behind. After years of hiding, they are miraculously rescued and taken to New Hope. On the surface, it appears to be a safe haven for survivors. But there are dark and twisted secrets lurking beneath that could have Amy and Baby paying with not only their freedom . . . but also their lives.

BUY NOW

————

**DOWN WITH THE SHINE by Kate Karyus Quinn**

**Only $1.99**

Think twice before you make a wish in this imaginative, twisted, and witty new novel from the author of *Another Little Piece.*

When Lennie brings a few jars of her uncles' moonshine to Michaela Gordon's house party, she has everyone who drinks it make a wish. It's tradition. So is the toast her uncles taught her: "May all your wishes come true, or at least just this one."

The thing is, those words aren't just a tradition. The next morning, every wish—no matter how crazy—comes true. And most of them turn out bad. But once granted, a wish can't be unmade . . .

**BUY NOW**

————

**AMONG THE SHADOWS: Thirteen Stories of Darkness & Light**

**Available through KindleUnlimited!**

Edited and with stories written by Demitria Lunetta and Kate Karyus Quinn

Even the lightest hearts have shaded corners to hide the black thoughts that come at night. Experience the darker side of YA as 13 authors explore the places that others prefer to leave among the shadows.

BUY NOW

————

**BETTY BITES BACK**

**FEMINIST FICTION TO FRIGHTEN THE PATRIARCHY!**

**Available through KindleUnlimited!**

Edited and with stories written by Demitria Lunetta and Kate Karyus Quinn

Behind every successful man is a strong woman... but in these stories, she might be about to plant a knife in his spine. The characters in this anthology are fed up - tired of being held back, held down, held accountable - by the misogyny of the system. They're ready to resist by biting back in their own individual ways, be it through magic, murder, technology, teeth, pitfalls and even... potlucks. Join sixteen writers as they explore feminism in fantasy, science-fiction, fractured fairy-tales, historical settings, and the all-too-familiar chauvinist contemporary world.

**BUY NOW**

## ABOUT THE AUTHORS

DEMITRIA LUNETTA is the author of the YA books THE FADE, BAD BLOOD, and the sci-fi duology, IN THE AFTER and IN THE END. She is also an editor and contributing author for the YA anthology, AMONG THE SHADOWS: 13 STORIES OF DARKNESS & LIGHT. Find her at www.demitrialunetta.com for news on upcoming projects and releases. Or join the newsletter list for DEMITRIA LUNETTA

KATE KARYUS QUINN is an avid reader and menthol chapstick addict with a BFA in theater and an MFA in film and television production. She lives in Buffalo, New York with her husband, three children, and one enormous dog. She has three young adult novels published with HarperTeen: ANOTHER LITTLE PIECE, (DON'T YOU) FORGET ABOUT ME, AND DOWN WITH THE SHINE. She also recently released her first adult novel, THE SHOW MUST GO ON, a romantic comedy. Find out more at www.katekaryusquinn.com and make sure you're receiving newsletters from KATE KARYUS QUINN

MARLEY LYNN is a lost child of the gods, who waits on the shores of Lake Erie for her parents to bring her home. In the meantime, she contents herself with reading, writing, and gardening. Find out more at www.MarleyLynn.com or sign up for MARLEY LYNN'S newsletter.

## ACKNOWLEDGMENTS

Thank you to Marin McGinnis for taking care of our copy edits!

Thank you to our cover designer Victoria @VC_BookCovers and Kate's husband, Andrew Quinn, for tweaking where necessary.

And, of course, a big thank you to our families for putting up with us crazy writers.

Made in the USA
Monee, IL
11 August 2021